SUDDEN DARKNESS

Sudden Darkness

L. R. ERDMANN

ARCHWAY
PUBLISHING

Archway Publishing books may be ordered
through booksellers or by contacting:

Archway Publishing
1663 Liberty Drive
Bloomington, IN 47403
www.archwaypublishing.com
1 (888) 242-5904

ISBN: 978-1-4808-1565-0 (sc)
ISBN: 978-1-4808-1566-7 (e)

Library of Congress Control Number: 2015902482

Print information available on the last page.

Archway Publishing rev. date: 3/3/2015

CONTENTS

ALICE JOHNSON WAS AN ATTRACTIVE BRUNETTE WITH A big family problem, and she needed help with it. She feared her brother was deep into satanic worship. He had been speaking of doing greater harm in private, but this time, she was afraid her brother had gone over the edge.

It was a warm and sunny day in Milwaukee. Alice stopped to open her purse. She reached inside to get the address of the man she was looking for. To her surprise, she was already very close to her destination. She spotted the name on the door, entered, and walked into a medium-sized lobby. After looking over the list on the wall, she found the name she was seeking. She walked over to the elevator as the door started to close, wondering if this PI could really help her with her brother.

Alice was registered nurse and worked at a fine hospital. She was thirty-six years old, of average height, slim, and took good care of herself. The elevator stopped, and the door opened at the correct floor. Alice slowly walked, inspecting the name on each door until she was halfway down the hallway. *This is it,* she thought and opened the door.

The room was deep in length and of average width, with a high ceiling. A window was open slightly, and a nice breeze filled the room. She noticed the man behind the desk, who was filling out paperwork. He didn't notice the door had opened at first, but he glanced up and saw her standing in front of the desk.

He returned his attention to his file and said, "I'll be right with you. Please have a seat and make yourself comfortable."

Alice watched him as he wrote in his file for a moment, and then she looked around the room more closely. There were pictures on both sides of the room, some of people she assumed were family and friends and others of a time spent in the military. There were filing cabinets on his right and other heavier cabinets on his left. His desk was messy, with notes in different areas, files, and a closed laptop. He also had a few plants on the floor on either side of the room, next to the filing cabinets.

"Okay, how may I help you?" he asked.

"Alice Johnson. I'm here for my appointment with you."

He introduced himself as Bill Radner. He was in his middle forties, about six feet tall, and had an athletic build. He ran his fingers through his dark-brown hair as he studied his client. He felt he was a good judge of character—he had to be in his line of work. Bill leaned back in his chair as he closed his file.

"From our telephone conversation, you are really concerned about your brother … ah, Adam, is that right, Ms. Johnson?"

"Yes, that is correct. Adam is my older brother, and as I told you on the phone, he is very well off, but his actions are very strange and not like him at all."

"Can you elaborate on this strangeness, please?" replied Bill.

"As I said, we were always close as we grew up. We went to the same college here in Milwaukee. I went into nursing and Adam into futures, but we were always close. But lately, he doesn't call or return calls. Here is that letter he sent me; it really makes no sense at all."

Bill leaned forward in his chair and took the letter. He leaned back before he began to read. As he took time to read it carefully, he could understand her concern and why she was in his office. The sentence that caught his attention read, "I'm sick of your childish clinging on to me and your love for all these sick, hypocritical people of the world." The letter was very hateful and was out of character from what she had said earlier about Adam and their relationship. He closed the letter and returned it to Alice.

She put the letter back into her purse.

"Well, Alice, that letter sounds like some kind of misunderstanding, or he's doing something behind the scenes he's not telling you about."

Alice was visually upset now, and her hurt was clearly evident to Bill, but he needed much more if he was to do anything. "You say your brother was giving you thirty-five thousand dollars every year as a Christmas gift, and you say that Adam is a very successful dealer on the commodities exchange in Chicago. You say that there has been no conflict up to this time between you and never has been."

"That is correct. Nothing has ever happened between us," answered Alice quickly.

"Well, you're going to have to tell me more about Adam, whatever about his private life that you do know, or all you have got is a misunderstanding. But the letter says we're all hypocritical fools."

Alice stared at Bill for a moment and then looked down at her hands and said, "About a year and a half ago, Adam met some men at the exchange who were Satanists, and they became close friends. Their numbers grew till now there is something like thirty or thirty-five of them. Adam used to tell me they found an old book that he said could release Satan into the world if they did the right ritual and all nonbelievers would be killed in Satan's name. Then the world would go into darkness. What does this all mean, Bill? I thought I still could change his heart."

A cult, thought Bill. *Damn it all!* He sat in silence for a moment, thinking. *If this is true, a lot of people will die for nothing at all.* He then thought of Bishop Mark Frazer. He did this work and had more information on the subject.

"Alice, is there anything else you can give me about your brother's background?"

"All I know is Adam has been more distant and now this."

Bill put his hands together and asked, "Do you feel he's normal in mental state?"

Alice responded, "Yes!"

Bill thought, *Most cults are little and don't do much, but the bigger ones can kill hundreds or more. Now these people have money, brains, and connections.* He thought back to his days on the police force and remembered what his lieutenant used to say. At this point, he still didn't have much to go on, but he could do some looking around and check on a few things. Business was slow, but the letter hinted at bigger problems, so he had time to do that much. "All right, this is what I'll do for you. First, I'll go around, ask some questions, get more information, and ask my experts about Satanist activities between Milwaukee and Chicago—this is my main area. And since I believe in good family ties, I will talk to Adam and settle him down some and maybe learn something here. Then, I'll go to the police for information, but I'll need names and addresses, so I'll have someplace to start on this. My fee is two hundred and twenty dollars a day plus expenses. If everything goes well here, I should have an answer for you in about three to four days."

Alice gave a faint smile and said, "Guess I came to the right man then."

"I'll be up front—so far, we don't have much here to go on, just a misunderstanding, if you see what I mean. I'll need names of some of these people and telephone or cell phone numbers or text information to start. Do you have them?"

Alice quickly opened her purse and handed all she had to Bill; he was surprised at this. Many clients needed a day or two to gather this much information. He got up from his chair and made copies of the information. He gave the originals back to her, as was his practice. "You really came prepared here, didn't you?"

"Yes, I did. I believe something is wrong here, and I want this thing over with. I went through his desk one day when he was out of the office. That's why I have it."

They went over some last-minute details of her case and other details of his business so everything was understood and then agreed to meet again at his office on Tuesday of the next week on her day off. As Bill watched Alice leave his office, he began to wonder if it was smart to take this case. *A family matter is a family matter, but if he is big-time, then he must be stopped,* he thought to himself.

Bill leaned forward in his chair to pick up the copies he had made and began to study them more closely. He noticed that some of the names sounded familiar, but he couldn't remember from where. He shook his head, trying to place the names; then it came to him. *How stupid of me!* he thought. *I read them in the business pages every so often.* Bill had been playing the futures market from time to time for a while; he always used the profits to fund his work when business was slow. He continued to look at the other information he had in front of him.

The thirty-seven cell phone numbers and other such information didn't help much. Then he noticed that all the addresses were within a block or two of each other; they all lived close together and all worked at the exchange. *How odd is that?* Bill wondered to himself. Bill turned on the laptop sitting on his desk and started to dig up more information, to see if there was more to it. After he had been searching the Internet for about two hours, the phone rang. Bill stopped and picked up the phone; it was his good friend John Cleveland on the other end.

Bill and John had been friends for about fifteen years. They had met when Bill was a detective on the police force. John had been a college mathematics professor in Milwaukee; he'd been retired for about five years. Bill had been allowing him to help him on some of his cases when he needed the extra help. John's wife had died about three years earlier of cancer, which left him all alone, because he had few family members for support and those he did have didn't help him much. So Bill helped John by allowing him to work with him from time to time when he needed extra manpower.

"Hey, John, what's happening?" he answered cheerfully.

"Well, Bill, it's been about a week since I last talked to you. How you been? Busy, I hope?" replied John.

"I'm doing fine, John. I just got myself a new case today—at least a short-term one," answered Bill. Quickly, he added, "The only thing here is there's something odd that I noticed, or maybe it's just the way I'm looking at it."

"What do you mean, Bill?" asked John, his attention spiked a little.

"Well, these people live in the suburbs of Chicago in upper-class communities, and they all live next to each other ..." Bill began.

"What are you saying, Bill? They're all next door to each other?" asked John.

"Yep. Everyone is almost next door. Some of these people paid huge sums to be next door to one another, John," answered Bill.

"Man, that is odd to say the least, Bill. I've lived in Milwaukee all my life, and that really doesn't happen much in a city this size," he said, with a little amazement in his voice.

"You can say that again!" returned Bill, his voice rising a little.

"You know, Bill, in a smaller community, that would seem odd, but in a large city like that ... Wow!" John replied, with his attention now heightened.

"Well, for now, John, this needs to be looked into, for sure, and see why, if it makes any sense at all," Bill said, with some serious thought in his voice.

"I take it you looked into the dollar amounts some of these people paid to be next door to each other, didn't you?" questioned John.

"Yes, I did and found that some paid far more than what the house was worth!" answered Bill.

"How many people are we talking about, Bill?"

"Thirty-seven. My client says she stole the information from her brother's desk," replied Bill.

"Thirty-seven? No, friend, that's too many; that is odd. I take it they all have high-paying jobs to do that?" John asked, his attention piquing. He quickly added, "Need any help, Bill?"

"Maybe," Bill said. "For now, I can do some looking here, and I think I want to talk to Mark Frazer to get more of a background point of view here on what we are looking at."

"Bishop Mark Frazer, the church's occult expert? My friend, what are you taking on?" returned John, who was really concerned by this time.

"Rich Satanist," he returned.

"Oh my God! Now you do have the bull by the tail!" returned John.

"What do you mean?" he asked.

"Well, before I retired about five years ago, you heard of this sort of thing from the staff from time to time and you brushed it off as stories. But then, as time goes by, it keeps coming back again, so you know it's real, but you do nothing," answered John carefully.

"Well, when I was on the force, back then, we ran into this once in a while—ritual killings—and sometimes those killings belonged to this group or that. But usually, they were small and not well organized enough, so they got caught. But this could be different in that they are well funded, larger, and maybe better organized to do this," answered Bill with thought in his voice. He again quickly added, "Anything else, John?"

"Just this—think twice before you enter into this," returned John.

Bill was silent for a second, taking it in. Then he said, "You really think so?"

"Yes, I do, friend!" said John.

"Why?"

"It's just my feeling and experience working with professors and so on that if you have the right people and skill and time, it works like electric lights," replied John.

"Well, that's true for most things, isn't it?" he asked.

"It's a lot like gambling, isn't it? Somebody has to win," returned John.

Bill knew that in life that everybody did some gambling. "You may have something there—the law of averages—but let's hope this is not the case, okay?" he answered.

There was a brief silence on the phone, and then John said, "Mark is the best man to bring you up to speed on this; his background for the church runs very good. I think I know someone who can help also."

"Who's that?" asked Bill.

"Oh, he works at the library, about six blocks away from me. The seedier crowd sometimes stops in and likes to talk to this librarian on occult subjects," answered John.

"Sound's good to me, friend; we can compare notes on this," he said.

"Well, I better close for now; it's running late for me here. I need to make dinner. Keep in touch, will you?" added John.

"You know I will, John. We always make a good team, and this could be another case to prove that," responded Bill.

Bill was thinking of the case of a runaway child where John helped.

"Then stay in touch, and have a good day," John said with confidence.

"You too, and have a good day too," said Bill as the phone went dead on the other side. He put down the phone and pondered what was just said.

Bill knew John was a well-rounded and steady man. His years as a professor in a large college and that connection to that many people helped too. The thought of the law of averages, which was talked of earlier, Bill decided to skip over for the time being.

Police in all large cities ran into this occult matter one day or another. He shook his head and thought, *The law of averages?* He looked at his desk and saw that he did have time to do some running around on this. Things had been slow lately. The stuff that usually came in wasn't there. The case to help a man prove he was innocent of robbery had fallen apart the day before. But it was enough to keep the bills paid for that week. It was getting late for him also. He looked at his watch—4:33 p.m. He picked up the phone and called Bishop Mark Frazer to make an appointment at his office. With that done, he again looked at his desk.

Maybe I do need this case, he thought to himself. *Gee, I haven't messed with Satanism stuff for a long time.* He took some time to clean up his desk and decided to call it a day and make a fresh start the next day. With everything set for the next day, he shut off the lights. The phone rang in his pocket. Bill answered, and the news caught his attention. In the conversation with his friend from the police department, it became clear that this was no small matter. As they closed and Bill put his cell phone away, he thought $95,000 worth of rifles and ammunition sold in Chicago was a big deal to somebody. But what had his attention was the name. It was one of the names on the list, the one that Alice had given him.

Was there a connection or something out of the blue? Bill locked up for the day, went to the elevator, and waited for it; his mind was busy now.

Bill was at his office early the next morning; he slowly went through the mail. He separated his mail and threw the junk away. After unlocking his desk and laying his work out for the day, again, he brought out the copies of Alice's information. The name of the man matched that of a top man at the exchange. Why he had bought $95,000 worth of rifles and ammunition was a puzzle to him. Bill decided to reach his friend at the police department to see if he could talk to him and find out what he knew. After a few rings, there was only a voice-mail message. "Tom, this is Bill Radner. I wonder if you'd leave me a message in my voice mail, or maybe you could stop by after work, so we can talk about something. Tom, have a good day then. Hope to hear from you soon, bye."

Bill looked at his watch and noticed the time. He thought to himself that if he wanted to drive across town to see Mark, he had better leave soon to be on time.

Bill slowly drove up the driveway to the church where he could park. This was a big church of the old design with tall red-brick steeples and big doorways. He thought those steeples touched the sky. He entered the church offices; there were already people moving around, several priests talking to staff or clients. Bill entered a hallway that led to Mark's office and came to the door. He walked in, and a secretary greeted him.

"Do you have an appointment, sir?" asked the secretary.

"Yes, I do. My name is Bill Radner," replied Bill.

"Yes, you do. Please have a seat, and the bishop will be with you shortly," returned the secretary.

Bill liked Mark Frazer. Mark was an active man of average height on the heavy, stocky side. His work for the church dealt with occult activities, and he was a very serious fisherman. They had gone fishing a couple of times a few years before. Mark proved he could find fish and big ones too.

Mark's office had wood trim everywhere; it sort of reminded Bill of something from the 1940s or around there. There was nobody in the room, except the secretary and him. He had plenty of time for this visit, and he took some time thinking of the type of questions he should be asking. After about ten minutes, the door opened and a woman stepped out. She was a middle-aged woman, well dressed, with neat, dark hair. Mark followed. They talked briefly and said their good-byes. Mark looked around his waiting room and spotted Bill.

"Hey, Bill, good to see you again. Come in. Come in," Mark said happily. He reached out his right hand to shake hands right away. They shook hands and greeted each other very warmly. "Bill, do I detect a little gray here and there, since we last met on the lake?" said Mark jokingly.

"Just a little gray hair, trying to keep up with you with fishing," replied Bill with a small laugh.

"Come in. Come in, my friend, and have a seat," said Mark as he closed the door behind them.

Mark's office was large and looked like an old library with lots of old wood in dark shades and a rich carpet of a lighter tone. His desk was the same, very sturdy and well made. Old light fixtures were here and there but in their proper places.

A window behind Mark's desk cast the morning sunlight into the room. The window curtains were tasteful and high quality.

"How you been, Bill? If I remember correctly, it's been a while since we went fishing together," said Mark happily.

"That does sound about right, Mark, and you did catch most of the fish that day," replied Bill. He smiled warmly.

"So why am I so lucky to have you here today?" he asked warmly.

Bill understood that Mark's time with him was short and he had to cut to the chase.

"Well, Mark, I need some information from you, if I may, about satanic religion or activity, between here and Chicago. It relates to a case I'm on," answered Bill.

Mark's smile faded a little. He leaned forward on his desk and put his hands together. "Bill, friend, this is only between you and me. It's gotten worse in the last ten years. Our reports state that those groups are lasting longer and are better organized. They're drawing more members than before. They haven't broken any real rules yet, nor have they been killing, but it's just a matter of time. You say you have a case about this? I will help you because I know you personally and as a friend," said Mark with a serious tone in his voice.

"Well, Mark, I handled it a few times on the police force as a detective, but it never really got out of control. Yes, there were a few ritual killings. I handled it. I led the department on those arrests, and it was messy, to say the least, but the department never really got down to the bottom of it or its real meaning," said Bill, offering some of what he knew.

"You say your department never really got down to its real meaning, just saying that it broke the law or if it was murder. And your captain wasn't sharing the real meaning; he just said that it was open and shut. Nothing other than what the law says about it, is that correct, Bill?" asked Mark seriously.

Bill leaned back in his chair, knowing he was on a sensitive subject and better answer correctly. "The department handled these special cases with care; some officers just thought of them as crazy cases or religious crazies; I just thought that it depended on your religious beliefs," Bill added carefully.

There was a moment of silence, and then Mark added, "You carefully chose your words, Bill. God is real, and so is the devil. These two powers are in play twenty-four hours a day, fighting for everything right, wrong, or anything that makes life worth living. One day, you feel up; the next day, you're down. You feel the spiritual battle for you, though some of it is just natural," stated Mark simply.

"Okay, Mark, but what is satanic religion and what does it mean in the end?" questioned Bill.

Mark knew this question was coming; he looked down at his hands and thought some more before answering. "Bill, listen carefully please. This thing is growing; as I said before, the person who gets into this is different than you and me. They are the kind of person who doesn't fit in society well. They see our sins and don't have a proper answer for them. Love is what they don't feel inside, so they find other things to fill up the void. They hate our sins, each of us, and the world. Satan, he looks for this type of person and tries to change the rest of us the same way. If they can't find love, they have lust; if they don't feel good inside, they can hate, and on and on. Too many of us today, if we can't buy it, we don't feel good. We have too much stuff in our lives today. The Satanists don't feel loved, but they do feel hate. In that group of theirs, they feel wanted, a part of something, somebody who says what they feel. They are hard nuts to crack, Bill," stated Mark the best he could.

Again, a moment of silence fell, each letting what was said settle in.

Bill then thought of his next question for Mark. "My client says that they found some old devil book that, with the proper ritual, will release Satan to this world and bring in a new age of darkness on us. Is this true?"

Again, there was silence, and then the bishop said, "Yes, it's true, but you didn't say which book, Bill."

"I don't know, Mark; my client didn't say the name of it. But is it possible for this to happen?" questioned Bill, with a little doubt.

Mark was now leaning back into his chair. He said, "The Vatican has many old satanic books in its library, and I've seen most of them myself. It is said that the Vatican has three satanic books of five that have not yet been copied. The worry is about the other two books, which are still out there somewhere, still on the loose. And these two books are trouble if they fall into the wrong hands, Bill."

This time, the silence was longer. But Bill now had his curiosity heightened some. He said, "You mean, if the wrong person really dives into this ritual, that's the end for all of us? Is that book that … w-w-well that evil?"

"Yes, it is, Bill!" stated Mark flatly. "We are talking about a war here, Bill, between two massive armies, and I don't want to think what will happen if we lose!" stated Mark again flatly. He looked up and saw the time on his wall clock behind Bill. He rose from his chair, as did Bill, and they shook hands in a friendly way and smiled warmly.

As Bill started to leave, Bishop Mark added, "I will be in touch with you now more often, my friend, and will help you in whatever capacity I can." Mark added cautiously, "One more thing, Bill, please find the name of that book, if you can. It might be important to all of us." A note of stress had appeared in his voice.

"Sure thing, Mark. I can do that for you," replied Bill with a warm smile.

Together, they left Mark's office and stood at the edge of the secretary's desk.

Mark then said, "When this project is finished, I hear they're catching some nice walleye on a certain lake I'm thinking of, Bill."

"That's a date, Bishop, and I'm going to hold you on that."

Quickly, he replied warmly, "Good, I will see to that also. Take care." Mark went back into his office.

As Bill was returning to his car, he knew he hadn't learned what he wanted to know. He knew Bishop Mark would help him but not that day. The bishop was on his team. *Mark did say he was going to be in touch with me now.* Bill returned to his office and once again sat in his chair. He got his cell phone out and checked for messages in the voice mail. There was one from Tom saying he would be in his office around 5:30 or 6:00 p.m.

The rest of the day, he called each of the names on Alice's list with no luck. But he did leave a message with as many as he could. The message Bill was leaving went like this: "Hello, I'm Bill Radner. I'm trying to reach Adam Johnson about a family matter. If you know him, please reach me at the number given. Thank you." Bill knew the exchange was a busy place at this time of day, but he knew that he had to start a dialogue with them with any calls that came later in the day.

The phone rang, and he answered it. When he finished, he recorded the call and subject matter. Again, he thought to himself, *Well, it's going to be a late night again.* Another married woman checking on her husband called. After a much-earned lunch break, this would give time for his cell phone to get busy. Bill knew he didn't have to meet the woman until 7:30 p.m. at her place. So he still had time; he went over the copies from Alice, hoping to find any connection with the names on the list. The phone rang, and Bill answered. It was another job for tomorrow night, same type of work as before, checking on a spouse. So he unlocked his heavy cabinets, took out his cameras and some listening gear, and started to get ready for that night.

ADAM JOHNSON WAS A BUSY TRADER AT THE COMMODITY exchange and loved his work. On busy days, he had little time to be talking to his friends. Adam was about six feet tall and had a slender build and trimmed dark-brown hair. Adam made his money as a successful trader. He knew the right people, made the right buys, and mostly learned from mistakes. Adam took little time for a social life; he was a driven type of person and had little time for such things as sports. At thirty-eight years of age, he did more to make himself a success than most people. But he did have one weakness, and that was making money—lots of it.

Adam's father and mother had passed away in a car accident when he was in his middle twenties. His sister Alice was the only real family he had left. Theirs was a small family, with most of his extended family in other states around the country. And he didn't have much contact with them either. Maybe a few Christmas cards were all. Now he did have a new passion in life, besides making money, and that was with his friends in studying satanic rituals.

It seemed to start innocently enough. He remembered just talking and laughing about it. A member and friend of his one day brought in a real old book on satanic rituals from a local specialty bookstore. And he told him of this book and that it was satanic and very rare. He left it at his apartment one day; it was in old Latin. He spent a lot of time trying to translate it, and with some help, he did translate it. Adam was very good with a computer, and he put all the information into his computer. When the book was returned to his friend, there was much to talk about with their friends. And from that time, with the same passion he had for making money, he pursued satanic rituals.

One night, out in the countryside, where no one would see them, on a friend's farm, eight of them, after weeks of studying the ritual, gave it a try. They had everything ready for that night; it was a great success and more. For they actually saw demons and a fog appear. They all heard the demons speak to them personally.

His followers slowly grew in number as time passed. Only serious members joined. Adam's passion for making money was still there. But now he had something new in his life, something dark and mysterious—something he really loved. They started out with simple rituals, like it was some kind of game to play with and then throw away. But what Adam and his followers found out later was it had a power to make them silent and secretive. With each new ritual they tried and succeeded at, the demons started to ask them for more and more—more blood from animals, then some of their own blood in the rituals, and then it was asking for a human life. The demons were getting stronger, and they were seeing them more and asking for more. Their loyalty to them was now being asked of them, and they had to prove it.

The rewards they received were theirs—more money,

more respect at work, and luxury items in their lives—but the price was also higher. Some just gave up, quit, and tried to walk away, but strangely, in some odd way, they met their end. It was all legal as far as the law was concerned, but they knew it was a warning to them. Each member's personality slowly started to change with time; they all became more negative with each passing year. And now Adam was asked to leave his sister Alice behind by his new spiritual master to prove himself worthy of Satan's loyalty. So Adam sent his sister the worst letter he could write, even though it pained him to do so.

He wrote that he didn't love her anymore and hadn't for some time. His life was his own, and he didn't need her in it anymore. He told her to go away and forget about him and take her God with her.

Adam knew she would wonder why and that she would find out. But at that time, in his heart, he just didn't have the right answer that would stop her, keep her from finding the truth. And this was what grieved him, for he still cared for her. But she loved her God too much to ever convert to his. It was closing time at the exchange. Adam was finishing up his last-minute details for the day. He went for his suit jacket and was slowly making his way out of the building.

Earl, a follower of his, moved up and said, "Hey, Adam, do you know that I have a message, asking about you?"

"Are you kidding me, Earl?" responded Adam, uninterested.

"Really, Adam. Some Bill Radner wants me to call back and talk about you," answered Earl.

"Let me see that!" ordered Adam as he grabbed the phone away. "Sure enough, it does," he said in a softer voice. He paused for a moment, thinking about what it meant; then, suddenly, it hit him—Alice. "Don't answer that, Earl. It's trouble; I'm sure of it!" stated Adam with some anger in his voice.

"What do you mean, man? It says it's a family matter," responded Earl, waving the phone in front of Adam.

"Do as I say, will you, Earl? I say it's trouble. Forget it!" snapped Adam sharply. Adam pushed past Earl and walked away; he had almost reached the door when two more of his followers stopped him with the same message on their phones. Adam told them the same thing he told Earl and angrily walked away.

He knew his sister was behind this thing, but who was Bill Radner and how was he in this? Adam was almost to his car when he spotted two of his followers with the same message on their phone. Now Adam was angry.

"Adam, every one of us has the same message. How can this be?" replied one of the two followers.

"I'm not sure yet, but I can think of who is behind it!" snapped Adam as he started to get into the car.

"What do you want us to do?" asked one of the members.

"Nothing, till I see you tomorrow, got that?" snapped Adam again. He started to drive away. Adam knew it was his sister, Alice. But who was this Bill Radner? Then he wondered, *How did she have so many names and telephone numbers—or anything else for that matter?* He had to think on this for a while. *Maybe this Bill is a new boyfriend of hers?* Adam returned to his apartment, unlocked the door, entered, and locked the door behind him. Normally, when he was home, he just kicked back and napped for half an hour. But because of Alice that day, he went to his prayer room in his apartment. It was a much smaller bedroom actually, which he had painted all black, including the window; on the wall opposite of him was a skull of a goat. The altar was in front of the skull. It was a really a small table, like a coffee table. It had black cloth over the top of it with two church candles that had oil in them, painted black also. He had found them at an antique shop not far from where he lived. Between the black candles was the incense dish. He lit the candles first and then the incense. He put the lighter away in his pocket and then stood straight and bowed in front of the skull. He started to chant in some old Latin dialect, which was really a blessing to Satan. What he was about to do was ask Satan for help. This was a way of showing loyalty to Satan and doing away with his problem.

Alice Johnson was having a busy day, not her best either. She'd had a patient go into cardiac arrest that morning just as she started duties. When things slowly went back to normal, she was behind in her routines. Alice was a good nurse and had handled pressure many times before. She had started with that hospital at the beginning of her career, and after so many years, it was hard to quit.

She liked running and exercising to stay fit, but mostly, it helped her with the pressure of the job. Alice, at this time, didn't have a boyfriend. She'd had some as time passed, but they never worked out. They weren't mature enough for her or fit her career either. At thirty-six years of age, she knew time was passing. Her job was in the way. It wasn't an easy decision for her, because of the many benefits she had earned along with time. Today, she was putting in a twelve-hour day, and the end of her day was near. Alice was at the nurses' station, going over a chart of a patient. A fellow nurse questioned her about one of her patients, and she told her the doctor was there now; she informed her about the patient's condition and medication. The head nurse stopped Alice as she was leaving the nurses' station and told her she could go home in an hour. The head nurse was explaining she'd done a good job handling her duties after that morning's cardiac arrest patient. The nurse was about to add something about the next day's duties when Alice suddenly felt weak and passed out in front of her.

Alice slowly woke up in a hospital bed with an IV running into her arm and a nurse standing by her bedside. Alice rubbed the back of her head as she looked around and said, "What happened to me? Why am I here?"

"You passed out, Alice. Don't you remember?" Nurse Reynolds answered.

"All I remember was listening to the head nurse, and now I'm here," said Alice, still feeling out of place.

"Just rest here for now, Alice. I'll ring for the doctor. He'll be here in a minute or two," answered the nurse.

Dr. Hoffman entered Alice's room; the nurse spoke briefly with the doctor and left. Dr. Hoffman was a tall, middle-aged man with graying hair. He had a professional attitude about him. "So how do we feel, Ms. Johnson?" asked Dr. Hoffman, studying her chart as he spoke.

"A little fuzzy, but fine otherwise," replied Alice.

"Oh, you hit the back of your head when you passed out on us. It will be fine," answered Dr. Hoffman, noticing her rubbing the back of her head. He continued, "We ran blood tests—all negative. The heart sounds good, blood pressure good … we gave you an ultrasound, negative. I was thinking maybe you were pregnant. You're not, and the blood test said that also. Anemia of some type, negative; we can do more. But you tell us more; you are a professional."

Alice thought for a moment and then said, "I don't know. Work has been fine. My lifestyle hasn't changed, and I'm sleeping and eating fine as well. There has been no real pressure in my life. Really, Doctor, I've been feeling really normal until now."

The doctor thought for a moment and then said, "Your tests seem to say the same thing as well." Then he added, questioning, "Do you feel there is any emotional problem that might be responsible?"

"Definitely not, Doctor! I keep my life in balance. I just want to get out of bed and go back to work, like you," stated Alice flatly. She knew that any troubling emotional problem could keep her out of work for weeks.

"Well, Alice, your coworkers all say the same thing as well. You've been very steady and emotionally balanced," stated Dr. Hoffman as he studied the chart closely. There was a moment of silence, and then the doctor added, "I think for now, Alice, we will give you five days off. During these five days, we would like to do some follow-up tests and go from there. But right now, all I can think of is rest."

Alice didn't know what to think for a moment; then she said, "You mean, I can go home, Doc?"

"Yes, Alice, you can go home," answered Dr. Hoffman, smiling faintly. "Now, Alice, when you're dressed and ready to go, Nurse Reynolds will give you a slip of paper, stating your visits with us over the next five days. And in the end, if nothing, maybe all you needed was some time off?" suggested

Dr. Hoffman, again with that faint smile. He nodded his head, turned, and left quietly.

Nurse Reynolds, after a moment, entered the doorway smiling. "Okay, Alice, I'll get the IV, and then you can get dressed. We are working on your visits with us."

Alice walked to the nurses' station, where Nurse Reynolds was standing. "Here you go, Alice. Now get some rest please?" said Nurse Reynolds, and she wished her well. They spoke for a few minutes, and Alice left for home.

BILL RADNER UNLOCKED HIS OFFICE DOOR SLOWLY AND entered, closing the door behind him. It was 10:00 a.m., and he was late. Being out half the night for a client was not his style. He was also carrying a small plastic bag with his left arm. It contained the morning mail and something to eat. He made himself some coffee and completed the usual task of dividing the mail and throwing half away. After several minutes, he was leaning back into his chair, slowly drinking coffee and reading the mail.

Suddenly, his cell phone rang, and he answered. John Cleveland was calling.

"Hi, Bill. Just thought I would give you a call this fine morning. How you doing there?"

"Good morning, John. Hey, could you stop over please? I will tell you then," returned Bill, wondering.

"Sure, Bill, no problem. Oh, give me a half hour on that," replied John.

John entered Bill's office, looking happy to be there, and made himself at home there.

Bill turned around from the window. He had been doing his paperwork earlier and reached a conclusion on his new case. "Hey, John, help yourself to some fresh coffee and some rolls," said Bill, happy to see his friend.

After a minute or two, they sat down in their chairs, enjoying the coffee and rolls. Bill started by saying, "I asked you here because I need your help. Would you be interested, John?" asked Bill nicely.

John sipped his hot coffee and then answered, "Sure, Bill. Just name it, and I'll do my best for you."

Bill started, "About three days ago, I picked up a new client, and her brother was a Satanist. Do you remember?"

"Yes, I do, and I thought it was a bad idea," stated John, nodding his head.

Bill leaned forward and rested his arms on his desk. "This case may be bigger than we first thought, John. At first, I thought it was a family matter, nothing more. But this is what happened; for two days, I text-messaged all thirty-seven followers and got no reply, except one follower called me and one friend. I have the phone calls recorded in my desk, and you can go over the notes. Both stated they each knew Adam as the leader and all thirty-seven of the followers. I played up the story about a family problem, and the family wanted Adam to be there. But then Kathy, a friend of a friend of the followers, was too smart for that line. She's afraid of them all and wants to help. So this is it, John, this is how it goes with them."

John interrupted Bill. "How do you know she's not lying to you, Bill?"

Bill thought for a moment and then added, "Gut feeling, John, gut feeling. For one, there's too much information we can learn; she works with them at the exchange, and she seems to know a lot about them. And two, she seems to be close to the upper levels of the group and knows Adam very well at that."

"But, Bill, she could be lying to you."

"That is where you come in, John. I want you to go to Chicago and talk to Kathy yourself, find out for yourself," answered Bill, looking John in the eye.

Bill continued, "First, Kathy stated they are recruiting thirteen women for a ceremony this coming Halloween night. It is supposed to be special. Second, this group just purchased ninety-five thousand dollars of rifles and ammunition, and they're locked in a warehouse a comfortable distance from the group. I got that from the police—the number of rifles and the amount of ammunition—and Kathy told me the same thing, without my asking her. John, I have the phone call recorded for you to listen to in your spare time. Kathy also told me clearly that she heard one of them say that they killed a twelve-year-old girl in an old, rundown warehouse along Lake Michigan. It was to be the first killing they have done to date. It was to be a new ritual they're trying, for the big deal on Halloween night. The police in Chicago told ours, and I got this from the police here that the dead twelve-year-old girl was nude, stabbed in ritual fashion, and had strange markings on her body, new to the police there. The hands and ankles were tied as well. There were blood drops on the ground in a circle, but—now get this, John—the body had no blood in it! And that came from the coroner's office; my PD friend Tom and I shared a line together. We called there!" added Bill, in a serious tone of voice.

John sat there for a moment; he looked at the ceiling, giving it serious thought. "You know, Bill, this is over your head. I hope you put some plan together to start with," said John, in a serious tone of voice as well.

Bill thought for a second, looking at his hands as he rubbed them together. Then he said, "It's not enough yet; in my opinion, we need to get solid evidence. There's too much hearsay. There's nothing solid to report to the police."

John was thinking it over quietly to himself; again, he looked at the ceiling and then back at Bill. "Bill, you're right. A good attorney would throw it out the window," he said, sadly agreeing.

Then he said, "You see the problem then, don't you? We know stuff, and we have some contacts, but nothing solid to run with; we're dead in the water."

"What about Alice—is that her name?" asked John quickly.

"Yes, it is," answered Bill.

"Well, when is she due here? We need much more from her," said John, agreeing.

"Tuesday sometime, I haven't heard from her yet," answered Bill. "Before I forget to answer you, yes, I do have a plan, but it's rough and some of the pieces don't fit yet," he added slowly, with concern. "It's about six weeks to Halloween, and I don't know if Alice wants to go that far with me. This would be the end of her brother and their group. They've started to kill now, and Kathy says they're already good at it. They clean up their tracks real good; they're neat. The police there in Chicago can't do any finger-pointing yet. There are too many of their kind there in a city of that size," said Bill, hashing it over in his mind.

There was a moment of silence in the room. John got up and poured himself a cup of coffee with Bill eyeing another roll. John looked at the time, 11:44 a.m., and he thought to himself, *I'm in no hurry.* Bill's phone rang, and he answered.

They talked for a while. A smile came to his face, and he looked pleased. He said good-bye.

John asked quickly, "That was Alice, wasn't it, Bill?"

"Yes, it was John. Tuesday at 10:00 a.m., just a little over a day from now," responded Bill.

Bill finally decided to eat the roll in front of him and took a big bite.

"What are you going to say to her, Bill?" asked John, wondering.

Bill looked at John and cleared his throat. "The truth, of course, but the hard part is getting her to see what must be done, and we are now at the first steps, with your trip to Chicago."

"Say, if I go to Chicago tomorrow morning, how would I know what Kathy looks like?" asked John with an eagerness in his voice. For the next forty-five minutes, they talked back and forth about Kathy and what she looked like and their case problems.

John was about to leave when Bill's phone rang. It was Kathy calling; they talked for about five minutes. John could tell it was Kathy, because they were talking addresses and clothes often. He could gather from listening that it was important because Bill was taking plenty of notes. Finally, they said their good-byes, and Bill looked really pleased. Bill rose from his chair, made a copy of the information, and handed it to John. Then he sat down, and they talked over the information and their plan for the following day. John made some notes as well and was on his way.

ADAM WAS IN HIS APARTMENT, RESTING IN HIS ARM-chair. The television was on, and the volume was low. His apartment was on the large side for Chicago, and it was in a good and solid area of the city. Being on the fifth floor, his apartment had a nice view of the city below. He had nice furniture; the walls were of a light shade of blue, but there were not many pictures. His lamps were expensive and added class to his apartment. Today was Sunday, and he had a slow walk in the nearby park and ate at a diner along the street. But at this moment, his thoughts were on the ritual killing of a twelve-year-old, blond, blue-eyed girl. He wasn't worried that he killed that girl; it was the ritual itself. It just wasn't quite right. It lacked something. It was good, but it lacked power. He got up from his armchair and went to his computer. He went over and over the ritual. Adam had the ritual in that old warehouse filmed, and he listened to it over and over. It came to him as to what was wrong. The incantation wasn't up to speed; it had promise, but there was not enough praise, not enough glory to Satan. He busied himself with writing down notes and again going over the film on the computer and taking more notes. Adam knew the police were all over that warehouse when they found the body. He himself had gone over the warehouse very carefully, leaving no trace of who was there. Halloween was coming, and his big ritual would be on that day. He now had the thirteen women he wanted for it, and every other night, his group of followers and he were there training them in their own homes. Everything had to be right; for on that night, Satan would be revealed to the world once again as master of the world.

Because of his part in it, he hoped for a top spot in his future. Adam felt that using that same warehouse again would be brilliant and gutsy. He would use the same ritual he had used a couple of days before, but he would revise the incantation for added effect. After some time at this, he felt pleased. Now all he needed was another young girl for the ritual. He thought again. He would put one of his spies out there for a while, pay him or her good for it, until the heat was off, and do the ritual. Just a nice sandy-blond, eleven- or twelve-year-old girl would do for the ritual. Adam laughed out loud when he was finished. All for Satan. He just finished putting everything away, so it would be safe. He went to get a drink from the refrigerator, and the doorbell rang. He walked over to the door, unlocked it, and opened it.

It was Jenny, one of his followers. He let her in, and she said, "Hello, Adam, do you have a moment please?"

"Sure thing, Jenny. What's on your mind?" replied Adam.

They walked over to where they wanted to sit, Adam back into his armchair and Jenny on the sofa. She started out by first bringing to his attention that some of the followers wanted to know when the next sacrifice was to be and how comfortable he was about having it at the same place. With a little amazement on his face and knowing he was just thinking that, he answered, "Yes, it will be fine to do it there again, Jenny, and tell the others it will be as soon as the police are finished there."

"Many think it's a big risk to do it there again. They could be laying a trap for us?" added Jenny with concern in her voice.

Adam studied her for a second and took a sip of his cold soda. "You're a good follower, Jenny, and I feel your concern is in the right place. Tell the others that I have a plan to take care of that. In fact, I plan to put it into effect very soon," stated Adam with a small smile on his lips.

Jenny trusted his judgment on details like this; she also felt he was a good leader of the group. She had been a member from the beginning. She saw the membership grow and was impressed by the order he kept and his attention to detail and discipline. Jenny saw the demons he brought up from nowhere and how he protected them in their circle. She had nothing but praise for him and his ability to lead, but she asked her question, "Adam, what will happen to us after Halloween night's ritual?"

Adam paused for a moment as he studied her on the sofa, looking at him. After some deep thought, he responded, "Tell the others and remember yourself, though our roles be different, I will always be your leader, now and forever."

They sat there quietly for a short time; he could see her concern lessen. A slow smile came to her lips, and she said, "I would like that, Adam; I trust your leadership and your skill as one. Satan was wise to pick you as a leader."

He saw that her loyalty was true, and he could rely on her and her position in the group.

"Well, Adam, I better go now and thank you for your

time and filling me in on your plans," said Jenny as she rose from the sofa. He walked her to the door and said good-bye. When he closed the door and locked it again, he stood there and smiled to himself. He was proud to have her as a member.

ALICE'S FIRST DAY OF TESTS PROVED NOTHING AT ALL. It was on a Saturday; the reason it was that day was she was an employee there, and they could run tests all day. Sunday was the same thing, nothing at all. That night, Alice was just relaxing all evening. She knew Monday would be the same thing. She kind of liked the little extra free time she now enjoyed. She had been doing some shopping and calling her girlfriends and a few of her distant family members. Normally, she didn't watch much television, but now she had more time for it. Alice had an upstairs apartment; it was a two-bedroom unit in an average neighborhood. She fixed up her apartment with bright colors on the wall, nice furniture in her price range, and a few nicer things here and there to look good. A commercial came on the television; she rose from her armchair to get a beer from the refrigerator. She opened the door of the refrigerator, reached for a beer, and spotted a slice of pizza on the shelf. With the beer and pizza, she returned and made herself comfortable. After she had watched some television, it was getting late and she was feeling a little tired. It was about 10:45 p.m., so she got ready for bed. Alice did her normal routine, getting ready for some good sleep. She slowly walked along her side of the bed, picked up the alarm clock, set it, and climbed into bed. Alice said a quiet prayer to herself and reached over, pausing once to check the clock. She turned the lamp off. Alice quickly fell asleep, but after a couple of hours, she was awakened from her sound sleep. The bed was shaking back and forth, not hard, but still enough to wake her.

Alice turned on the light, and the bed was still shaking back and forth.

"Oh my God, what is this?" cried Alice out loud.

After a minute or two, it stopped shaking, and all was quiet again. Fear was on Alice's face. In all her life, this had never happened before. Alice got out of bed quickly; she shook the bed violently but nothing like before. She turned on the clock radio; there was music playing, so she tried another station—more music. Alice was thinking that maybe Milwaukee had had a small earthquake. It did happen, but it was really rare. It should have been on the radio. So she turned the lights of her apartment on. After looking around, she thought all was normal. Alice was now confused. She walked into kitchen side of her apartment, opened the refrigerator, and grabbed a beer. She popped it open and took a big drink. It made her feel better, and it helped to settle her nerves.

Alice sat in her armchair, sipping her beer; she pondered what had just happened to her. Then a thought came to her mind—maybe it was one of those waking dreams. She had heard of them in college, at nursing school, and they did seem real. Then she remembered, sipping her beer again, that the light was on and the bed was still shaking. *Maybe I do have an emotional problem I'm not aware of,* she thought. *No, there's nothing wrong with me, maybe the devil; I doubt it. I know what I*

saw, and I know what I felt. I better keep this to myself tomorrow.
The psychiatrist would be taking a turn with her, and his or
her word was final. She finished her beer and went back to
bed. The rest of the night was normal.

The next morning, John Cleveland left Milwaukee about
8:00 a.m. for Chicago. The car was full of gas, and the traffic
was heavy in the south-bound lane to Chicago. A couple of
hours later, he was in Chicago and the traffic was no better.
The first thing on the to-do list was to find this rare bookshop
in downtown Chicago to find that book for Bishop Frazer.
The shop was important because it was close to all the members living in that area, and he wanted to buy the book for
Bishop Mark Frazer, if possible. John's GPS was on and working well. After some time and a few bad words, he found the
shop and parked. It was somewhat of a large building on a
busy street, but it was clearly marked. He was quickly waited
on by an elderly woman wearing glasses. John told her what
he wanted, and she led him to the back of the store. There was
a door, which she unlocked, and they went in. She asked, "Sir,
are sure you want ancient books on Satan worship?"

"Yes, I do. I'm a retired college professor from Milwaukee,
and I'm currently studying it. Thank you," replied John in a
professional tone of voice.

"We only have two books here on that subject; one is
newer, from the mid-1700s, and the other, we are not sure.
All we know is that it's older than the other and it's written
in very early Latin. We've only had one person interested in
it since we purchased the book from another professor from

New York," said the clerk with knowledge in her voice. She turned, pulled out a book from the shelf, and set it on the table. She pulled out the other and set it on the table beside the other. "These are the two books I was telling you about. The one on the left is newer, and the one on the right is the older," said the clerk in a businesslike tone of voice.

John paused for a second, looking at the two books. The two books showed age and wear. The older book had two straps sealing it shut. "You said only one person studied the older book?" questioned John with interest.

"That is correct, sir. A man, I believe from Chicago here," stated the clerk, trusting her memory.

John opened the newer book first, with great care so as not to rip any pages, and saw that he could read some of it. He could read some Latin but not much. "May I see the other please?" he asked nicely, wanting the clerk to open it for him.

The clerk carefully opened each strap and presented it to him. John opened the book and started to page through it. It was very old Latin, with pages of text and old pictures and ideograms. He closed the book and smiled at the clerk. He said in a businesslike tone, "What's the book called?"

"*Black Passages*, sir!" responded the elderly clerk.

John could feel the excitement grow within him. Could this be the book? "How much do you want for it, ma'am?" asked John with much interest.

She slowly returned the books back to their shelves and said, "Follow me, please."

After they left the room, she locked the door. They continued to the front of the store. She went behind the desk and entered the name of the book on the computer. After a minute or so, she said, "Fifteen thousand for that book, sir."

"Can you tell anything at all about this book that might be useful for my studies?" asked John with interest.

John Cleveland questioned her for some time, for she seemed knowledgeable in her work. She asked why he was writing so much down. All he could tell her was it was for full record keeping. When she went to get another book on the same subject, he wrote down her name while she was gone. The other book she came back with was of no value to him. Finally, she wanted to know if he wanted the book. John told her he wanted to make a phone call first. So she went back to her duties, while he made his call. Bill answered his call from John, and John explained everything to him on the phone in detail. Bill had to think too, for he knew that Bishop Mark Frazer would buy it from him; the Vatican would want that book.

After some serious thinking, Bill said, "Fine, John, get that book. We need it!"

John knew they needed evidence, and Bill explained the church's position on the book. John noticed the elderly clerk doing her duties and waved her over. Right away, she started to go to pick up the book in the back of the store, and John said, "Yes, I'm buying it, please."

The elderly clerk looked a little surprised at first, and then John told her to wrap it nicely.

When everything was done, John owned a very expensive old book—for a little while anyway. He left the rare book store and went back to his car. He opened the trunk of the car, carefully laid it in there, and covered it up with anything he could find. He drove away, feeling good about it, for now they had possible evidence. John pulled over for a minute to find Adam Johnson's address. Once he located it on the computer, he went there.

John took a small camcorder with him and went inside. The building was an apartment building but was well cared for. It was close to a park and was in nice neighborhood, and the people were friendly. John walked inside to a very neat lobby; he went to the board on the wall and found Adam Johnson's name and room number. He noticed the elevator, crossed the lobby, and got in. Shortly, he was on the fifth floor of the building. He slowly walked down the hallway and located his room. John was careful that nobody was present. He picked the lock and let himself in, closing the door behind him. "Boy, my apartment, doesn't look like this one!" he said softly. Quickly, he went to film everything, every room and anything he could think of, including the black room in detail. His filming didn't take ten minutes; he looked out the door carefully and locked it behind himself. In another three minutes, he was by his car. He carefully wrote down the address and time of visit.

His next mission on the list was to film as much of the followers' houses as possible. He set his GPS to the neighborhood and left quickly. In about ten minutes, he was there. He checked the map of Chicago to see how far the street went. John busied himself with the mounting bracket and started filming all the houses of the followers and the streets they lived on.

With that done, it was time now for the warehouse where the little girl was killed. Again with the GPS, John found the address of that warehouse, but he was slowly using up his time. Finding the warehouse was not as easy as he had thought it would be. When he found it, there were two police cars still there, so he filmed what he could and left. John went to the financial side of town where Adam Johnson worked.

Once inside the exchange building, he carefully asked around for Adam Johnson, who was on the floor trading. Once Adam had been pointed out to him, he filmed him carefully, with no one watching or noticing him doing so. He tried to get closer but was stopped by security. After being told to leave the trading area, John left with no dispute. Once at his car, he recorded everything. Now the only job to do was to find Kathy's apartment and wait.

After some driving and looking, he finally found it. He located a good restaurant and waited his time out. John finished his meal and had some coffee, stalling for time. First, he read the paper, and then he ate dessert, read some more of the paper, and then ate more dessert. Finally, it was time; he took care of his bill and left. He walked over to his car in a parking area, paid for maximum time, and then slowly walked across the street to Kathy's apartment building. He looked at his watch and thought she should be there any minute. He entered the building and waited in the lobby. While waiting, he pulled the notes out of his pocket. He kept going over the notes, so he knew what questions to ask. He looked up; a red-headed woman entered the lobby wearing a red tie.

She was in her thirties and well dressed. John was not good at starting a conversation so he said carefully, "Excuse me, please; are you Kathy?"

She turned quickly and spotted John sitting there. "Yes, I'm Kathy. Who are you?" She seemed a little startled.

"I'm with Bill Radner. I believe we were to meet today at this time," answered John carefully.

A little more relaxed, she responded, "You're with Bill Radner? Who are you then?"

"I'm John Cleveland. I work with Bill Radner on some of

his cases. I'm here to represent him today," stated John the best way he could.

Not sure yet, she opened her purse and reached in. She pulled out a cell phone and dialed. After a moment, she was talking to Bill on the phone. She questioned Bill, wanting to confirm John was with him. She was satisfied by what Bill told her, thanked him, and hung up. "Well, John, you're the real deal then, aren't you?" stated Kathy with some sharpness but a faint smile.

John got up and followed Kathy into the elevator. She entered the floor she wanted, and the doors closed. She turned to John and said, "I was expecting Bill today, so forgive me if I didn't trust you at first."

"That's fine with me, Kathy. I do understand your position here," responded John, feeling more relaxed as well. They reached their floor, and the door opened.

Kathy added, "In this city, a woman can't be too careful nowadays."

They walked out of the elevator and proceeded down the hallway together. They came to her apartment. She let them in. She turned on the lights and the stereo. "Would you like a drink or some coffee, John?" asked Kathy, becoming more relaxed.

John had had plenty of coffee at the restaurant but then decided, "Beer, if you have it, please?"

Kathy gave John his beer and then busied herself making coffee. "Oh, John, give me a minute please. I want to change first," added Kathy, as she went into her bedroom and closed the door.

Kathy's apartment was of average size but well furnished. The walls were white. On one, above the television, there were pictures of family and others. The furniture was nice and neat and of a modern style, and the stereo was also of a high-end design and on the expensive side. He liked her apartment; it felt like home. The arrangement was good. The music that was playing was modern but nice, not too loud or too hard. As he was sitting and looking around, he noticed a crucifix above his head. He hadn't noticed it before. Kathy came out of the bedroom and entered the kitchen of her apartment. She was wearing workout clothes to feel more comfortable in her home. She poured herself a cup of coffee and then sat across from John.

They had a really nice conversation that went on for some length of time. John noticed the time and then asked to use the restroom. When he came back and sat down, he said, "If you don't mind, please, I think we should start?"

"Sure, John, no problem," replied Kathy, agreeing with him. "Let me do something first though," she said as she went to the kitchen. She took something from the freezer, removed it from the box, and put it into the oven. She came back. "Dinner, on me?" she said and smiled.

"Sounds good to me, Kathy," said John nicely. He reached into his pocket, pulled out a recorder, and turned it on. "Is this recorder fine with you, Kathy?" he asked nicely as he looked at her.

"Yes, it's fine with me. I kind of figured this much," answered Kathy calmly.

John reached into his pocket and then came out with his notes again. He studied them for a second and then started with the necessary information on the recorder—date, time, day, the person he was with, and where. "Okay, Kathy, we understand that you came forward with information concerning Adam Johnson?" stated John, opening.

"Yes, I did!" answered Kathy in a direct tone of voice.

"Can you tell us how you came to know Adam Johnson, from the beginning to the present?" questioned John nicely, so as not to make her nervous.

She answered, "I have known Adam Johnson from almost my first day at the exchange. He trained me in my job there and to the present; at that time, he was a pleasant man to know. He was in the Satanist group at that time already. He really started to change when they learned of that book of rituals. It was like he was obsessed with it and talked constantly of it to his group. I don't work directly with him but around him. The past year, he's practiced many of the blood rituals. I know this from some of his followers. One is a man named Clifford. He likes to talk of it to me when no one is around and gets really excited when something happens. He just has to tell someone like me all about it. Clifford is the one who told me that they had purchased the weapons. But I learned of the human sacrifice when I walked in on some of his members talking of it among themselves. They didn't see me. I was lucky that day. There is another person there who would like to help you, but not at this time, not till I can tell her it's safe to do so." After that lengthy answer to his question, it was apparent she knew a good deal about Adam.

"What do you know about a satanic book that he and his group are using in their cult?" he asked.

"From what I've been told by Clifford Hoover, a cult follower at work, like I said before, a friend of his bought Adam a book on satanic rituals. I don't know the person's name—really, I don't, but Clifford told me that Adam translated it and has the entire book in detail in his computer. And when he had finished copying and translating, Adam returned the book to this person. Now Clifford doesn't always tell me much; in fact, I haven't talked to him for day or so now," answered Kathy, acting a little nervous.

"You're doing fine, Kathy. The next question is how was the group different since the book?" asked John carefully.

Kathy paused to do some thinking and answered slowly, "They became very much more secretive. Before, I could walk up to one of them and just talk, like anyone—no more. They became more serious around each other, like ... like something was heavy on their minds. That's the only way I can put it. If you're with the group at the exchange, they would talk freely to each other, but if you're not, you're nobody now. Another thing, my source that I get my information from is slowly drying up. I think it's weird, man. Adam's temper is now much more visible than before. The last couple of weeks, without asking, they have been murmuring around each other about something big that is about to happen on Halloween night. I was lucky to overhear some followers in the restroom, when they thought they were alone. I waited till they left before I came out and went back to work," stated Kathy with concern in her voice.

"You're doing fine, Kathy, just hang in there with us," said John, trying to keep her steady and calm.

Kathy got up with her cup and went to the kitchen. She refreshed her coffee and came back. She took a sip and put the cup down. With a faint smile, she said, "I'm ready for another question."

"If you can, please, what did you hear, if anything, about a ritual killing just recently?" John could tell from her face she knew that the question would come but was not expecting it so early.

With some pausing and pondering, she said slowly, "It was after the killing, and it was at the end of the day. I was picking up the paperwork from each of the traders on the floor. You know that we are largely electronic today, but there is still some paperwork yet. I was gone from my desk, which is just down from the trading floor. I was gone longer than usual that day; it was a busier-than-average day. When I made my way back to my office, it was quiet enough. I was close enough to my office to hear people talking in it. There were two persons in my office, and I saw them too. One said, 'That ritual went off sweet last night, didn't it, friend?' And the other said, 'That girl died nicely for Satan.' When I heard that, I hid quickly, before I was spotted by anyone. From where I was hiding, I saw two followers come out of my office, and they were acting very casual about it."

"Could you point them out from a lineup, Kathy?" said John in an official tone.

"Yes, I could. Very easy for me, I was not that far away, uh, thirty feet," stated Kathy nodding her head, approving of what she just said.

Enough time had passed already that the smell of her dinner was starting to fill the apartment. Kathy noticed John's reaction to it and said in a friendly tone, "Smells good, doesn't it, John?"

John nodded to the reply and said, "Has it been that long already?"

Kathy looked at the clock in the kitchen and said, "Fifteen more minutes, John."

John continued his questioning with another question about the weapons and Adam Johnson personally, and then he asked for the names of the followers, and she answered very well. John switched off the recorder when Kathy went to the kitchen.

"What's for dinner, Kathy?" asked John jokingly.

"Lasagna and would you like something to go with it?" questioned Kathy with his interest in mind.

John paused for a second and then replied, "Do you have maybe a salad in the refrigerator?"

"Why, yes, I do. I think that would go fine with the lasagna," returned Kathy, agreeing with his idea.

"Anything I can do to help you?" asked John.

"No, you had a busy day so far, and you must have a long drive back again," returned Kathy, going into the cupboards. She set the kitchen nook for them and took out the lasagna to let it cool for a minute. She busied herself with the details of their dinner. John watched with interest. It reminded him of when his wife was alive, not too many years ago. He lowered his head, looking at his hands, and remembered.

The stereo was still playing rather nice music. Finally, Kathy said, "All set here, John. Let's eat."

The meal was great, and they enjoyed each other's company. John noticed in her personally that she was lonely. After dinner, she did her kitchen routines and again sat across from John for more questioning. The time went by fast after that; he asked all the questions Bill wanted and a few of his own. Kathy's knowledge of the cult group was better than he had thought it would be, for she seemed to understand its structure. It was getting late now. John had to be getting back. John thanked her for her help with Bill and everything and left. He returned to his car, feeling happy about the day. He did his paperwork and proceeded to make his way home. Once he made his way back to the interstate, he headed back to

Milwaukee. On the way back to Milwaukee, he found his cell phone and called Bill. After five or six rings, he answered, and he continued to explain how the day went for him. He was a little impressed that John had so much to tell him. He wanted to be sure to bring the book with him the following morning when Alice was there. He told John that he wanted Alice to feel she'd gotten her money's worth in the work done for her. John questioned Bill about the cost of the book.

Tuesday morning was cooler and cloudier in Milwaukee; you could say it was a somewhat dreary day. Bill was early that morning, and he was feeling rather up for the day. By chance, he had called Adam Johnson the previous night after John called. He played up the family matter story, but Adam got very angry on the phone. He did agree to see his sister Alice for a short time. Adam stated on the phone that he would be in Park River in northern Wisconsin at his property and then gave some vague directions. Bill tried to weasel more information out of him but had no luck in that quest. Adam gradually got angrier on the phone and then hung up on Bill.

Bill was at the door of his office. He unlocked the door, went to his desk, and placed his plastic bag on it. It had the usual stuff inside—mail and something to eat. He slowly went about his normal routine and made some coffee for the morning. Bill turned on the radio as the smell of hot coffee started to fill the office air. Bill was in his chair, casually doing his routine, when John tapped on the door. He just walked in and tapped on his desk. Bill looked up and said, "Morning, John. Hey, I have some fresh coffee made. Help yourself."

"Thank you, Bill. I think I will. It smells good," replied John, quickly helping himself.

Bill just threw his junk mail into the wastepaper basket by his desk.

He took one more look at the bills and said, "Oh shit, man, I hate bills."

John sipped his coffee carefully and added, "I know the feeling, Bill, but there's nothing we can do about it."

Bill, a little frustrated, threw them on the desk, rose from his chair, and poured himself some coffee. Watching Bill, John casually said with some humor in his voice, "Are they really that bad?"

Bill sat down in his chair again, set his cup down, and picked up a bill. With frustration in his voice, he said, "I can pay the bills all right, but there's not much profit this week."

"When you're self-employed, like you are, my friend, it does happen," answered John, joking.

Bill rose from his chair, opened his filing cabinet, brought out some day-old rolls to share with John, and set them on the desk. They helped themselves, and Bill started explaining business to John for the morning. Bill and John shared their stories of what they had been doing up until this morning. John sipped his coffee quickly and stated to Bill, "If Alice feels she didn't get her money's worth, she's nuts."

Bill nodded with agreement, drank a little coffee, and added, "I think so too, John, but I'm afraid it's not what she wants to hear about her brother. Like I said earlier, I tried to settle the family matter with Adam, and it's a no-sale."

John sipped a little more coffee and then looked at Bill and responded, "So you're telling me she may storm out of here?"

Bill studied John quickly and said, "Yes, but she'll be back soon. The radio, newspaper, and television will tell her she made a mistake. Her brother is a murderer and a madman. John, I've been in this business for a long time now. I met these people many times when I was a detective on the police force. Other detectives and I hunted down murderers who liked blood. Once they taste blood and like it, they won't stop. They want more and more. It's a drug to them; they got to have more. This man will kill again and very soon. He's smart and gutsy, and something tells me he'll try the same place again."

"Why there, Bill? It's crawling with police; I have it on film from yesterday. What makes you think there, man?" said a startled John, stress in his voice.

Bill nodded slowly, drank a little coffee, and said carefully, "Experience, John, the police in Chicago are great men and women, but they can't be everywhere. They can't do what we do. We have the time and experience to track faster and follow up on every lead we get here. They can't afford to like we can. This man will kill at the same place. That's his fingerprint; it's brilliant, and it's gutsy. We need evidence. That's it, John, our man made clear."

Silence filled the room for a moment. They stared at each other, and then John added with thought, "You're very certain on this, aren't you, Bill?"

Bill quickly added, "Absolutely!"

Another pause fell between the two men. John was about to say something when Bill's phone rang.

"Hello?" answered Bill. He listened to the person on line. "Really?" He listened again for about a minute and said, "Thank you very much for that information," and hung up.

Bill stared ahead in serious thought and then said, "That was Amy on the line; she is our other informant at the exchange, and she works with many of the followers on the floor. She took a quick second from work there to inform us. They're moving all the rifles and ammunition to Park River next week by an unmarked truck. And get this, John—they're planning another ritual killing soon."

John looked a little startled and said, "Where?"

"She's in deep cover for us, John. I will tell you her full name in a minute, but she did hint it was to be the same place," answered Bill, with a smile coming to his lips.

They were helping themselves to another roll when the door opened and Alice walked in.

She was a little early for her appointment. John rose and gave her the chair. He finished his jelly roll.

"I hope you don't mind that I'm early, Bill?" responded Alice, looking somewhat tired in appearance.

John quickly said, "Bill, I'll get the package, okay?"

"Sure thing," said Bill.

"I don't think I met your partner, Bill," said Alice as she turned to see him leaving.

"Oh, he's just a friend who helps me here and there," responded Bill, studying Alice with concern.

Alice looked down as she rested her small purse on her lap. She started by saying, "So what's happening with my case?"

Bill, not sure where to start, began, "I talked to Adam for you, as promised, and he said he will see you briefly. I also came to the conclusion I would like to make this trip with you, at my expense, to protect you if necessary. From my talk with him on the phone, he sounds a lot like what he wrote in that letter you gave. He would not state the reason on the phone as to why, but his attitude toward you is not promising."

At this time, John reentered the office with the package in hand.

Alice watched him carefully, as he stood behind the desk with Bill. "What's that he's got there?" she asked with much concern in her voice.

At this time, Bill carefully and skillfully told her, "Your brother and followers have already killed a girl in Chicago and are planning a second soon. Together, they have purchased weapons as well, and we've learned they're well organized."

Alice was more than upset; she was angry. She looked Bill in the eyes. She wasn't getting up from her chair, so Bill didn't answer right away. The office was silent for a while, and then Alice said sharply, "I want to see some proof! I want to see some Goddamn proof! My brother is no murderer! He's … he's not a lunatic or something!" If Alice had been a fire, the whole building would have gone up in smoke.

Again, there was silence. Bill was using his experience to calm her anger, to help her see what he knew as truth.

After a lengthy pause, Bill nodded to John to unwrap the package. John carefully opened the package and picked up the book. He held it up before him to show her. She stared at it for a moment, passed out, and rolled out of the chair onto the floor.

"John! Get some smelling salts and some water, please, quickly!" ordered Bill, with surprise in his voice.

John went to get what was asked of him. Bill was trying to lift her head and gently tapped her on the cheeks to revive her. John came back with the smelling salts and water. John made the smelling salts ready and gave them to Bill, and he waved them under her nose. Slowly, she came to and murmured something about a bed shaking again. Bill and John looked at each other, trying to understand what that meant.

She looked around in a foggy state and slowly fixed her attention on Bill. Again, she said, "Bill, my bed has been shaking the last two nights. It's been shaking."

Bill and John slowly and carefully lifted her back to her feet. John gave her a drink of water. They carefully watched her until she was mostly recovered. When they felt she would be all right, they went back behind the desk. Bill now remembered what Bishop Mark Frazer had said about demonic attacks against people. The bed shaking was just part of that. It was to wear people down until they made a mistake and died or were killed. Bill sat again behind his desk, John at his side, and continued to watch her as she finally sat down in the chair again. She then stooped down, picked up her purse, and again placed it on her lap.

"What happened, Alice? Why did you pass out on us?" asked Bill with some care.

She leaned forward and set the glass on his desk.

"That book, it's evil! Put that book away, so I don't see it!"

Bill chose his words carefully. "Your brother is using this evil now to kill you. That book is pure evil, Alice, and you know it too. And he has that book in his apartment, on a computer, Alice! I have a friend; he's a bishop in the Catholic Church here in town, and he wants to help you. Your bed shaking is no accident; it's not mental illness. Your brother is trying to kill you with that book, and slowly, you will die because of your brother."

Alice shook her head back and forth, trying not to hear.

She replied, "You're both mad! How can my brother kill me with a book, unless he hits me with it?"

Quickly, Bill explained, "You've heard of metaphysics, Alice? I'm sure you have. You have a rational mind. It's black and white to you, isn't it? I'm sure in nursing school they touched on it for you to learn. People today are black-and-white people like you, Alice. They only see the supernatural on television. Nothing bad happens to them. People don't believe in the devil today. People live, and people die. It's been that way for a long time, hasn't it? For you see, Alice, there is a God and there is a devil, and we're here in the middle. If we can't explain it away, it probably didn't happen. Now tell us, Alice, about your bed shaking, from the beginning will you?"

Alice sat there a while, silent. She couldn't believe what she was hearing. Bill and John waited and watched her. Alice just shook her head back and forth slowly. They told her their story again. Finally, Alice thought to herself, *Why not? I have nothing to lose.* So she explained everything from the time she was last there to the present. John looked at Bill. Their eyes met. They were thinking the same thing. Alice wondered what they were thinking, and it made her a little nervous.

John then said, "We do believe you, Alice, and we're glad you did tell us. I have known Bill for a long time now. Bill worked on the Milwaukee police force as a detective for a lot of years. He has handled ritual killers before. He worked with the best and handled the worst you can think of. Your case, Alice, is one in a million. We are not talking just flesh and blood, dear. The Catholic Church is interested in your case, so think hard, Alice. Your life is in the balance. You see, a normal ritual killer makes lots of mistakes. Your brother doesn't. Mental illness is behind most of it, but not your brother's actions. He has made a choice. Your bed shaking is an example. The mental tests you passed are another example. The physical you had is another. But your bed shakes all by itself, and you pass out when you see an evil book. Explain that to us, and let us help you. Please, I'm pleading with you."

She was confused by all of this. How could an everyday person like herself be involved in something this strange? She thought a moment and said, "So what's your next move, Bill? I hope it's not as weird as what you're telling me."

He thought for a moment and said, "Yes, maybe for you, but when you get your answer, it won't be such a surprise." He picked up his cell and called Bishop Mark Frazer. When the conversation was over, he said, "Bring the book. We're going to see the bishop."

Alice was shocked by this. She wanted to say something but couldn't.

They reached the church offices and started to the office door. Alice was quieter now than she had been in the car. She was still finding it hard to believe all of this. Bill and John just kept saying to her, "Trust us, and you will see for yourself."

They walked down the hallways until they reached the bishop's office door.

Alice said, "I hope you two are right about this, because I think you two are working too hard."

The secretary recognized Bill, and they went straight into the bishop's personal office. They opened the door and entered, as the bishop was just rounding his desk.

The bishop saw Bill and said, "Bill, glad you could make it so fast." He turned and greeted John with a handshake. Then he noticed Alice. He stepped over and greeted her. "And what's your name, young lady?"

Alice responded, "Alice Johnson, Bishop Frazer."

Bishop Frazer then saw that John was carrying a package. "You have it, don't you?" He turned to Bill, amazed to find it so fast. "Why didn't you call when you found it?"

"That's partly the reason why we're here today, Bishop, but the other reason is Alice. John and I both believe that she is under attack from her brother's demons," stated Bill to answer his question.

Bishop Frazer turned and walked slowly around his desk. He sat down and looked up at Bill with concern on his face. "Let me guess—that book is attacking Alice here from an incantation her brother put on her."

Bill turned and looked at Alice and John and then back at the bishop. He studied the man's face for a second and said, "Yes, sir, and if you want to see for yourself, open the package, please."

Bishop Mark Frazer had studied the occult most of his years in the church. He had seen different effects on different people. His experience with the occult led him to be cautious when opening the package in front of him. He carefully unwrapped the package and then spotted the name of the book. "*Black Passages!*" he said out loud. There was shock on his face at the sight in front of him. "I'll gladly pay whatever price you paid for it right now!" said a shocked bishop.

"Mark, please hold the book up so Alice can clearly see it," requested Bill, knowing what would happen.

Cautiously, John held it up, and Alice quickly passed out. A sudden wind blew hard, and half the books on the shelf next to John fell on the floor. The men in the room were shocked by what had just happened. Bill knelt down and pulled smelling salts out of his pocket. He waved them under her nose until she slowly came to again. Bishop Frazer quickly covered the book, so as not to have another incident. He then quickly joined Bill and John in easing Alice into a chair.

Alice's fogginess cleared slowly, and she saw Bishop Frazer studying her closely. As she looked around at everybody with her, she noticed the books on the floor. "Did I do all of this? I don't remember anything," Alice asked slowly, confused.

The bishop turned, poured Alice a glass of water from a pitcher on the desk, and offered it to her. She drank slowly, still amazed at what she saw. The secretary entered the room and was shocked at all the books on the floor.

"What happened in here, sir? I heard a strong wind, and then I heard books hitting the floor," said a startled secretary, looking at the books on the floor.

The bishop slowly walked up to her and whispered something in her ear. She nodded, agreeing slowly to what he said, and left. The bishop returned to his chair and sat down slowly. He looked at the covered book in front of him. Then he lifted his eyes to the three on the other side of his desk. He nodded his head as he decided what to do with this problem in front of him. He sat quietly in his chair, now drawing on his experience, choosing his words carefully.

Bill interrupted suddenly, "Sir, I didn't know all of this would happen here, like this. The first time, she just passed out in front of us."

The bishop nodded and waved his right hand, telling them not to worry about it. Bill, John, and Alice looked at each other and wondered what he was about to say to them. The bishop leaned forward and rested on his desk. He said with much concern in his voice, "Bill, you were right in bringing her here today." He paused and said to Alice, "You are in grave danger, my dear. The power against you is growing much stronger by the hour. Your brother is trying to kill you with the power of demons. Dear, it would look like an accident, but you would be killed by the devil himself. Based on my many years of serving the church and studying the occult, I believe you are in serious, grave danger, dear! If you don't agree with Bill after this, that's your business. But before you leave here today, with all my power, will, and the grace of God, I will set you free of this."

Alice leaned back in her chair, trying to absorb all of it. Were Bill and John really right? "Are you saying, sir, that my brother sent the devil to kill me? Did I hear you correctly?" asked Alice, disbelief in her voice. She sat there a minute in the chair, quiet. The three men patiently waited for her next question. They looked at each other and wondered. Suddenly, she started sobbing in a painful way. John tried to console her as she cried. They felt her pain inside themselves, but there was nothing they could do for her. After several minutes, she slowly regained her composure. The bishop offered her a tissue to wipe the tears away. "I'm sorry, Bishop, and everybody. I know you're right, but I'm finding it so hard to believe it myself. I never thought of my brother this way. I never thought he would turn into this or be this evil," answered Alice, her voice breaking some.

"You're very brave, dear. Most people right now in your place would just leave, but not you. You have a good mind and a strong heart for what is right and true," added the bishop, smiling some as he looked at them.

Bill then asked the bishop for advice. "What do you plan to do next, Mark?"

Bishop Frazer got up from his chair and walked around his desk to join them. "We are going to the church now, friends. It should be ready for us at this minute. Then I'm going to do a blessing to rid you of the demons around you and a blessing especially for you, Alice," stated Bishop Frazer with authority.

They left his personal office and walked into the waiting room. The secretary said, "It's ready."

The bishop nodded to her. Two men they passed in the hallway walked into his office.

Bishop Frazer said, "They're here to clean up the mess."

The hallway was long with several turns along the way. They stepped outside and walked the distance to the church. They entered through the rear side door at the back of the church. Bishop Frazer quickly noticed that everything was indeed ready for them.

"Bill, John, each one of you, take one of those large containers of holy water," commanded the bishop, getting into his proper gown. Everybody followed the bishop single file out of the room and into the altar area. The bishop suggested that they place the holy water on the altar and then stand six feet in front of it. Bill, John, and Alice looked at each other, not sure what was going to happen. The church inside was large, and the lamps hung from the ceiling on long chains. This was an old church, but it was in excellent condition.

The stained-glass windows are beautiful, Alice thought.

The bishop opened the book, paged to what he wanted, and started a blessing over the water on the altar. It was in Latin, and John understood some of it. When finished with the blessing, he walked in front of the altar and knelt before the cross of Jesus. Then he got up and turned his attention to

Bill and John. He told them to join him on his right and then whispered to them to do something he wanted at the right time.

Alice stood there quietly, but she was nervous, not sure what was next. Alice never had been much of a churchgoer in her life. She believed in God but never attended church much.

The bishop turned his attention to Alice. "This will now be a deliverance from evil demons attacking you, Alice," stated Bishop Frazer with authority.

Bill and John looked at each for a moment, and then Bill walked over and picked up one of the two jars of holy water. Then he slowly walked to the right of the bishop. Suddenly, Bishop Frazer spoke in Latin, holding his arms slightly above his head in a blessing over Alice. Alice started to feel sick to her stomach but stood there trying to listen to him. She held her stomach, feeling sicker; they heard a soft growling in the church. Alice heard it too, even though she felt sick to her stomach.

Bill and John looked at each other, and it was getting louder. It was easy to hear it. The bishop spoke more loudly and with greater authority in Latin. The growling got louder. Any doubt in Alice's mind was now gone. Now she felt really sick, and she could hear the growling above her. As this continued, the bishop's voice rose higher and he spoke with even greater authority, until at the back of the church, where one would normally enter, the doors started to shake. Alice could hear it behind her. Bill and John turned to look at each other, and they didn't know what to think. Bill had seen many strange things in his life but never this. After what seemed like several minutes, the doors began to shake violently. Alice was now really stricken. She began to bow forward, grabbing her stomach. She started to cry again from the pain inside her. It was intense now, but the bishop continued with even greater authority and his voice rose higher. The growling was very loud, almost deafening, and finally, Alice collapsed on the floor.

"Bill, the holy water!" demanded Bishop Frazer.

Bill quickly gave him the container, and he poured it all over Alice, who was on her back on the floor. Now, the growling was painful to the ears. The lamps hanging from the ceiling were swaying back and forth. The doors were shaking so violently by then they were about to come off the hinges. With that done, the bishop gave the container back to Bill and continued his prayer with even greater authority. Finally, a dark mist appeared above Alice, and it quickly went for the doors. The doors flew open with a loud crash. Bill and John stood there, not believing what they saw, and stared at each other in awe. But Bishop Frazer was not done yet. He turned and told Bill to get the other holy water. Bill told John to pick it up, for he was next it. John picked it up, and they passed it to Bishop Frazer. The church was quiet now, like it had been before. He started over again, for another ten minutes, but all was quiet. He finally lowered his arms and just stood there and watched Alice lying on the floor. Slowly, he walked over to her, and Bill and John followed. They rolled Alice onto her back carefully, and the bishop said another blessing over her in Latin. With the three of them kneeling over her, she slowly regained consciousness. She wondered why she was wet. They explained all that had happened to them and to her, while she was unconscious.

"How do you feel now, Alice, since you have been cleansed of all evil influences around you?" asked Bishop Frazer.

Now the cleansing part was over? She was lying there and

looking at each one of them. She said, "You know, somehow, I feel better than I have for a long time. I only wish I was drier than I am now," responded Alice, a smile breaking on her lips.

They helped her to her feet, John now wondering to himself, *Why the extra time over her?* He asked, as they again walked up to the altar, "Bishop, why the extra prayer time over her, when she was unconscious?"

The bishop answered, as he went behind the altar, "When dealing with something evil, you have to be sure it's really gone."

He then asked Alice to stand in front of the altar and Bill and John off to the side. He said to Alice, "Now, Alice, please answer the questions of confession of faith with, I do, and then we will proceed."

The bishop then asked a series of questions, and she said, "I do," to all of them.

The bishop just smiled widely and proudly and said happily, "Alice, you are now a child of the living God. Congratulations, Alice." And then he added, "The devil can still tempt you, my dear, but you and God's Spirit are always greater than Satan's power. Always remember that, my dear."

Alice stood there smiling proudly as Bill and John gave her a hug. The bishop came around and hugged her as well. "Now, Alice, all we have left is your special blessing, and we're finished here today. Are you ready, Alice?"

"Yes, Bishop, I'm ready," replied Alice happily to everyone there.

The bishop performed the blessing on Alice, and Bill and John, as before, witnessed it.

Two women came up from behind them to clean up the water on the floor.

John nodded to them as they started to mop. He asked, "What's with the other holy water?"

The bishop turned as he was leading them off the altar floor. "Oh, that's just in case, John; there could have been more than one dark spirit in her."

They left the altar, and Bill picked up the containers as they went to the room in the back. Once they were finished there, they again walked back to the bishop's office. Bill, thinking of what had just happened back there in the church, asked Bishop Frazer, "Mark, did Alice really have a devil inside her or around her?"

The bishop, understanding the question, glanced at Bill as they walked back to his office. "Good question, Bill. You were watching, I see. They were around her, Bill, not in her. When I poured the holy water on her, it fell on the demons. They were very strong around her, and the dark mist you saw rise from her was the main one; he's the real bad guy. What saved Alice here in this was the minimum amount of faith she had in God. And that's what really saved her in this picture. I could get more into this, but to keep it simple, she had some faith but not enough to save her from this, for what is God's is God's and what is the devil's is the devil's."

Bill nodded approvingly to the answer he received from the bishop. They returned to the office building from where they had first started and entered. They stopped by a closed door. The bishop entered and quickly returned with a large towel. He gave it to Alice to wrap up in, and then they continued back to his office. They were talking among themselves on the way back. Single file, they entered his personal office. Alice sat in her chair there, Bill and John at her side. The bishop walked around his desk and then sat down. After he made himself comfortable in his chair, he reached down to the right side. He opened the bottom drawer, pulled out a small booklet, and closed the drawer. Then the bishop gave the booklet to Alice and said nicely, "This is for you, Alice. Do read it carefully. This has information on your new life in Christ. Draw close to him. You're not Catholic yet, but you're a real Christian."

John was curious about that evil book on his desk, if it would bother Alice anymore. John asked the bishop, "Bishop, would you please lift that book up? I want to see if there is any more effect on her."

The bishop a little surprised by his request, lifted up the evil book and showed Alice once more. There was no effect on her at all. Bill noticed that all the books that were once on the floor were again back on the shelf.

The bishop, a little unnerved by John's request, thought about paying them for the book. He opened the top drawer and pulled out his checkbook to pay for it. Bill noticed the checkbook on Mark's desk and said, "Sir, please make that out for John Cleveland."

The bishop glanced up at Bill and said, "I'm glad you mentioned that. I almost started to make it out in your name." With the check written out, he reached over the desk and handed it over to John, who was happy to receive it.

Bill was thinking he had better say something now or it could be too late. "Bishop, the book is yours now, but we would like to have access to it for possible police evidence. We know of one killing in Chicago, and another will soon happen because of that book. We need your word, if the police ask any questions?"

The bishop studied Bill for a second and put the checkbook

away. He pondered the question and said, "You're absolutely correct, Bill, in saying that. I shouldn't get ahead of myself. You say, Bill, there could be a second murder, so soon?"

Bill quickly responded, "Yes, sir, our sources, who are close to them, tell us that there will be a second ritual killing as soon as things quiet down for them."

The bishop shook his head in disbelief and said with a little pain in his voice, "Remember what I said earlier when we met here, when you were just asking questions? A book like this in the wrong hands, the damage it could do to us? Then let's pray he doesn't go to the Web."

Bill quickly said, "Yes, you did, sir, and we also know, and you agree, we only have six weeks to stop them."

The bishop leaned back in his chair and pondered a second. "Halloween, isn't it, Bill?"

The four of them all knew that it was a big celebration for a lot of occult activities. There was moment of silence in the room, and then Alice spoke up. "If there is anything else here that should be said, I would like some dry clothes."

Everyone chuckled and agreed with that. The bishop added, "Give it to Bill or John there when you're finished with it. I know it will be returned."

They all shook hands and left politely. The traffic was increasing on their way back to Bill's office. Alice and Bill talked at her car for several minutes and said their good-byes. John stood next to Bill's car and wondered what they were talking about. Bill returned to John, as Alice pulled away onto the street, and watched her drive away.

"We saw a lot today, Bill, didn't we?" stated John as he watched Alice drive away.

"Yes, we did, John, and more than I thought at that," added Bill, now thinking of something else.

The two men made their way back to Bill's office on the next floor. They spoke little in the elevator. Finally, the door opened, and they returned to Bill's office.

ADAM JOHNSON WAS ON THE TRADING FLOOR, AND HE
was busy. A lot of business was going through his hands
that day. After an hour or two in the morning, he could
tell how the day usually would go after. Adam was at the moment making some big sales for other people he had receipts
for. The day was going right for him. He had his right arm up
and had made a sale. Suddenly, a very sharp pain stabbed his
lower abdomen and made him double over. He grabbed his
stomach quickly, for the pain was great. He tried to straighten
up slowly and looked down at his right hand—blood! It was
also on his other hand as well when he lifted it off his stomach. Slightly bent over from the pain, he kept his hands on
his stomach and quickly ran off the trading floor and into a
nearby restroom. Some of the traders noticed him as he ran
off. It was unusual for Adam to be off the floor at this time
in the late morning. The restroom he went to had no one in
it at the time. The blood was covering his shirt on his lower
abdomen. He pulled the shirt out of his pants and unbuttoned
it. He reached for some paper towels and ran some water over
them. He started to clean up with the wet towels. He cursed
profusely because of the pain. When he cleaned up the blood

and tried to make the bleeding stop with the cold water, he noticed three deep scratch marks across his lower abdomen. They went horizontally above his belt line. Adam couldn't imagine what had caused them. In pain and not knowing what had just happened to him, he looked up at the lights and gritted his teeth. He looked down at his abdomen and saw he was still bleeding. He reached for more paper towels and wet them. He reached into his pants pocket and pulled out his cell phone. He dialed his manager to come to the restroom.

After three long minutes, the manager joined him there. He was roughly the same age as Adam and about the same height. He took one look at Adam and said, "What on earth happened to you, Adam?" He saw the wounds on Adam's abdomen and noted the amount of blood.

"I'm fine. I'm fine. It was just a nasty accident I had with some equipment!" answered Adam, trying to brush it off as nothing.

Not happy with the answer he received, he sharply replied, "You must have been swirling around out there on the floor with someone holding a rusty nail to you!"

Adam, knowing he didn't buy his story, thought quickly and replied with some sharpness, "I tell you I fucked up, man. I was careless in the pushing and shoving, and I cut myself a number of times!"

The manager, knowing he wasn't going to get anything from Adam, stated, "You better go home for the day and heal up for tomorrow morning. Give me your slips for today's trading."

After handing over the slips, Adam braced himself against the sink and looked in the mirror. He saw the manager shaking his head as he left the restroom. He was now thinking to himself, *I'll hear about it tomorrow morning for sure.* He knew he couldn't work like this; his jacket couldn't hide everything. He was still bleeding some yet. It would eventually go through his jacket.

Since the paper towel was soaked, he stopped the bleeding the best he could for the time being and tucked his shirt into his pants again. He wrapped paper towels around himself a couple of times, trying to hide the blood. He knew he would look funny to anyone who saw him—at least they wouldn't see the blood. He left the restroom and got some quick looks from many of his colleagues, until he put his jacket on and left the building. Back at his car, he got in, closed the door, and found his keys. He stopped suddenly. *What the hell happened in there today?* he pondered to himself. *I better pray to Satan for knowledge.* He started the car and left, a little shaken by what had just happened to him. He headed for his apartment, only half his attention on his driving, but he made his way home safely.

Later, Alice Johnson returned safely home as well. She removed her wet clothing and quickly washed it. She had a stereo playing softly in the background, but her mind was on what had happened that morning. How did Bill and John know she needed that kind of help? What happened to her was like something on television. She heard the bishop say to Bill that the evil spirits were around her but not in her. Because of Adam, in a day or two, she would probably have been dead. Was her brother that twisted now? And would he really do this to her too? She pondered these questions quietly to herself, but after several hours, the answer was the same every time—yes! Her reasoning was if someone chased her, she would know it, or if someone got in her face suddenly and she ran away, she would know it. This was perfect; this was supposed to look like an accident and raise no questions. *But why kill me?* She felt sorry for her brother at that time. For so many years together growing up, they were each other's best friend. Each trusted the other and in so many different ways! She remembered her dad and mom, after they died in a car accident, how close she and Adam were and how they watched out for one another. Even after they grew up and went to different jobs and different cities to work, they were always close to each other. Who were these rotten people he worked with, who twisted her brother so badly in the first place? This thought made her angry every time it crossed her mind.

Well, I made some new friends today, she thought, *and some real good ones too.* She was thinking of an old movie she had seen on television. It said something about love always being greater than hate, but she couldn't think of the words. She had to work the following afternoon. She remembered what Bill had said at the car, that she'd need two days off so they could see her brother up north. So she picked up the phone and called work. They were just making out the schedule on her floor. Quickly, she requested two days off in a row. "For a family matter," she told the person on the phone.

After a couple of minutes of waiting on the line, she was cleared to have those days off, but she had to work the grave-yard shift to get them. She thanked the nurse on the phone and hung up; she then wrote that week's schedule on the calendar.

She called Bill on the phone and passed the word along to him.

Bill said, "That will be very good," because it was late enough in the week to arrange work there for him. After a few other things, Alice told Bill she was stopping by to pay him for his time to the present, to keep everything fair and right with the books. When Bill finished talking to her, they hung up. Alice went to change to go to the bank and Bill's.

Bill and John had just entered the office. Bill quickly made a fresh pot of coffee, and John made himself at home in his chair.

John suddenly stated, "You know, since I retired from my position, I've seen movies with something like that on television but never in real life, Bill, never."

Bill glanced at John as he picked the coffeepot up. "You're right, John. We saw more in one hour than we would normally see in our whole lives," Bill replied with wonder, shaking his head. His voice was rising in tone. He made his way to his chair and sat down, John casually watching him.

"Why didn't you tell me that Mark did that sort of thing?" John asked, with interest in his voice.

Bill searched for an answer to the question and found one in his memory. "Well, first, I thought you knew that. And second, Mark made me promise not to ever talk about it to anyone."

John quickly added, "But we often work together, and you never said anything to me."

Bill suspected this was a sensitive subject and decided to

handle it with care. "Sometimes, it's important to talk about it at the time and not before. Your job has the same rules," he responded as gently as he could.

John sat there thinking it over, just hashing it over, but not liking the answer. John was remembering all the times on the college staff when he had been told not to say anything to anyone about important issues. Now, he had just heard it from Bill on something similar. He knew he was right, but he didn't like it.

Bill gently added, "Like I said, I thought you already knew, John."

John could see clearly that he wasn't bluffing about this and decided to let it slide. He didn't want to make it into something it wasn't. "All right, Bill, but please do a better job of letting me know," John stated, upset.

Bill thought he had better clarify his dealings with the bishop.

"John, the bishop is the main person working for the church region of Wisconsin, doing exorcisms. He also does church studies on all occult activities in the state and area. That's why he studies occult subjects as much as he does. His job there is secret in nature and kept from the everyday public, like you and me, so when he tells me not to talk, I listen."

John could understand Bill's position better and why he wasn't totally informed about this person. "So I see, Bill. It wasn't that you didn't trust me; it was more secret in nature from the beginning. If I was in your position, I would probably have done the same as well," responded John, with a bit of relief in his voice.

Bill nodded his head, showing his approval in the matter. There was a moment of silence in the office, as Bill slowly rose from his chair and set up for coffee and sandwiches. John was still a little quiet yet about the matter but was returning to his usual self.

Bill was thinking to himself, *A matter this big proves who your friends are in life—if handled correctly from the beginning.*

John was thinking something similar.

They each helped themselves to sandwiches, and peace filled the room again. After some time of enjoying themselves, John said, "Do you want to see that information you wanted?"

"Yes, John. Why not? We have plenty of time," responded Bill. He finished his coffee.

John sipped his coffee quickly and set it on the desk. He left to get his computer. Meanwhile, Bill cleared a spot on his desk so they both could watch easily. John returned in about five minutes with his computer and the camcorder as well. Bill had already moved his chair in front of the desk. Together, they watched the computer, as John explained the details of what had been recorded. John's recordings were just about finished when Bill's cell phone rang. John quickly stopped the computer; it was Alice on the phone. They talked in detail about her schedule at work, and she made a full payment to Bill. Before she hung up, Alice told him that she would be there in about an hour. Bill then hung up, and he and John continued with the computer. When they finished with the computer and closed the laptop, John pulled his recorder out of his pocket and set it on the desk. He turned it on.

It was Kathy's and John's voices on the recorder. As it played, John filled Bill in if there was a question. Bill was going over John's notes as it played. Bill nodded, approving of the work done for him. Almost an hour went by as they listened to Kathy's interview.

Alice knocked and entered Bill's office.

"What's happening here?" Alice questioned.

John saw the confusion on her face and explained, "We are going over evidence of your brother's activities in Chicago."

Bill, hearing John explaining a little more than he should, then added, "Ah yes, that's correct, but if you want to hear of your brother's activities, it's on the recorder on the desk."

John started the recorder where they had left off, and Alice listened to Kathy's voice. As she listened to several questions being asked, her expression changed and some hurt appeared on her face. John took the recorder from her hand and turned it off.

"You were right from the beginning about my brother; it's really true," Alice responded with some pain in her voice.

Bill added, "It's a terrible thing when someone you love deeply goes bad. Perhaps you would care to tell us of any weakness you know of in him. But the hurt you feel inside lasts a long time and is slow to go away."

Alice nodded, agreeing with what Bill said. John offered her a seat.

There was a moment of silence in the office. Bill broke the icy silence by stating, "I believe you have some days off next week that we can work with?"

Alice nodded slowly. Inside, she was pushing the hurt aside and moving on. "I made out my schedule of my days off next week. Will they work for us?" asked Alice as she gave the paper to Bill.

Bill opened the top drawer of his desk and pulled out a folder. He opened it and studied his schedule closely. He was busy through Wednesday. He again looked at Alice and remarked happily, "Yes, Alice, Thursday and Friday are fine with me."

A faint smile appeared on Alice's face again, and she added, "We can leave Wednesday morning if you want?"

Bill indicated that he couldn't and said, "I have a case Wednesday night, and then I'm done." He then continued by explaining his case Wednesday night. The two hashed it out and finally agreed that when Bill finished his case on Wednesday night, he was to call Alice and John and they would meet him at his office. Then, they would all drive up north. Thursday morning was the time set for an appointment with her older brother. Bill really didn't like it at all, but then he again looked at her schedule; she had the graveyard shift Friday night into Saturday. "All right, we can do it that way if you want, but you're driving up there into the night. And John and I are sleeping along the way to your brother's place. We will need our rest too," said Bill, with some concern about Alice and her rest as well.

Alice, seeing that it was settled, picked up her purse and quickly opened it. She pulled out some money. "I would like to settle up with you today, Bill, and we can start fresh again," answered Alice, feeling confident in herself.

Bill reached into another drawer and pulled out her file, the one he had taken out of the filing cabinet earlier. He told her the amount, and she paid him cash. In her file, he marked "paid" and dated it for record keeping. He opened another drawer and pulled out a metal box. He put the money inside, locked it, and put it away. With that done, he leaned back into his chair and then stated carefully, "From this point on, Alice, when something comes up on your case and we work on it, you will be charged for it. You understand? I don't mean incoming telephone calls about your case; I mean actual work done on it. We have about six weeks to end this case with your brother. I'm not going to rob you with six weeks' of time. You will now just pay for work done and expenses, okay?"

She thought for a second and nodded approvingly. "That sounds fair to me, and we will stay in touch, will we?"

"Absolutely, count on it, Alice," replied Bill, smiling in a friendly way at her to give her some confidence. Alice rose from her chair, thanked Bill and John for what they had already done, and left quietly. The door closed behind her, and the office was quiet for a second.

They once again made themselves comfortable and looked at each other, wondering who would say it first. Bill looked down at his hands and rubbed them. "Right now, we don't have anything solid, John. My friend at the police station can't get his hands on anything for me at this time. I haven't heard from our informants today yet, so there's nothing. I've been on the computer here, but we need to talk to the bishop. Otherwise, we're at a dead end for right now, and at this moment, I'm out of fresh ideas."

John thought of some possible angles for a second but came up dry. Finally, he said to Bill, "Hard cases like this, with little information, dry up fast, don't they?"

Bill nodded approvingly, as he looked at some hard choices.

Bill then added. "Let's play that recorder again, John, and see if we missed anything on that."

For the next two hours, they listened to it closely.

Finally, Bill rose from his chair and smiled a little as he poured the last of the coffee into his cup. He poured the rest out and turned off the coffeemaker. Bill decided to think out loud. "It's been under our noses all the time, John. All those expensive rifles and ammunition? And who is to deliver them to Park River in northern Wisconsin?" Bill found his cell phone and made a call suddenly; he had an idea. He was calling Kathy and then Amy, and he was just leaving a message on their phones.

John just sat there watching as Bill busied himself with calls. When finished calling, he put the phone down. Bill smiled to himself and paced the floor, looking at other ideas, some of which could get him in trouble and others that were just not that good. "John, you may be going back to Chicago soon and to Kathy's place. If the information is good enough, I want you to find the location of those rifles. Then we will go there again and tag them with locaters so we can track them to the square foot!" explained Bill carefully, walking back and forth.

John, not sure what good that would do, then said, "What good is that, Bill? We'll be out of range most of the time. It may only be good if we're on the property of Adam's place." As John finished saying that, he saw the idea of it. "You mean we may be going to Adam's place to find those rifles?" He now saw that would be evidence as well.

Bill nodded and said, "Yes, permits and who sold them—you'll need permits for all of that. We'll need to see if he has that. No average man can do that at one time without permits. We'll have to go there, John, and see. Adam might have bought them all underground from a gunrunner there, and maybe the police there don't have a clue of it either. By putting a locater on them when we are up north, maybe it will be possible to break in and get a better look," said Bill, now going over some of the details in his head.

John could understand what he was thinking, and most of it made sense.

No average person could just go downtown and buy that much at one time. Too many people would raise eyebrows and ask questions. A gunrunner made sense to him. This was what they did all the time, and as long as you paid cash and kept your mouth shut, no problem. Being at Adam's place, that was another. This would possibly mean night work and silent alarms or dogs. He didn't know what Bill was thinking on that subject, but he was thinking something. John asked, "At Adam's place there, how are we going to find the basement and not be seen in it?"

Bill stopped pacing the floor and said after some thinking, "We are going to play the whole thing by ear. Adam is too smart for something usual in this case. There are only two real ways to do this. We let Alice show us when we go there next week, or we go there first and find it ourselves."

John quickly added, for he wanted to hear it for himself, "If we go there first, then what about possible dogs or silent alarms, like most wealthy people have?"

Bill was still thinking over his first plan, the one that John described, and then answered, "First, we use the locator, and if they're there, then there has to be a back door. I also think, if possible, we will use the heat device, to see if he has some other underground cellar and where. And if it is in the house, there has to be a back door with a lock to pick. It's smart to test it first for electrical alarms."

"That's great, Bill, but what about dogs?" remarked John.

Bill laughed a little about that and said, "A little sleepy meat will do for that!"

John laughed to himself; he just then remembered another time they had put dogs to sleep for a couple of hours. Then John checked the box to see if there were any more sandwiches in it. John didn't ask Bill about plan B; that was all play it by ear there, and he knew that.

Bill returned and sat down in his chair. He turned his laptop computer on and decided to check if Adam had permits for what he had bought. John, seeing he was working now, decided to call it a day. "Hey, Bill, I think I'll call it a day then," said John, rising from his chair and giving a weak wave.

"Sure thing, John. See you tomorrow then," replied Bill as he glanced at John.

Bill spent hours on his laptop computer and looked up many things he needed to know about Adam Johnson. He made careful notes on anything he found that would help him. The thing was Adam didn't start a church for his group of followers. Bill knew, in rare cases, that they filed for a license with the state and made it legal. Bill also noticed that he didn't file as a militia, even with that many rifles and that much ammunition. Bill then searched the police records for known gunrunners in Chicago and Milwaukee. On that, he found only a few, and with that information, he made careful notes on them. And the last thing for the day, he checked for all warehouses that were close to their location and found five. Bill knew he better quit for the day. He had to work late that night on something else, and he decided to take a quick nap for it.

When Bill woke up after his nap, he went to the restroom down the hallway to freshen up for the night. He readied everything and carefully put his equipment in his travel bag. He was about to leave when his phone rang. It was Amy on the line. They talked for about ten minutes. She had great information for him. Bill hurried to make as many notes as he could when they hung up. It was about the movement of the rifles and some of the next ritual. Bill finished his notes and smiled about some of the information he had been looking at earlier. He started to leave and was about to lock up his office when the phone rang again. This time, it was Kathy, and she shared pretty much said the same information as Amy did. But Kathy had something else to share with Bill, and that was there at Park River. She stated on the phone that Clifford had told her the shipment was to his house property and he was to keep the shipment there. When they finally hung up, he had to stop and wonder to himself. That church cellar had to be big for that many members. Could it be that there was another passage in or out? The next morning, Bill arrived late at his office, and John was waiting for him. They both went in together, and as usual, Bill did his routine before they really got into talking.

They both made themselves comfortable with their coffee and sandwiches.

"Any word from our informants yesterday, Bill?" opened John.

Bill had to wait a second, because he was chewing his sandwich. "Yes, John; in fact, they both called yesterday! From what they said last night—Kathy was clearer on it than Amy—the rifles and stuff are at a member's garage right now. You see, Amy heard part of it from a few in the restroom at the exchange. And Kathy heard it at work also, when Clifford and Adam were talking about it at the end of the day, and they were moving them very soon. And with that, at this time, John, I don't think you need to go to Chicago."

John felt a little relief at that news, for he hated all that downtown traffic.

After a moment of silence, Bill then added, "But, John,

you're going up north and staking out Adam's place, and if possible, tag those rifles. I really think it will be done at night for best cover."

"You want them tagged, don't you, Bill?" answered John quickly. He looked a little surprised.

"Yes, John, and for only one reason, Kathy and Amy both said that there is an underground church up there, and we need to find it. Then we can plan from there and figure our attack with some leverage in mind," stated Bill as carefully as possible, so as not to upset John.

John looked for another roll to eat and found one that looked good. He was now thinking to himself that it had been a long time since he had been up north. A change of scenery would be nice, and this job wasn't hard, just a lot of waiting and timing. John knew that Bill had been booked every night for some time and was into the near future. "Well, that sounds good to me, Bill. I hope you have directions. You know I get lost fairly easy up north," said John, joking a little.

"I know, John. Just watch out for those big mosquitos they have there; they can drain you in five minutes if you're not careful," answered Bill, starting to laugh a little with that reply.

The rest of the morning was quiet for Bill. Later in the afternoon, the phone on Bill's desk rang. With that call, Bill had a new client to deal with. This client was charged with murder but claimed she didn't do it. She claimed her boyfriend did kill that person. The client also claimed she was being framed, because they were breaking up and he was upset with her. When they hung up, Bill knew he would start that one in the morning. Most of those only took two or three days to solve, because it was done in haste and not well thought out. But Bill did make a call to the police station and checked with Tom, a friend of his, for further information on it, just to compare notes. It was later in the afternoon when Amy called again. She informed Bill the rifles were to be moved on Saturday morning and early because of the distance. When they hung up, Bill knew that John had better be there Friday night, for safety. Bill then called John and told him about the new case. He also told him to come in the afternoon, but he would call first so he knew when he was there. John didn't have anything new to add, so they closed after a few minutes.

It was now late Wednesday morning, and Bill was somewhat drained of energy. He'd gotten into a big fight with a client over his findings on his report. At 2:30 in the morning, the woman's husband was cheating all right, but not with the woman he was reported to be cheating with. After that big fight, her husband fought him over the matter, and it got physical. He didn't want his wife to know that he was having an affair with her best friend. The whole thing was a mess indeed, and he was glad it was over. Bill knew it was a mess from the beginning, but he didn't know it would end so badly.

He did his usual routine and had just finished sorting the mail for the day when John came in. John was in a perky mood this morning and was looking forward to a long ride up north. Bill, however, just wanted some hot coffee. When they finally made themselves comfortable, John then really noticed Bill for the first time.

"Bill, what happened to you last night?" asked John, noticing some red marks on his face.

Bill carefully drank his coffee and then added, "Don't worry; I didn't hurt the truck." He then quickly told his story to John about early that morning and how it ended. John chuckled out loud a little and shook his head as he sipped his coffee.

"I hope you won that one, Bill," responded John, as he was reaching into the box of rolls.

"I sure did, my friend, and I bet he feels worse than I do this morning!" said Bill, a little upset by that remark as he also reached into the box of rolls.

Then John added, joking, "I hope you got paid for that, as well?"

Bill, feeling a little irritation under the skin with that remark, then said, "It's in my pocket yet, if you want to see, and I have the paperwork as well completed."

John was sensing Bill's irritation from the previous night; he thought of something different to talk about. John was thinking how the murder case went or if it was still going. "Bill, is your new client finished or still going yet?"

Bill, trying to quiet his mind from the previous night, slowly answered, "I finished it yesterday afternoon. The client did murder that person; the evidence clearly showed it was her. And I made her finally admit to it. The boyfriend's alibi proved to be correct and solid. I gave her to Tom to book and put a feather in his hat."

After an hour, John left Bill's office and went home. He got things ready for that night's trip up north. Bill did some bookkeeping and saw he had a good week. Slowly, Bill made some notes for Thursday with Adam and then worked on getting his gear together, including an extra night camera and a listening dish, just in case. Bill was planning for the worst and something extra if the opportunity presented itself. The phone rang, and he answered. After a few minutes, he had a new client, but he was careful to note that he couldn't start until Saturday morning. That was fine with the client. After he gave the client all the details of how he worked, they closed and hung up together. Bill smiled to himself; he liked this kind of client. He was to be on a mystery hunt and find lost papers for his client. This could take some time and effort. It all depended on what he learned and how fast. After a few minutes and proper filing of the new case, he went back to packing his gear. When he was finished with that, he turned on the laptop computer and went over John's pictures of Adam's apartment. He spent extra time with Adam's worship room. The room was largely empty but very black and oddly dark inside. Bill wondered about the altar; it was covered with a black cloth that extended over the sides halfway down the legs. Bill had been wondering for some time now about the ritual dagger that killed that little girl. His information from the coroner in Chicago didn't leave him much at all, other than it was that type of dagger. He knew that he didn't say much to John about it, because any one of the thirty-seven members could have it. Who and where did one ask or look? It could have been one of the leaders in the group or Adam himself. Right then, he had two informants working on it but no leads as yet. This would be great evidence for him, and those fingerprints would tie it up. Bill nodded his head, wondering about Adam. *This man is good, real good.* Bill loved a good mystery to solve; now he had a real one.

Bill picked up his phone and called a distant friend, who was a PI like Bill. His friend answered. They talked for many minutes about the past and the good times. Finally, he got to the point. He wondered why he had called. Bill explained his case a little to his friend there and wondered what the police had come up with yet and about the dagger. Nothing at all had been done so far. A special group was set up and was looking into it. Bill asked about any leads or hints his friend had heard and got nothing. All he said was, "You're on a tough one," and hung up. Bill turned off his phone, leaned back in his chair, and thought.

He ran his fingers through his hair and wondered, *Why can't I get any leads?*

Bill ran his fingers through his hair again and had an idea. *When we get back from up north or when we are there, bug it.* Adam's apartment needed to be bugged as well. Bill knew this type of evidence had some legal costs to it; breaking into an apartment to do it took some explaining—mostly with the Constitutional right to privacy and then other laws that went with it. The evidence would be no help in court. The support of the police department on this would be a big help, but with the lack of evidence, that would be a zero. Then Bill thought of a transmitter in the apartment to Amy's or Kathy's apartment. It should be short range and high frequency so it was not listened to by anyone else. It could then be attached to a re-corder, and he could mark important points of it. Bill thought a second. *Damn it. That's big bucks to buy. They just don't give that away.* So he just sat there thinking. The minutes passed by, and then it hit him. He would make it! Then he thought of who could do it. He leaned forward and grabbed his phone. He went through his phone book and called. The phone rang on the other end for some time, and then someone answered.

The mother answered, and Bill responded and said he wanted to talk to Jimmy. After several moments, Jimmy came to the line and said, "Hello?" and Bill introduced himself. Once Jimmy understood it was Bill, they started talking.

Bill knew Jimmy from several years back, when Jimmy

was picked up stealing from electronics stores. Bill arrested Jimmy at a store that the storekeeper had hired him to protect one night. He took the kid aside and talked to him. He asked him why he was doing it. Bill discovered that the kid was a near genius with electronic stuff and could build just about anything. Bill did run him downtown, for booking, but asked the police to give him a break. Jimmy heard that there at the station, for Bill asked for help for troubled teens. This placed Jimmy in an electronics school for troubled teens. Bill and Jimmy talked for some time and renewed their friendship. After a while, Bill explained why he had called and told Jimmy what he wanted. Jimmy explained it would be somewhat expensive to build. Because it was high frequency, the transmitter and receiver must be set together so it would be unlikely for others to listen in. Jimmy also believed he could have it made in ten to fifteen days because he had a lot of equipment and the parts at his house. Bill explained that a range of about ten miles would be good for his needs. Jimmy felt that it would be easy enough to build. Bill told him to be at home around 6:30 p.m. that night and he would give him five hundred dollars to start. Jimmy was happy with that, and they hung up.

Bill leaned back in his chair and smiled a little. He knew he had just saved a lot of money. Jimmy was good, and it would be done right. With that tool in his hands, he could get a better drop on Adam and figure out his business and structure and who was where. There was no word yet on the thirteen women, who were to play their role in the Halloween ritual. So far, they had no names, just thirteen women.

After that thought, Bill took a nap for that night and waited for the phone to ring. Bill woke up and got ready. He went to Jimmy's first and paid and thanked him. He ate and went to his client's where he started another night of work. At 1:15 a.m. Thursday morning, Bill called Alice first and told her to meet him at his office. Then he called John and said the same thing to him. He got back to his office about twenty minutes later, and they were waiting. Bill wanted to take his car for insurance reasons, but John insisted they take his because it was bigger. Alice looked fresh standing there, waiting to see which car they would take. Alice's car was on the small side, Bill's car was in the middle, and John had a full-sized car.

"Alice, can you drive this size car all right?" asked Bill, joking.

"Sure, Bill. It's just a matter of finding everything," stated Alice, with confidence, and she smiled some.

Bill opened the trunk of his car, as John opened the trunk of his. Bill carefully placed his gear in John's car and made another trip to his for more gear. Then he locked it up. The last of the equipment was in his gear bag, which he placed in the trunk of the car. John closed it and gave Alice the keys to the car. He opened the back door and entered. Bill thought to himself, *I like the front anyway.*

Alice made herself comfortable in the driver's seat and looked things over for a second. "Okay, I think I got it now, so let's go, huh, Bill?" said Alice. She smiled at Bill and then John. She backed out of the driveway and onto the street, heading for the main road out of the city and to the interstate. Bill and Alice talked for some time as they made their way. They were still talking when they reached the interstate and left the city. Alice glanced at Bill and said, "You better get some rest, Bill; I can take it from here."

Bill looked for the switch to let the seat back. "You're right, Alice. We have some way to go from here."

Bill found a position that worked for him with the seat. He was leaning way back now. He said to Alice, "I'm glad you're driving tonight, because I'm beat."

Alice glanced at Bill, who was trying to sleep, and said, "I know, Bill; I saw that right away at the office."

Bill nodded to Alice and drifted off to sleep.

With Alice now driving into the night, she glanced at Bill, who was very much asleep. And she knew John was asleep in the backseat. He had begun snoring lightly before they reached the city limits. She drove steadily and without stopping until she reached Park River.

Bill was sleeping fast when something told him the car wasn't moving and he jerked awake. With his left hand, he rubbed both eyes and yawned. *This isn't any place I know of,* he was now thinking. He looked into the backseat and saw John was still asleep. Bill looked at his watch. It was 8:12 a.m., and all he knew was they were at some gas station. Bill looked out the side window and could see that the trees were in full color and this was a smaller city. Looking at the main road that ran into the city, he noted there wasn't that much traffic. He looked again at the front of the gas station. He could make out Alice paying for something and talking to the clerk there. Alice opened the door carefully and was carrying something with both hands as she left. Bill could hear John starting to move around in the backseat. He was starting to wake up. Bill opened his car door and stepped out to help Alice with what she was carrying. As Bill approached Alice, he asked, "Alice, where are we? Is this Park River?"

Alice, a little surprised by the question, shook her head and said, "Bill, this is Park River. I bought some coffee and four egg-cheese-and-sausage biscuits, and I even filled up the car with gas."

Bill stopped suddenly, really surprised by what she had done for them. He asked politely, "Do I owe you anything or partly?"

"No, Bill, this is on me. I'm just glad you're willing to help me like this," said Alice, handing over the coffee to Bill.

Together, they reached the car; they noticed John looking out the window, seeming groggy. Alice and Bill looked at each other and had a small laugh together. They got back into the car, as she gave them their coffee and two biscuits each.

John, wondering what she was going to eat, said, "Aren't you going to eat something too?"

Alice looked in the rearview mirror at John and said, "John, I ate inside the gas station while you were sleeping."

Bill noticed the time and then said to Alice. "We better get going to make our appointment."

Alice, noticing the time, nodded in agreement with Bill. She started the car and pulled out onto the street, heading north through town. John and Bill both thanked Alice for the food and gas, as they continued toward Adam's place. As they drove through town, Bill noticed that the town was nothing like Milwaukee with the buildings and the hustle of that city. This was freer, slower, and simpler, easy to manage.

"Bill, aren't the trees up here just beautiful, with all their colors glowing so brightly?" said Alice, with the glow of wonder in her voice.

Bill nodded and had to agree with that. "You're right, Alice. This is great, and just look at that; it's never this good by us there."

John in the backseat was just taking it in and sipping his coffee. He noticed that she drove two miles north and then turned left to head west on a blacktopped road. "Alice, how far from here to Adam's?" asked John.

"About fifteen miles, John, and it will be on the right side of the road," stated Alice as she looked into the mirror.

The road had small round hills along it. Sometimes, there were open fields on one side or the other. But mostly, it was trees, and they were in full color, for this time of year, the pine trees that were mixed in kind of set off the trees' colors. There were a few houses and one or two small farms along the way, but it was mostly wooded land. Bill, seeing that there were no fences, asked Alice to stop the car for a minute, and she did. Bill and John both ran into the woods until they couldn't be seen from the road. Alice smiled. *Coffee, that stuff does it every time.* Bill and John made their way back to the car and got in.

"Pretty serious, I could see," said Alice, laughing a little as she drove away again.

After ten minutes heading west, she slowed down and pointed at a crossroad. "Here, we're here." She slowed way down and said, "This woods here is my brother's. He has 320 acres of woods. His land is half a section from this road; from that intersection to the next one is a mile, and it's a mile deep to the next. My brother has a road cut into the woods, back there, with a steel gate, and it runs just behind his house, where he lives. He used to hunt deer when he was younger. I don't know if he still does. He doesn't say anymore." As she slowly drove forward, they spotted a clearing on the north side of the road. They went closer. It was a large yard.

"My brother's house, my good friends," stated Alice, pointing toward it. Bill and John were in awe of it. It was a two-story southern-style mansion with black shutters on the windows and huge columns on either side of the front entryway of the house. An old-style chandelier hung above the front door. The yard was huge as well and well taken care of, with a six-car garage on the west side of the asphalt driveway. The two driveways ran down to the house in front of it and back past the garage and then to the road, if one was going west. On top of the house were three satellite dishes pointing up at the sky. All of it was beautiful in size and grandeur and well taken care of. Bill couldn't believe in his heart Adam was throwing it all away.

John just sat in the back, like he was watching a movie or something. Alice took the first driveway in and stopped the car in front of the house. "Alice, that house; it's maybe two million dollars by itself, not counting everything else," stated John, figuring it out in his mind.

They all got out of the car and took a few steps toward the house. Each one was looking at the others and trying to look his or her best before entering. Finally, they walked toward the house and stopped at the front door. Bill rang the doorbell, thinking how grand this house was in size and care. Adam opened the door, greeted them, invited them inside, and closed the door behind them. The foyer they were standing in was tasteful and expensive in design.

Adam could tell the two men were in love with his house. So he went out of his way to show them the front living room to the left. It was a huge room; the walls were something of an eggshell blue, not too dark. There was a large gas-burning fireplace on the opposite wall from them. All the furnishings were very tasteful and nice, with a rich, thick light-colored carpet. "Adam, I'm impressed with your taste, in design and grandeur," stated a taken-in John, beaming with a smile and a pleasant voice.

Bill stood looking around slowly, taking it all in and marveling at the luxury he saw around him. Alice, having been there many times in the past, enjoyed it as well. Adam then led them gently across the foyer and into his office. He closed the door behind them. His office was large in size as well, with off-white walls. There was a leather sofa that could seat four people at a time in front of the large desk. His desk was a dark cherry wood and had two computer monitors on it, two telephones, and many papers. Adam pleasantly asked them to sit down on the sofa, and he walked around his desk and sat as well. Bill quickly noticed that he had everything he needed to run his trades electronically from there and more.

"You're very well set up here to do your work here, Adam," commented Bill, agreeing Adam had an eye for detail.

"Oh yes. Oh, I'm sorry, I didn't catch your name," added Adam, rising from his chair to shake Bill's hand. They shook hands, and both sat down. He introduced himself to John, and they shook hands. He said hello to his sister, smiled, and sat down again.

"You changed your office since I was last here a year ago, Adam," said Alice, carefully looking around as she sat on the sofa with Bill and John.

"Oh yes, Alice. I did with a few floor plants, all new office equipment, a special phone line to work, and a few different pictures on the wall," stated Adam, seeing that she approved of some of his changes. "So how can I help you today?" he asked, starting to show his business side.

Bill, thinking they better get down to business, stated, "I'm Bill Radner, and I'm Alice's private investigator from

Milwaukee. I'm here to be a third party, to settle what seems to be a terrible family misunderstanding between you and her."

Adam leaned back into his chair, studying Bill carefully, and said, "I didn't think PIs got into family matters, just other matters."

Bill quickly answered, "We do when the letter that you sent may show harm or mistreatment. So I'm here as a third party to settle it for her and you!"

Adam was still leaning deep into his chair, studying Bill, trying to figure him out. He said, "It's none of your business. She'll get her Christmas gift each Christmas but not me anymore, and that's that!" Adam's demeanor suddenly changed dramatically. His temperament shifted to angry for no reason. Why?

Seeing her brother change so suddenly caught Alice off guard. She answered with some fear in her voice, "What did I do to you? Why all this hate toward me? I did nothing, nothing at all!"

"You make me sick; all that love you feel for me, I can drown in it! All I want is some room to breathe. I don't have time to be a father figure to you and hold you up. So I wrote that letter, to get you out of my hair for a while so I can breathe!" snapped Adam with much hatred in his voice. His voice was loud enough to be heard in the next room.

Bill, with his right arm, gestured for Adam to calm down. Adam was watching Bill and saw that he was mediating their differences. He calmed himself a little. Bill could see he was hiding something; Adam wasn't letting out the real reason. Bill then calmly responded to the little pause in the room by saying, "You talk of needing more room to breathe, so what is she doing that you feel so badly about?"

Adam just glared at Bill, who to him sounded more and more like a mediator all the time. "Sisterly love is one thing, but I'm drowning in love. I can't explain it well. Just leave me alone, all three of you! Get out *now*!" snapped Adam bitterly, his voice rising higher than before with his finger pointing to the door.

Alice, shaken by it all, was moved to tears suddenly. She rose from the sofa and left the room.

Bill and John rose to their feet, nodded to Adam, and left as well. Alice sobbed in the foyer. She said, "I've heard enough here. Get me out of here!"

John opened the door for them, and they let themselves out. Alice gave the keys back to John, as the two men tried to comfort her. Once they were in the car, John drove away slowly and up to the road again. They noticed a man outside walking around. When they were out of sight of the house, Bill told John to pull over and stop. Between the two of them, Alice started to feel better. With Alice slowly starting to get her composure back, the tears stopped.

Bill looked at John a second and said, "That was uncalled for, John. I don't know what's eating him, but I plan to find out some today."

Bill slowly turned his attention toward Alice and added in a softer voice, "Is there another way into that house, where we will not be seen?"

At first, Alice looked a little startled by the question, and then her strength grew inside and she answered, "Why, yes, there is. There's a tunnel that Adam built years ago that runs into the woods. I haven't been in it for a long time, but it should still be there yet." Alice proceeded to tell them how to find it and which road to take. With that information, John drove up the road and took the first left turn, along Adam's property. They drove slowly until they came to the steel gate she'd spoken of earlier and stopped. John could see that it was being used but not much recently. Then Alice remembered and told Bill about the padlock on it. She didn't have a key.

John and Bill looked at each other for a second and then Alice, who now wondered what they were thinking. Bill then said to John in a determined voice, "Open the trunk, John. I can fix that problem."

John pushed a button on the dashboard, and the trunk opened in the back. Bill got out of the car and walked to the rear of the car. He went through his gear and then walked across the road to the steel gate, carrying something in his left hand. John just smiled and then looked at Alice. He knew he had a bolt cutter in his hand. After a few seconds with the cutter, Bill began to open the gate and motioned for John to drive in. Once John was on Adam's road in the woods, Bill closed the gate behind them and made it look as if the padlock was still on. Bill returned to the car, got in, and closed the door.

"Okay, Alice, give us some idea how far we have to go, before we are up to this tunnel?" said Bill, sounding determined, putting a plan together. He wanted to hear more.

Alice then stated, "Follow the road till you start to see the house through the woods and stop."

John drove slowly up the road, which was uneven and narrow, with tree branches rubbing against the car. The fall colors of the trees around them made them enjoy it a little. After some time, they could finally see the house just starting to be visible from the car. They stopped and looked. With the car idling, Bill looked around them and told John to back up a little to be safe. Bill was thinking if they could see the house, anyone in it could see them. The woods around them had a lot of undergrowth, which should offer some protection as they walked around.

Bill looked at Alice and with interest in his voice asked, "Alice, how close are we to the tunnel from here?"

Alice, looking ahead of them, thought hard and said, "Not too far, Bill. When you see the tree stand on the right, as we walk up this road, there's a small clearing there, and the tunnel is next to an artificial tree about ten feet tall. It looks real. The tunnel is left of the small clearing."

John looked at Bill, and seeing his face, he shut off the car and opened the trunk.

"Alice, we are going find that tunnel and go in. Any information is now important for our safety from here on," responded Bill, reassuring her with a faint smile. They all got out of the car and closed their doors quietly. John locked the car. Bill put one of the bags that had his gear in it on his back. John did the same and closed the trunk softly. They walked carefully up the road for some time until they came to a small clearing, and Alice spotted the tree stand on the right. Bill believed in stealth and quietness and keeping one eye on those watching.

The undergrowth had taken over the clearing some, but it was still there. The three stopped and looked around. John pointed out that they couldn't see the house from there.

"That's not a problem, John; we are very close to it from here. It should be on the south side of the clearing. There's a tree, about ten feet tall, and the tunnel is next to it," stated Alice with confidence in her voice. She started walking south of the clearing. They all looked for any tree ten feet tall. After about thirty minutes or more of searching, they stopped looking.

"You're sure it's here in this area, Alice?" asked John as he wiped the sweat off his forehead.

Alice, feeling the frustration as well, sat down on a fallen tree and looked at the sky; it was partly sunny and comfortable out. There were several trees ten or more feet tall around her. She reached down and picked up a stick. Looking at it, she started gently hitting the fallen tree she was sitting on. Finally, out of frustration, she threw the stick at one of the trees and hit it. She watched it hit the tree, but the sound wasn't right. John heard it too as he tried each tree, searching the area. John walked up to the tree and tapped it again. He gave a big smile toward Alice sitting there. Bill walked up to John and tapped the tree firmly. "You're right!" They smiled at Alice as she rose from the fallen tree in disbelief at first.

Alice joined them and tapped the tree as well. "It's artificial, guys, just like I said it was!" She beamed in excitement. They looked down at the ground around them for any sign of tunnel markings to get in. After several minutes, they realized that it hadn't been used in years.

Bill stopped and thought about it for a second. This was a good thing and a bad thing. The bad thing was if they opened it, it would be visible the next time for anyone there. Bill looked around again and could barely see the house. Then Bill noticed that they were farther from the clearing than they thought. He took the bag off his back and looked for the GPS device. Once he found it, he set it for this location; he quickly made a note of it and put it in his pocket. John and Alice watched him as he did this. They looked at each other, and she slowly began to remember something about a hidden switch that opened the tunnel. Bill stood there, looking around. He wondered why the tunnel was there. It was in the middle of nowhere. "Alice, why is this tunnel here at all?" asked Bill, for it was unknown to him.

"My brother, when he first made his money and then got into all that Satan stuff, had a lot wild ideas. Dreamed like he was a young kid—great adventures he could have. We know now that was just fun and games." Alice paused for a moment.

John had stopped looking, listening to her, and added, "Who built this thing? Do you have a name for us?" Slowly, he looked at Bill and Alice for an answer.

Alice with her hands on the artificial tree paused to think for a moment. She shook her head and said, "If I remember correctly, I think he died shortly after that; he was an old man, John. I remember him saying that this was the biggest job he ever had in his life."

Again, they all went over it, looking for some switch to open the tunnel. Then Bill remembered the device he put into his bag. He quickly took off his bag and checked, but it was not there. "John, remove your travel bag," said Bill, now with an excited voice, as he watched John start to remove the bag from his back. Bill dug through the bag and found it.

This device measured changes in electrical current like in alarm systems. "Alice, is there power in that tunnel?" asked Bill and waited for an answer.

"Why, yes, Bill, but that was back then," answered Alice, responding to the question. She carefully watched Bill with the device in his hands.

"Good, Alice, that's all I wanted to hear," replied Bill, as he finished with the settings. He ran the device up and down the tree, until he found power in the tree. He tried to find the switch, and the device made a beeping sound. Bill looked carefully at the bark of the artificial tree and opened the panel that hid the switch. He turned off the device and handed it over to John to put away. The switch was about five feet off the ground. He waited until John was ready. "This might take some power from us, John. This hasn't been opened for some time. Alice, you have the switch?" asked Bill, wondering where it would open. He watched everyone get ready.

Bill nodded his head to Alice as she pushed the button. At first, nothing happened; then they could hear a faint pump running. The ground opened slowly, with a dull sound, to the south of the tree in a grassy clearing. It wasn't a large opening—about three or four feet wide and about seven feet long. It opened on one side, with about three inches of soil on top of it. John and Bill gave Alice a friendly hug for being sound in her information. They slowly walked up to it and gazed in.

"Wow, that air smells bad!" said John, waving his hand in front of his face. There was no argument there from Bill or Alice.

"Well, we better make ourselves at home, for a minute or two, till the air gets better down there," replied Bill, now thinking about other things before they went in.

"ALICE, IN THAT TUNNEL THERE, THERE IS NO ALARM OR anything on the other side that says this door is open?" asked Bill, now a little concerned about this passageway.

She was quiet for a moment and then answered, "I remember there was a light on the other side. It turned on when the door was open. But I don't remember any buzzer or anything like that."

"Good, then for now, we're safe yet," responded Bill, looking for a place to sit awhile.

They all found a place to sit. Bill went through his bag and gave each one a flashlight and then a candy bar for something to eat as they waited. He located his night-vision goggles and a night camera to film everything inside. He gave that to John, who had used it before on other cases with him. After about fifteen minutes, Bill stood up and said, "Everybody to the restroom now; there's no chance in there."

Everybody got up and went in different directions. John was back first.

After several minutes, the others had all returned. John then said, "The air is going to be bad in there and get worse the farther we go, so be warned."

They nodded in agreement, and Bill led the way in. Bill turned on his flashlight first; then the others followed suit. The steps, concrete and damp by appearance, were some distance down into the tunnel. There was a light switch on the wall to his right at the bottom of the steps. Also at the bottom of the steps was an electric hydraulic pump and switch that opened the door of the tunnel. Bill was thinking to himself, *this man thought of everything.* Bill put on his night goggles for better vision and shut off his flashlight. Bill noticed with his goggles on that there were drains every so often to catch the water. The air was very damp and somewhat cold in there, and there were cobwebs everywhere. But the floor was at least dry and safe to walk on. The walls were made of concrete blocks, and the width was about six feet wide, maybe a little more. The ceiling height was seven feet or a little more. They carefully made their way into the tunnel, with Bill clearing the way through the cobwebs. After what seemed like forever for them, they made their way to the other side, where there was indeed a small light shining in the darkness.

But that small light only shone into more blackness ahead. Bill, with his night-vision goggles, saw that there was a clear plastic curtain hanging at the opening of that tunnel. He could tell that the air on that side of the tunnel was fresher and slightly less damp. He also saw that on the other side of that curtain was a large, empty space with large metal drums and boxes. Alice's and John's flashlights bothered him, keeping him from seeing more. Bill reached to his goggles and shut them off for the time being.

He then turned to them and whispered, "There is a curtain at the end of this tunnel, and with that small light above this tunnel on the other side, I can see large metal drums and boxes ahead."

John and Alice nodded that they understood. Slowly, they made their way to the curtain. Bill wasn't using his flashlight at that time. He could see enough with theirs. Bill stopped again and turned to them, whispering, "Now shut off your flashlights and wait here. I'm going through the curtains and see if anyone is waiting for us."

They nodded again and shut off their flashlights.

Bill reached up and turned on his goggles in the blackness all around them. As he passed through the curtains, he knew they would have already been seen in this blackness. It was a bit of carelessness on his part, but somehow, he felt he would get away with it that day. He slowly walked past the large drums and then the boxes. Bill was now thinking how large the room was. *It's like a warehouse inside here.*

He looked up. It had a high ceiling, and that meant that they were far underground. The tunnel sloped some from that room. This was interesting to Bill, because he would never have thought of that before. Bill saw that the walls were again made of concrete blocks and could now see that there were center poles to support the ceiling. He could estimate the room to be something of a square and sixty or seventy feet in all directions. As Bill walked by what he felt was the southern wall, he found another tunnel and a room inside it. He carefully stood there a minute, to see more clearly and to wait, in case anyone was hiding. The quietness of this underground room was unnerving. One could hear a drop of water hit the ground fifty feet away. He looked back across the room and could see the small light shining and the curtain and the other things. But nothing moved or gave any hint of another person.

Slowly and carefully, he stepped forward into the other tunnel. On his left was the other room, and on his right was just one straight wall up those stairs and to the house above. Bill was listening for any sound, as he walked slowly toward the room on the left. As he reached that room, he could now see it was a locker room with two rows of lockers facing each other. The ceiling in this room was a normal eight feet high, as was the hallway to those stairs. The room was not deep or fancy; it appeared to be just a changing room for his members. There were some benches so they could sit and change. Bill carefully checked many of the lockers, but they were all empty. Bill went out the other side quietly but encountered nothing but blackness. He went to the stairs and looked up. He saw only a faint light from under the door at the top that said this was the house. So he went up the steps to the door and found when he opened it that he was inside the house. He was in some hallway of the house, and he could hear people in other rooms talking. He couldn't make out anything they were saying, so he closed the door silently and went down the steps. Bill walked past the locker room and stopped short of the large room.

Then Bill noticed a round structure. It was about four feet high and had a pulpit and an altar in front of it. This made Bill think at first, *How did I miss all of this?* He backtracked and then could see that some of it was hidden with boxes stacked up. Bill walked up to the round structure and looked inside it with his night goggles. He could see no bottom to it, just blackness at the farthest point. Bill, somewhat amazed by this discovery, shook his head. Bill went back to the curtain, reached up, and unscrewed the light. With the light out, he went back to his friends and told them everything he knew. Together, they carefully covered their flashlights for minimum light.

Bill and John went out to explore the west wall of the large room and found the rifles and the ammunition. Bill reached into John's backpack and brought out the night camera. He had John take pictures of it all. This was great evidence for them. Bill told John this paid for the gas. While John took pictures, Alice was looking at the round structure. Bill whispered to Alice to go into his backpack and bring out his light sticks. She opened his pack and reached inside, fishing about until she found three. She gave them to Bill. He shook one up and started it. It gave out a nice glow in the blackness. Together, they looked into the structure. Bill dropped a light stick to see how deep it was. It fell farther and farther into it until it was not visible anymore. He readied the other two light sticks and dropped them together. The same thing as before happened. Bill and Alice took a few steps and stopped.

Bill whispered to Alice, "Was this structure here before, the last time you were here?"

Alice thought and quickly whispered, "No, Bill, this thing was only talked about then. Adam once said that there was a natural geological fault on his property, and he was going to use it."

Bill thought for a moment and then whispered, "This must have been built for his grand ceremony this Halloween!"

Alice looked a little shocked by that knowledge. John walked slowly toward them, and Bill pointed to him, indicating what he wanted. Bill and Alice walked over to the drums and looked at them. All he could see was some type of hydraulic oil covered with clear plastic.

Bill and Alice looked at the cardboard boxes. They each went through several. Some had old gowns in them from years past. Others were boxes of receipts for work done to the property and other things. There was a large box for light fixtures, and others for some type of ventilation stuff. The only boxes of interest were the house and property receipts. But Bill didn't have time for them just then. He again looked at the ceiling. He was wondering why the air was different there. On either side of this large room was some type of ventilation ducts. They were big enough for a larger area, but they were silent just then. Bill thought that was odd.

John returned from taking his pictures and asked Bill if he wanted him to do anything else. Bill shook his head no and then pointed to the walls on either side. "Take pictures of that."

John took pictures of the walls on either side. When he finished and put the camera away, he whispered to Bill, "Why am I taking pictures of the walls here?"

Bill smiled carefully and whispered, "That's for the bishop, John. Mark might have an idea about them, and it might help to ruin Adam's party."

They looked for Alice then. They noticed her going through other boxes. She seemed to find something that held her attention. The men walked up to her, and John tapped her on the shoulder to let her know they were behind her. They looked at what she had in her hand, and that caught their attention as well. It was an old ceremonial sword. Bill looked more closely inside the box and noticed that there were others as well. Bill wanted John to film this evidence. Bill was looking for his ink pen, as John made the camera ready.

"Alice, look and see if there are any daggers in there,

please," Bill whispered softly as he finally found his pen. Bill bent down and wrote something on the side of the box of swords and then made a note of it on his notepad.

Alice looked carefully inside the box but couldn't find any daggers. She whispered to the men with her, "There are no daggers in that box, but they could be in one of the others."

With the discovery made, Bill felt it was time to leave; they were almost up to the pulpit when Bill stopped. Bill was thinking that there might be an old sermon left there, and he wanted to read the content of it. John and Alice watched with patience, as Bill looked for other evidence. There wasn't a whole lot of anything, so he lifted up the paper pad. There was a sermon.

"John, the camera, please!" whispered Bill, somewhat loudly, for this was good luck for him.

John again readied the camera and took several photos of the sermon. He whispered, "Anything else you want, Bill?"

"No, I think that's it for today, John. I think we did well on this trip for one day. We better not press our luck," whispered Bill, starting to think they had better get back to the car.

Bill placed the pad back as it was before with the sermon under it. Bill quickly made a note of his finding in his notebook. Together, they met Alice, who was waiting for them. They went through the curtains with John leading the way out. They were quiet as they went through the tunnel; they could all see that there was light at the end of the tunnel. When they reached the other end, Bill took the lead, just in case this was a trick. By the electric pump, he found a short hydraulic hose he could use for protection. Bill left the other two at the bottom of the steps as he made his way up. When he reached ground level, he carefully looked around and listened even more carefully. Suddenly, he raced outside and turned to see if anyone was behind the open door. There was no one there. Bill felt relief with that knowledge, and he scanned his surroundings carefully. Then he waved for the others to come up. When they were outside, Bill went back down, placed his hose where he had found it, and went out again.

"You gave us a little scare there, Bill. You looked as if you were expecting the worst," said Alice, a little fear in her voice.

Bill, seeing the concern on her face, answered with care, "In my line of work, when you're evidence hunting like we were, somebody can hit you hard on the head, Alice."

Alice smiled at his response and now understood his meaning. John was carefully reading the vegetation around the hole, so they could close the door. They watched him for a moment, as John readied the opening.

"Need any help, John?" asked Bill, seeing what he could do to help.

"No, it was fairly simple this time. Only some of the roots needed trimming and readying," replied John as he was finishing up his work. Alice walked over to the tree and waited for John to finish. Bill walked over to the door and noticed that almost none of the vegetation had fallen off the door. Bill was thinking there must have been some kind of mesh to hold the roots in place. John finished and stood up, and Bill nodded to Alice to close the lid. When the lid closed tightly, it made little noise at all. There was an outline indicating where it was. Bill and John spread leaves over the edges, so it was much less noticeable. When they finished, they smiled at each other, for it looked good.

They slowly made their way to the clearing again and looked back to where they had been. The house was not to be seen because of the trees and undergrowth. John noticed the time they had spent there and said to them, "Jeez, you know how much time we spent there?"

"No, John, how much time was it?" answered Alice, now thinking of it some.

"Almost two hours in all!" answered John with amazement in his voice.

Bill gave John a pat on the shoulder and said warmly, "Good sleuthing takes time, my friends; it takes time."

As they walked back to the car, they again took time to enjoy the fall colors everywhere. The sky was still partly cloudy, and the sun was warm on their faces. Once they reached the car, John opened the trunk. Bill and John removed their backpacks.

"Feels good to get that weight off, doesn't it?" remarked Bill, stretching out a little as John did the same.

John looked at the trunk to be sure that all the gear would travel safely back to Park River for the night. Alice was starting to show that she had been up all night.

John looked over the car as he was unlocking it. He looked at her. "Alice, you think you have enough energy for something to eat before calling it a day?" he wondered as he opened the door on his side and then all the others.

Alice noticed the time and slowly looked at them. She said a little weakly, "That might be a good idea, as long as we don't overdo it." She climbed in the front passenger side, and Bill got in the back. John was driving.

"Alice, we will get you what you need for some good, restful sleep. You had a good day, overall, today," said Bill in a complimentary sort of way.

John backed out as carefully as he could without scratching the car.

When they reached the gate, Bill got out of the car, opened the gate, and closed it after John drove out. Bill once again made the padlock look as if everything was fine with it. The three of them felt it would not be a good idea to be in a restaurant. They probably didn't smell that good anymore after being in that tunnel. So they decided to go to a hamburger place, go through the drive-through, and eat at the motel. They got three rooms for the night, even though it was early afternoon. The man argued it was too early yet. The manager agreed to some extra cash, and then it was fine.

Once they had eaten their lunch together, Alice called it a day. The next morning, John and Bill had fresh clothes. It was about 6:00 a.m., and Alice was knocking at their doors. Bill was in John's motel room, drinking coffee and deciding who was driving that day. They let Alice in; she was looking much better for the day.

"Well, that small lunch and some sound sleep has done wonders for you, kid," joked Bill, immediately noticing the big change in her.

"I know. I was really tired after all of that. I really did need some sleep," added Alice, beaming with new energy for the day.

Once they had taken care of their rooms with the manager, they were on their way. It was about 2:00 p.m. when they reached Bill's office. Once Alice had her small travel bag again, she gave each one a brief hug, said she'd be in touch, and drove away. Bill and John watched her drive away and then picked up their gear and closed the trunk.

"You know, Bill, we did have a good day with her yesterday."

Bill, making his backpack comfortable, said, "You're right, John; she's really a very good person all the way around."

The two friends made their way back to the office and set down their backpacks.

"Well, John, I think I'm going to unpack this stuff and check the mail and the phone and call it a day early. It is getting late to be really starting something at this time," said Bill as he looked around and then glanced at his watch for a moment.

John thought about it a second and decided he had nothing pressing at home. He said, "Well, if you don't mind, I'll give you a hand with this and we'll both call it a day."

Bill nodded at John, and the men went to work making things ready for the next day.

Twelve days later, it was a much chillier late morning for Bill. Bill was doing his bookkeeping for the middle of October to see how the business was doing on paper. So far, it had been a slow morning, so he thought he would get that done early. He did get one call for work that night; the client wanted her husband checked on. When he finished his bookkeeping, he thought to himself, *So far so good yet.* His phone rang. It was Jimmy on the line. Jimmy informed Bill that his transmitter was finished and ready to go. Bill told him that he would pick it up right away. Quickly, Bill wondered what he owed him yet, and he wrote it down and hung up.

Jimmy presented Bill with his new transmitter and receiver set. Bill could tell Jimmy was really pleased that he could help him like this. Jimmy went over all the features and how to work it properly. Jimmy was also proud of how to mark each important message and play it back when he wanted. What Bill liked about it was that it was small, light, and easy to use and understand. He thanked Jimmy, told him that he'd be in touch again someday, and left.

Bill turned on the car radio. As he drove back to his office, traffic was normal for the noon hour. The news was on the radio. The reporter stated that another body had been found at a warehouse by Lake Michigan. It was the same warehouse that had been involved in a ritual murder a month earlier, and Chicago Police were at a loss to explain it.

Bill shut off the radio angrily and hit his steering wheel the same way. "Damn, that no good, rotten bastard!" stormed Bill. He swore bitterly after that. Bill decided when he got to his office he'd called Bishop Frazer for any other advice he might have on this.

Bill came out of the elevator and spotted John at his office door. "You heard, Bill? The news, I mean?" asked John carefully, at the same time eyeing the package.

Bill unlocked the door. They entered, and John closed it as Bill went quickly to his desk. He picked up his phone and called Bishop Frazer. The secretary told him he was out at that time. Bill asked her to have him call back when he could and to tell him that it was important. Then, he gave his name and telephone number. When the secretary finished and they hung up, Bill said to John, "Yes, I heard it on the radio, coming here. Now I know why he ate Alice's butt off for no reason. He was planning another killing as we left!"

Bill quickly called his PI friend in Chicago. After a few rings, he answered. Bill introduced himself and explained what he wanted to know. "Oh, Bill, my friend, that will cost you seventy-five dollars for that one."

Angrily, Bill agreed to the price for the information.

"Well, my friends at that department say that these Satan boys are really good—I mean damn good. No traces at all, fingerprints, or stuff, or anything at all. The girl was eleven years old, blond, nude, ritual markings on the body, killed in a ritual way. But get this, friend, there was no blood in the body at all."

In disbelief, Bill said, "What? No blood? Is that what you said?"

"Yep, no blood at all in her. They found blood drops in a circle where they stood, but that was all, man. I tell you they're really good. Their special committee is at a loss on this one, man. Man, these Satan boys are so good; they can't point the finger at anyone in town here. They just don't fit anything they have on file here at all. Hell, they're pointing the fingers at themselves. These cats are pros, man. Hell, they must be trained like Special Forces somewhere. No one's seen them or noticed them—hell, man, no one's coming or going to the warehouse. One thing though, they walked up behind a police spotter and gave him something that put him to sleep. No one saw anything, man. And like I said earlier, Bill, no one is a suspect yet. They simply don't know where to look!" stated Bill's friend with a flare that was all his own.

Bill glanced at John and said, "Anything else, friend?"

His paused and then added, "No, friend. That's it in a nutshell, man. Bye the way, man, if you're on to this cat, man, you better be way smarter than the rest of us here or this cat will run away." They talked a little more, and Bill also added that his money was on its way. Then they hung up.

Bill ran his fingers through his hair. He was trying to make sense of it all. Adam Johnson, at that time, was playing a brilliant game and then some. Bill knew his little bit of evidence was never going to be enough to hold the man on anything. John was thinking what Bill was thinking. Again running his fingers through his hair, Bill turned toward the window and looked out, trying to find something big enough to hold Adam. For some reason, Bill was thinking of a tractor pull. As the tractor raced down a course, the weight got heavier until it stopped the tractor. Bill thought, *Adam is not a tractor, but the idea is the same.* Bill turned from the window toward John and said, "John, we are going to Chicago early tomorrow morning, but first, I'll set it up with Kathy. So this receiver will be set up before she goes to work. And then we go to Adam's place and set up this transmitter in this bag. And while you set up the transmitter, I'll be looking for that dagger. I hope it has some blood on it for DNA!" stated Bill with some bitterness in his voice.

When Bill said that, John's eyes got bigger for a second because it caught him by surprise. John was wondering what the man on the phone had said to him to fire him up like that. John stepped forward and then rested himself on Bill's desk. He said, "So what do you know now that you didn't know ten minutes ago?"

Bill paused and studied John's gaze. "We are the only ones who know who the killer is and why at this time. We are also going after the biggest fish to have on a line. I was just an average detective on the force back then, but today, I must be better than that if I want this fish, John."

John straightened up and saw the serious look on Bill's face; he hadn't seen it in a long time. "Okay, Bill, I'm in on this with you. What's your plan? Let's get to work on it," responded John. He then pulled up a nearby chair and readied himself.

Bill spelled out a simple plan. First, they would use Bishop Frazer's knowledge to find out what Adam would do next, before Halloween. Bill pointed out that he must be one step ahead of Adam to make it work. Bill was so serious about it. Even if it meant filming the whole damn thing for evidence, that was what they must do to catch him and his followers. Bill told John the hard part was persuading the police there in Chicago. "They're going to want proof, and we what have is not enough yet. The only way then would be to go to Park River and try to convince them with the evidence. We must have patience, and wait for the right time to jump on it." Bill went on, "I don't blame them in Chicago; right now, they're under a lot of pressure there. Hell, everyone under a rock is saying they have an angle on this thing. Getting their proper attention is going to be hard without solid proof, where no one can argue it or have it thrown out of court by some fast-talking lawyer."

Later in the afternoon, Bill called Kathy on the phone. All the news was of their latest ritual killing. But what she gave in detail on the phone was of no help to Bill. Bill told her of his plan to be there early enough to be set up at her place, before her work time. She told Bill that would be fine with her. When they had finished, it was set. After they had hung up, Bill was pleased with her and her desire to help. Bill then called Amy in Chicago, and after they had finished, it was pretty much the same except for Clifford Hoover, who seemed to be one of Adam's key men. Amy explained the dagger was moved from leader to leader. This was what Bill feared; locating it for evidence was going to be much harder than he'd thought. Both informants agreed with Bill's friend in Chicago, that they were at a loss for evidence and clues.

Bill was now thinking that Adam Johnson was no average man at all. Adam was as cunning as he was smart. Bill knew that he had to be both but only better. The next morning, Bill and John left for Chicago at 4:30 a.m. It was still dark out, and the city was fairly quiet. Bill had everything he needed to put his plan in place in his car. John was dozing lightly as Bill drove. While he drove, Bill was looking at different plans and ideas. He did come up with several different ideas, but he decided on one. Mostly because of money and manpower, he decided to keep it simple and straightforward.

Bill and John rang the doorbell at Kathy's place. The door opened slowly. Kathy was in a white robe. She was familiar with John immediately. She said, "You must be Bill Radner. We spoke on the phone last afternoon."

She let them in and asked them to join her at the kitchen nook. She went into the kitchen, set some cups in front of them, and poured them some coffee. After several cups of coffee and some pastry, Bill went to his business side. Bill didn't want to take too much of her morning time. Bill and John explained everything about their receiver, how it worked, and what they wanted her to do. When they finished, Kathy looked at it and then at them. "This is really simple. Sure, I can do this for you. I don't have a problem with this," replied Kathy, looking really sure of herself. Then she smiled.

Bill and John felt really comfortable with Kathy; she was very competent and able to do it. Kathy told them to make themselves at home while she got ready for work. Bill and John watched television and drank coffee. After about forty-five minutes, Kathy reappeared from her bedroom. She looked very professional. Bill and John were surprised by her transformation in that short time.

John rose to his feet and made his way toward her. He said politely, "Kathy, I would follow you anywhere."

Kathy really liked what he said and gave him a very

warm expression. "That's really nice of you, John, and I think I would like that."

Bill was still sitting there with his coffee, watching the magic between John and Kathy. They had something special that many people didn't have in their relationships. And that was magic, the force that brought two people together and kept them together.

Bill, not wanting to ruin the show, reminded them of the time.

"You're right, Bill, and thanks for reminding me of that!" responded Kathy, knowing he was right and they better get going. Kathy went over, looked at the receiver, and turned it on, and then they all left. Together, they went to the elevator and then out of the building.

Bill was following John's directions to Adam's place. This was going to take some time, because the downtown traffic was heavy at that time of day. After much time and trouble, they made it to Adam's apartment building and parked. Bill, wanting to use his time carefully, decided to wait and play it safe.

"What's your plan here, Bill?" asked John, wondering about the waiting time.

Bill noticed the time as they started to wait. "It's 8:15, John. Adam only left a little over a half hour ago."

"I know that he's on the fifth floor up there, but I don't want to make his neighbors suspicious. I think we'll wait fifteen minutes, and then we'll go."

John was a little impatient about this but kept it to himself. He knew Bill was right in waiting, for he was watching the people leave until things went back to normal. After about twenty minutes, Bill said, "Okay, John, let's go and do this."

They made their way toward the building, into the lobby, and then onto the elevator. The door closed, and Bill said, "You have the room number, John?"

"Yes, I do, Bill," responded John, pulling out his notepad.

The door opened, and John led the way down the hallway and stopped at Adam's apartment. Bill picked the lock, and then they were in. Bill gently closed the door behind them. He scanned the place for the first time.

"Hey, this is really nice, John," said Bill, whispering, as he looked it over.

"I said that too, Bill, when I first came here," replied John in a whisper.

John carefully looked at all the furniture, deciding which piece would be the best place for the transmitter. Bill went to each room until he found the altar room. He pulled out a small flashlight, turned it on, and went to the altar where he knelt to see if there was a drawer and the dagger there. He felt by the legs against the black cloth and thought, *There it is.* Bill carefully lifted the cloth on the altar, and there was a drawer. Bill smiled.

Bill reached into his left pocket, pulled out some heavy latex gloves, and put them on. Then he pulled open the drawer; there was a thin black sponge rubber mat where the dagger had been. But it wasn't there, just an impression. Bill quickly pulled out a can of luminal and a small black light of sorts and turned it on. "This light will show if there is blood on the mat. It should shine out brightly." Going over the mat, he found only a few tiny specks of it. *Damn,* thought Bill, *not enough to do anything here. Damn, I need more than that for a sample test!* He gently closed the drawer and put the cloth back as before. Everything looked good. He then ran his light over the cloth, looking for any traces there but found none. He then went around the altar, looking on the carpet for traces—still none. *Damn, that man is good.* Bill then left that room and went into his bedroom. He carefully looked there. Bill spent extra time in the closet, looking for gowns, and found none. He looked in the dresser drawers and under the bed and found nothing. Bill ran his black light wherever he could, looking for bloodstains. He found nothing. Bill went to the bathroom and checked everything—nothing.

John placed the transmitter under an end table; he used duct tape to attach it. He was careful enough to use plenty so it would stay a long time. Bill had just finished the bathroom when John found him.

"I think we are through here, don't you, Bill?" asked John, whispering carefully to Bill.

"Yes, I do too, John, there isn't anything here. We could look all day and find nothing here," whispered Bill with a note of frustration in his voice.

Bill checked everything one last time. He wasn't going to leave anything with this man. Bill double-checked the transmitter to make sure it was running. Bill and John met at the front door and carefully scanned the apartment for anything out of place. It all looked fine. But they couldn't leave just yet; there was someone in the hallway outside. The person was talking to some neighbor in the hallway. They waited about ten minutes before it was clear. John locked the door and checked it; it was good. John noticed the gloves on Bill. Bill quickly removed them and put them in his left pocket. Once in the elevator with the door closed, they wondered if they could finally relax a little. They were walking back to the car when Bill thought of something.

"You know, John, it just hit me now; who does their cleaning here?" asked Bill, thinking out loud.

John then looked at Bill, and after studying that thought, he said, "Ah, I see your thinking here, Bill, not bad. How do you get rid of bloodstains, unless you burn the robe each time and make a new one? They could have a member who does this each time?"

Bill then said, "I think, while we're here, we will check with fabric shops close to here and the members and find who's selling the most black fabric and to whom?"

John was thinking, *That's not a bad idea, but the police maybe thought the same thing as well.*

They got into the car, and Bill looked for his smartphone in the center armrest and found it. When it was up and running, Bill went on the Internet, looking for fabric shops in the area. He found two that were close. John recorded the information in his notebook. Then he looked for dry cleaners and Laundromats in the area and found three that were close and one a little farther but still close enough. John recorded them in his notepad as well. Bill was about to start the car but then stopped and said, "John, use my smartphone and look for occult shops close to here. They may sell black fabric as well to good customers."

Bill quietly waited for John to look the information up. It took about ten to fifteen minutes. John looked at Bill and said, "That took some time, Bill. My search on the Web included fabric, and the search engine took longer. But there is one close to here … In fact, my map says it's about a mile away from here."

"Really, John, then let's go and see for ourselves. Maybe we both look good in black clothes?" joked Bill, trying to ease the tension some. Bill set the GPS device, and they left in that direction. They reached the shop quickly and parked the car. They entered; it was big inside with lots of merchandise for different beliefs. A woman came up to them; she was wearing somewhat odd clothing but was polite.

John made the pitch. He told her that they wanted to buy five yards of very good black cloth and sew it into two black robes. The lady hesitated and asked them if they were from the police department. John flatly denied it and again asked her for the cloth. She then asked for the manager to come up and talk to them. The manager was about forty years of age and of average height and weight with a touch of gray in his hair. He wore wire-rimmed glasses. He started with what he could do for them, and again, John gave his pitch about black gowns and how much he wanted. The manager hesitated as well and told them, "Only our best customers, sir, with whom we have long-term relationships. We run a legal business here. Are you from the police department? If not, leave now!"

Bill, seeing this was going nowhere fast, pulled out his badge and showed the manager. He studied it and then said, "A private investigator, well, you're not the public, but you're not quite the police."

Bill, having heard that line before, said to the manager, "All we have for you is one question: do you know Adam Johnson?"

The manager knew Adam personally as a customer but did not want to say; it was store policy. He then said, "As a store, we are not at liberty to disclose our customers to any-one, unless you show me a police officer and a warrant."

Bill knew he'd better back off because he was only legal in Wisconsin, but he now knew that Adam was a regular there.

"Sir, you will probably see us again and with the same question as well," stated Bill flatly; then they both left the store.

Once outside the store, they went to the car and got in.

"John, mark this store as suspect, and let's go to the city hall," stated Bill, now knowing what he could do. John set the GPS to city hall, and they drove away to downtown Chicago. Once inside city hall, Bill asked a clerk whom he should see about property. He wanted to find the owner of a store. The clerk picked up a phone and then told them to wait there. A few minutes later, a well-dressed woman greeted them and led them to a desk. They sat down.

The woman started with the question, "So you're interested in property here in the city?"

Bill gave the name of the property and then stated he would like the name of the owner, so they could talk with him about a sale. There was a computer on the desk; she entered the name of the business and then said, "I know Mr. Varney personally. He owns that occult store. He is a very private man, but I suppose you could call him on his private line if you wish, sir?"

Bill, seeing an opening there, said politely, "That would be fine, thank you."

She recorded the number on a piece of paper and gave it to Bill. Bill politely thanked her, and she said, "Do you have other property you would like as well?"

"We do actually, but for now, we will start with Mr. Varney," replied Bill, in a professional tone of voice, and then he smiled nicely.

Once they left the building and were back in their car, Bill said to John, "Ready your computer, John, and get that disk out of the glove compartment."

John handed over the computer to Bill and then the disk. Bill put the disk into the computer, and his program started.

"What are you doing, Bill?" asked John, watching.

"I'm going to get Mr. Varney's address, John. And since we have Wifi here from this building, we will use the Internet," stated Bill as he worked. He entered all his information quickly. In a few seconds, Mr. Varney's address appeared on the computer. And John wrote it down on his notepad.

"I've never seen you do this before, Bill," said John in disbelief.

"I think we will get something to eat. We'll be busy for some time after." Bill entered information on the computer about restaurants on this street. "Oh good, John; it's just up the road there," responded Bill, looking pleased with the address on the screen.

When they returned to the car, after finishing their meal, Bill picked up his phone and called Mr. Varney.

After several rings, Mr. Varney answered. Bill explained to him that he was a private investigator and then mentioned that one of his customers at the store might be involved in a crime and that he was looking into it. All he wanted was a few simple answers to some questions. Mr. Varney hesitated at first and then wondered if this would hurt his business reputation. Bill answered that it wouldn't, for he just wanted information.

Again, Mr. Varney hesitated, and then he said the police had been there twice in the last few days asking questions.

Bill replied, "This is about a customer and not what's in the news."

Mr. Varney agreed to that.

He then asked Mr. Varney his two questions. They were

about Adam Johnson personally and whether there were any recent purchases. Bill then gave him his telephone number and said he would wait for his call. Mr. Varney agreed to that, and they hung up.

John, listening to this conversation, was amazed by what had just happened and said, "You sneaky old fox you, Bill. How in the world did you make that look easy?" with disbelief in his voice.

Bill just sat there pleased with himself. He said carefully, "You tell the truth, John, but not the whole truth. We just want to collect the facts."

They waited in the car for about twenty minutes when Bill's phone rang. It was Mr. Varney again on the line. He told Bill that Adam Johnson was a very good customer and he had bought twenty-five gowns for women, twenty-five gowns for men, and ten custom made for himself. Mr. Varney again stated he wanted no trouble from him. Bill promised that he would not give him any problems in the future; all he was looking for was information. Mr. Varney sounded a little more at ease and said good-bye.

Bill relayed the information to John, and John carefully wrote it all down on his pad. When he finished writing, John wondered what was next. "With that done, what's next on the list?"

Bill was now thinking about those weapons Adam had bought. "We should see a gunrunner. Maybe we can get lucky there too, but remember, John, these are rough people."

John went over his notes and located the closest gunrunner on the list he received from Bill and set the GPS. They left. Traffic was again starting to get heavier, for it was later in the day. This was somewhat of a rundown area of town, most likely not safe at night. They found the address and got out of the car. John once again gave Bill the name of the man in charge as they entered the building. They entered the office, or what looked like an office to them. Bill introduced himself to a very hard-looking man behind a rough-looking desk. Bill carefully stated he only wanted some information and then they would leave. The man behind the desk shouted at a man in the other room, and three men came into the room. Each of the three men looked meaner than the other. Bill sized up his situation and said firmly that he wanted to speak to a Mr. Rabbit. The really hellish-looking man said, "Ah, I'm he. What do you want?"

Bill then firmly stated he wanted to know if they had sold hundreds of rifles and ammunition to an Adam Johnson. The reply was, "What's that to you? Are you a copper?"

Bill showed his badge and said that he was a PI, looking into Adam Johnson. Suddenly, the three men fiercely attacked Bill and John. The fight was short, with two on Bill and one on John. John took a hard one on the chin and was out; then the man turned to Bill and kicked him in the stomach. All they knew next when they came to was they were lying on the hood of their car.

John came to first and shook Bill. Slowly, he came to. They painfully got into the car and left without saying a word to each other. The men there had worked them over really well, and Bill could feel in his chest that he had been kicked a couple of times. John looked into the passenger-side mirror and saw that he had welts on his face. Bill, looking at John at a stoplight, said, "I would take it that we found the gunrunner who sold Adam that stuff, no need to go further?"

John turned his attention from the mirror and nodded to Bill in agreement.

Bill then said to John, "I think we've had enough fun for one day. Let's fill up and go back home."

On the north side of the city, they filled up and then made their way back to Milwaukee.

"Jeez, Bill, what did they hit us with besides their fists?" asked John, starting to feel sore all over.

Bill then glanced at John carefully and said, "That's all, John, but they were very mean about it."

When they reached Bill's office, Bill cleaned out his car. Once he was back in his office, Bill and John quietly put everything away for the night.

"Would you like some coffee, John?" asked Bill nicely as he finished putting everything away.

"Well, it's getting late, Bill, but why not?" answered John, feeling plenty sore from the day.

Bill readied the coffee maker and started it brewing. Bill returned to his desk and sat down with John watching casually. Bill checked his answering machine. There were several calls on it. One call was from Bishop Frazer, and they both listened to it.

"Sorry, Bill, I was out of town on church business. Call me as soon as you can. Thank you."

The last call was from Alice, wondering how their day went in Chicago. After about three cups each and a fair amount of friendly talk, John left for the day.

It was about 5:30 p.m., and he closed for the day.

Bill arrived at his office at 9:00 a.m. the next day and went about his usual routine. He placed a call to Bishop Frazer, and his call went through right away. After about twenty minutes on the phone, they hung up. Bill leaned back in his chair, feeling fairly sore from the previous day's pounding by those men in Chicago. He also took some painkillers for his chest, which was plenty sore from being kicked.

There was a knock at the door, and John appeared, moving stiffly, as he fixed a cup of coffee. "You talked to Bishop Frazer already, Bill?" asked John as he sat down to enjoy his morning coffee.

Bill paused; it wasn't very good news. So Bill started with the best news first and then told him the rest of it.

"Well, John, first, he was up in south-central Wisconsin doing church business for several days; he didn't say what for. He's been reading that book of yours, John, and thinks he knows what Adam is trying to do next. He told me that if he's right in thinking this, we all could be in trouble! The bishop thinks Adam has to do three ritual killings to qualify for a ritual on Halloween night, plus another ritual killing, after Satan is released from hell. There will also be thirteen women who will become pregnant that night, and their young will be joint rulers of the earth. But Satan's child will rule directly with Satan himself. So that's four killings altogether, and then the world dies, so to speak!"

John was starting to wonder what they had gotten themselves into.

"Well, Bill, I know what we saw and heard in the church that day with Alice and the rest of us. But do you really believe that stopping Adam and his merry followers will save the world too?" asked John as he looked at Bill steadily.

Bill sat and thought about his answer and then said, "John, my friend, we will never know if this is true or not.

Science has come a long way from the Dark Ages. It's made our lives better and, for the most part, healthier, but honestly, I don't think science will ever come to answering the really hard questions."

John was now seeing where this was going; he said, "So you're saying that there is a God and a devil, heaven and hell, but the vast majority of us live our lives just fine without it in our lives?"

Bill knew that was what most people really thought. He replied, "Well, John, most people do feel that way, but most religions will tell you that there is something after death. Science will tell you it's just the chemicals in your mind at work there. I don't believe that; if our lives here on this earth are to mean something, then we must move on to the next. I want to move on for something good and better."

John, after hearing that statement, was thinking metaphysics and other possible theories he'd heard on that subject. John now knew Bill was a believer, and Bill was his friend and a good man to be with. He thought he would just let it alone. "All I know is we are talking four murders by this madman, Bill, and I'm with you. I'm not a religious man, but we must stop him and them!" answered John, finding his coffee had gotten cold in all of this. John, after refreshing his coffee, turned and said, "Did you call Alice by the way?"

"Oh, it's too soon at this time of day for that, maybe a little later. If she worked all night, I don't want to wake her just now," replied Bill as he rose from his chair to refresh his coffee.

John then continued, "Our stockpile of evidence on Adam is starting to grow now, and that's good, but we still need the murder weapon to tie it up good."

Bill nodded and agreed with that, but at the same time, he hadn't yet heard from Kathy. If there were to be three murders before the big deal, he wanted to know it beforehand and not after. They still had a little over two weeks to wrap it all up and put Adam and his followers away for good.

The next morning, Bill opened his office as usual and did his routine. He noticed his answering machine had messages on it. There were two messages for his services and one from Kathy. Bill wrote down the numbers for work and the necessary information and then moved on to Kathy's message. "Bill, there is to be another ritual murder very soon and within the week. The location is not set yet, but this time on the south side of town, in some rundown part, and before I forget to tell you, it's to be around eight or nine at night."

Bill saved the message for John so he could hear it too. Bill picked up the phone to call Bishop Frazer to report the new information to him. Bill reached the secretary and asked her to have the bishop call him toward the end of the day and hung up. Bill was on his computer, checking out the south side of Chicago, when his friend Tom entered the office.

"Hey, Tom, good to see you again. Have a seat, will you? How have you been?" Bill greeted him happily, and they shook hands warmly.

Tom poured himself a cup of coffee and sat down. Tom started by saying, "Rumor has it you're looking into the ritual killings in Chicago. Is that right, Bill?"

"Yes, Tom, we have a few leads in that direction right now," answered Bill, wondering where this was heading.

Tom tried the coffee and found it to be fair. He replied, "My department downtown received a message that you harassed those gunrunners two days ago. They claimed you showed your badge to them and wanted to know what was going on."

Bill, leaning back into his chair, wondered who this was. He said, "Which one? I did a couple of times."

Tom, now not sure what to say, decided to proceed anyway. "Those badasses sell illegal weapons. That place has been staked out for months. We were told they put the two of you on the car hood to dry out."

Bill could hear, by Tom's tone of voice, that the captain down there didn't like it. "Yes, we were there; we were following a lead that took us there. What of it?" asked Bill, in a similar tone of voice.

Tom, knowing Bill well enough to know he had been a good cop in the past, then stated firmly, "Well, you could have told me of this adventure you took on yourself. I would have told you what kind of apes these men were! The captain was really on my ass for this, but I told him nothing, because I wanted to hear it from you first!"

Bill thought quickly and then replied, "So that's the entire thing the captain said? He didn't like my adventure. I have information, Tom—almost a hundred thousand dollars' worth of weapons and ammunition were sold illegally. And I did check it out."

Tom was surprised by this and answered roughly, "So why didn't you tell me, before you took your joyride?"

Bill was now thinking he had better be careful. "Because I was trying to find out to whom and to where; that's why."

Tom shook his head and waved his arms. Then he said, "Okay, okay, I get the picture. We haven't heard that end of it. But you say there was a lead on this; did I hear you straight on that?"

Bill was thinking that the storm was now breaking, and he answered, "Yes, I have information that the weapons are to be moved to northern Wisconsin, but we don't know why yet or for what."

Tom knew that Bill was hiding something and really didn't want to say right then, but he knew he would when he knew more about it.

"All right, Bill. I understand that you have more digging to do on this. Just don't go on any more adventures like this without informing me first," said Tom flatly; he then finished his coffee.

"That's fair, Tom. You can count on that one," responded Bill with some respect.

Tom gave a faint smile and then left, a little disappointed, because he didn't get the answers he wanted, but he did learn of a sale he hadn't known about. Bill spun his chair around to look out the window for a moment and blew a sigh of relief from that little fight.

Bill didn't want to upset his friend any more than he had to, for they had been friends a long time. As Bill looked out the window, it was business as usual. All was well on the surface, but it hid the pain of the troubles we all face. Bill spun his chair back to his desk and opened his laptop. He began where he had left off. Bill knew that side of Chicago and up to the state line. He knew there were a million places to do this sort of thing and get away with it. As he looked at the map of Chicago, looked at the size of it all, he felt Milwaukee was big enough for him and smiled to himself a little.

It was about noon, and Bill had just finished a call with a new client. The client had burglary problems and wanted him to figure out a way to solve them for him. Bill was about to go out for lunch when Alice entered his office. First, she wanted to settle up for now on her bill and then maybe get something to eat with him. With the bookwork done, she now had her receipt, and they left together. She drove them to a small restaurant, and they sat in the back so they could talk about her case. Once they had been served their meal, Bill brought up everything she needed to know and what John and he had been doing on the case.

"You have been busy, Bill; in fact, you now know it's been more than a week?" said Alice, with some surprise in her voice.

"Bishop Frazer is supposed to call later this afternoon, for I know he wants to play a bigger role in this case. I am beginning to feel he wants to do something. I don't know what, but I know he's planning something," stated Bill, waiting for some reaction from her. "You seem to need a small army with you, Bill. But how do you plan to use it?" Alice was now questioning what his next move would be.

Bill thought it was a fair question. He said, "It depends on two things, Alice, first, what the bishop says, and second, on what I hear from our informants. It's something like a good chess game; you watch every move and then decide."

Alice was starting to think it was sounding more complicated all the time. "Do you feel you can have this all done by Halloween or before?" Alice was looking for a clearer answer.

"Yes, I do. In fact, the more we know in advance, the more we know about how to deal with it," stated Bill with some confidence in his voice.

"You will keep me well-informed, I hope?" wondered Alice, not wanting to be left out.

After they had their dessert and more coffee, Bill told Alice what he felt was the motive behind Adam's actions.

Alice slowly leaned forward on the table and said, "If I heard you correctly, Bill, you're calling my brother a madman, aren't you?" Alice questioned some of his points of view.

"No, Alice, I'm not at all. In fact, I think your brother is brilliant, but he's following some type of plan here. What it is, we'll just have to see," answered Bill with some care.

Alice sat back; she studied him for a second and said, "So you're saying that he's following some type of game plan. That almost makes me think he's after something, in spite of what he's done already."

Bill nodded, approving of her thoughts, but said nothing, for he was wondering about her deeper thoughts. He studied her a little more and then said, "Adam is trying to be like any great engineer; he needs a plan to follow, to improve upon and make better. As an engineer, the goal is to finish it ahead of time and have it built correctly for the one he's building it for."

Alice did not fully grasp what he said but understood the job of an engineer. She shook her head and said, "I'm starting to see that you are beginning to get into Adam's head and you're looking around to see how you can stop him, aren't you?"

Again, Bill nodded approval of her statement and carefully said, "That's correct, Alice; I've been with you on this case long enough that I'm starting to understand him better and how he reasons, and I will stop him."

Alice was now seeing that she had picked the right man for the job; all he needed was to understand him and then make his plan.

"You know, Bill, for a while, I was starting to have some doubts about you, but not now. From what you say, you'll need a small army, which you're trying to build. You really have something in mind, don't you?"

Bill nodded again, approving of her statement, but said nothing. Alice could now see in Bill something of a warrior, a man who, even if he failed in the beginning, would rise up in the end and become the champion. With that thought in her mind, she gave him a small smile and then nodded that she understood.

She dropped Bill off at his office, and they waved at each other. Then she left. Once inside his office, he readied himself for that night again. A little after 4:30 p.m., Bill picked up the phone. It was Kathy, and she told him of the location, the building and street, and the time of the next ritual killing. The day was to be October 18. She said that she had heard it from the transmitter. Bill then quickly asked her several questions and carefully recorded all her information. After a few more minutes, Bill thanked her a lot and then said good-bye. About twenty minutes later, Amy called and said something similar. Again, after several other questions, Amy proved to be valuable in her cover, and again, he thanked her very much and said good-bye. Bill completed his notes and was about to get ready. The phone rang again. It was Bishop Frazer on the line. After they exchanged greetings, the bishop got to his point for calling.

"Bill, I'm going to take some time off from my church duties and work with you on this case, if you don't mind. This is too big, and I can fill you in as it gets closer to Halloween."

Bill was shocked but somewhat happy to hear this. Bill informed the bishop of the latest information and the day and time. The bishop told Bill that was very likely to be his third ritual killing that soon. And then he added that both Adam and he had much to do to get ready for Halloween. They talked for some time, and then they hung up together. Bill added to the notes of this case, and now Bishop Frazer was on the team and would be working steadily with him. Bill finished his notes and paused to take it all in. He wondered what would happen next. He looked out the window behind him to catch his breath and think a little, as to what to do now. Bill looked at his options and tried to decide what move would be better in this game. Bill paused for about ten minutes.

When John entered the office and saw Bill staring out the window, he said, "Earth to Bill, Earth to Bill?"

Bill now slowly turned to look at John. "Oh, John, it's you, good. I need to talk to you," stated Bill; something was on his mind.

John was starting to see that Bill was thinking hard on something, and he was going to be a part of it.

"The bishop has just joined our team, and I welcome it, now that I think of it. We are going to Chicago on the fifteenth of October, and we are going to do two things. We're going to the police there and talk to them about this, and we are going to find where the next murder is to be and the bishop will be with us," stated Bill, still thinking that telling the police there might be pointless.

"Going to the police there in Chicago, I think it might be hit or miss, Bill; they might be bombarded with people saying this or that."

Bill nodded and said, "I know, but I feel it's the right thing to do, if I do it right and can make them see the point of this."

John made himself a cup of coffee and sipped some of it. "I still think it's a long, long shot, friend," he said, pointing to Bill. John sipped some of his coffee and then added, "Anyway, we'll be looking at the next murder site first and not after the fact. This time, we'll be ready, right, Bill?"

Bill nodded, approving of that, but now he was thinking of Tom at the station. Bill decided to call Tom on the phone in front of John. Tom answered, and then Bill told him of his plan, what he was about to do. Tom felt it was fine and thanked him for telling him about it, but he felt it was a no-sale.

Bill questioned him on it, but Tom felt it lacked solid evidence. After another minute or so, they both hung up.

Bill did have the answer he was looking for now; this gave him free reign to plan his attack. Confidence appeared on Bill's face, and John was watching the change in front of him.

"Well, what did he say, Bill?" wondered John.

Bill loved this moment, for now his hands were free to prove his point.

"We are going to Chicago, John, and whether they believe us or not makes no difference to me. We are going after Adam and his gang of merry men, and you are going to be part of it!" stated Bill flatly, now with confidence and determination in his voice.

T HE SUN WAS SLOWLY BREAKING THE HORIZON ON THE
fifteenth of October as the three men got into Bill's car.
John had the camera, and Bishop Frazer was in the backseat. City traffic was just starting to pick up for the day, so
leaving the city for the interstate was not hard to do yet. They
all knew that when they reached Chicago, things would be
very different. Bill knew from experience where the police
department was; it was just getting there that would be hard
in heavy traffic. On the way to Chicago on the interstate, the
three of them made for good company. As they approached
the city, the traffic was getting serious, and the men decided
to take a break from it all, have a good breakfast, and let the
traffic settle down some. They pulled off from the interstate
at an exit. Bishop Frazer knew of a good hotel and restaurant at this exit. As they were enjoying their meal together,
Bishop Frazer wanted to know about their visit to the police.
Bill explained his idea of stating their evidence to them, as
to who and why, and his plan to get Adam and his followers.
The bishop got it right away when he heard it and clapped his
hands together. Finally, John got it when the bishop told it a
slightly different way.

The bishop said as he shook his head, "Son, and my good friend, you're in the right place at the right time."

John sat there a little shocked at himself—that he didn't get it the first time. "You mean, Bill, by telling the authorities and having them turn you down, you cleared yourself, so you can investigate freely?" responded John, still amazed at Bill's cleverness and the twist he put in it.

The bishop continued to enjoy his meal. He was proud of Bill's clever reasoning. The bishop was also thinking of John, who sat across from him. He was a very intelligent man, but the bishop also saw that those people usually worked well with set ideas and didn't reason well outside the box. Bill felt comfortable with his longtime friends but still wondered why the bishop was taking time off for this.

Bill then nicely questioned the bishop, "Mark, how did you explain to the church that your work here needed your full attention?"

Mark cleared his throat of the toast he had just eaten and then added, "Well, Bill, Adam and his followers are following a very dark satanic plan here. You are going to need my knowledge and experience from time to time, to stay ahead of them, and I really want to help."

"Thank you, Mark. I know I can count on that, very much, and I think we are forming a very strong team that will get the job done," stated Bill with some pride in his voice.

After they finished their meal, Bill went to the lobby of the hotel and checked on the prices of rooms for the night while the rest went to refresh themselves. After that, they continued into the city. The traffic was better along the way, as they went into the heart of the city. Finally, they arrived at the police department, parked their car, and got out. When they were at the desk, John talked to an officer behind the desk and said that they would like to see someone about the ritual killings because they had some information. The officer turned, picked up the phone, entered that department, and waited for a reply. Then the officer told them to wait there and someone would come out and see them.

Several minutes passed, and they watched many people come and go. Finally, a plainclothes officer greeted them. "Hello, I'm Lieutenant Wilson. You say that you may have some information for us? Will you please follow me to my office?"

They followed the officer down the hallway and into a somewhat small office. He closed the door behind them. The room had plenty of filing cabinets and a window that looked out to the main floor where many other officers were working. The desk was full of files and papers and looked a little out of control.

The lieutenant sat behind his desk and made himself comfortable. He got to the point of their visit. "You say you have information on these ritual killings? Well, we get five to ten calls each day, all stating the same thing. So if you don't mind me saying, this better be good."

Bill and John pleaded their case very well. Bill showed the lieutenant his badge and explained that he was a PI. He gave him their client's name and address. Bishop Frazer joined in by stating the church's position on this and these men's investigation. Bill showed the names of the followers and their leader. The lieutenant picked up a phone, and shortly after, an officer took the names to run them through the computer for follow-up information. The three men offered all their information, including about the rifles and ammunition that were now in Park River. When they finished their plea with the officer, they stood silent and waited for the lieutenant to say something. He was still taking notes on what they were saying. The lieutenant then added, "So you say that the next ritual killing is to be on the eighteenth of the month, on the south side, and at this address, is that right?"

"Yes," said Bill, seeing the lieutenant's concern. He told him again of his informant's information about the next killing. He told him that they would leave no trace, like the rest, and that the body would have no blood inside it.

The lieutenant looked surprised by that comment and was about to say something when an officer entered the room with the information and returned Bill's notes to him. The lieutenant looked over the information closely and seemed frustrated at the findings. "You almost had me on this one, but this report states that each of the ten people we looked up has no record. So are you saying that this Adam Johnson and followers took a course on professional killing and are moonlighting as murderers?"

The three now knew they had hit a dead end, and all there was left was to wait and leave. But then John stated, "What we told you is the truth, sir; it's not much, we know that, but Adam is brilliant and trained his followers well. You have no profile on anyone this good. We are not crazy; we've been following him almost three weeks, and we have this much already, though it's not much. On the eighteenth of the month, or the nineteenth, when you find the body of a young girl, dead and nude, remember we told you so."

The lieutenant sat there silently in his chair. He knew they had no profile to fit these killings. He also knew that Bill did have information that was correct for the crime scene and the ritual markings on the body. The lieutenant stated, "You three have offered the most information to date and a little proof. I can't take this to the captain and argue for you. If you're right about the eighteenth, we will take this further, and you will be hearing from us. Is that understood? Now let me show you out."

Once they had left the building and were standing by the car, they stood around each other, and the bishop said, "You know something, that actually went better than I thought. Maybe, if I may say so, maybe we planted a seed there, and it will serve us later?"

Bill and John looked at each other and then the bishop. John then said, "You mean that little speech I gave there at the end, about profile and date?"

Bill and Mark both nodded to that. Then Bill said, "They didn't toss us out; they walked us out. I think Mark is right on this thing. You noticed the lieutenant; he never raised his voice at us, like so many lieutenants do at bad reports from people. I remember doing that myself in the past; when a story sounds bad, it probably is."

They got into the car, set the GPS to their next stop, and drove away. Once they got on the expressway south, they were making good time. They didn't speak much to each other, for they just watched the city go by. Once they were getting close to Indiana, there were more signs of it. "Well, we're getting close now; the GPS wants us to take this exit. I better take it," said Bill.

He then drove toward the exit off the main expressway. As they drove down this street, they were in some old industrial area of town. Many of the buildings hadn't been used in years and were in a state of decay. Bill followed the GPS until they came to the building and stopped. It was a very large building with many broken windows and four floors to it. The front door was gone. It should have led into the main part of the building. The office part of the building was off to their left, and they were feeling a little nervous about going inside.

Bill had John open the trunk and find his revolver just in case. Bill didn't like carrying it around much. Once Bill had his gun, they entered the building cautiously; only drug users, runaways, and others who had fallen out of the safety net would be there. Once inside, they found that it was an old, abandoned manufacturing building. This building needed to be torn down; there was no hope of fixing it. The rooms were large, and most of the machinery was still there. There were cobwebs everywhere; they ran down from the ceiling. There was the sound of some distant water dripping. They spent some time going from floor to floor, searching as much as they could. Finally, they went back to the main floor of the building. Bill asked Mark for his take on it. The bishop gave Bill an idea of what he would want in a place like that. They looked some more, going from room to room. The bishop then stopped them and said, "This is it—it's perfect, it's large, and it has something that looks like an altar for the ritual. It's fairly clear, perfect." The room seemed to be where some manufacturing had taken place; it had worktables of a sort. There was a small maintenance shop in the back and an exit to the outside. There were few windows in this room, so their lighting would not be seen. The floor of the room's only entry showed no evidence of traffic in years, for there was dust everywhere.

The three men used their GPS to lock in on the location, and John took careful notes of it. They then went to the roof to get some tactical positions, so they would not be noticed in their coming. Then they went to the main level again, for more tactical positions there. Bill was thinking there could be at least twenty to thirty of them for this ritual, and the rest were going to be guards. John found some old paper, and Bill drew on it where he figured they would be and where they must be if they wanted to save the girl. John also pointed out some other possible tactical positions, and Bill circled them on the paper.

Sometime later, when they were satisfied with their work there, they left the building and went home for the day. On the eighteenth of October, Bill, John, and Bishop Mark Frazer readied Bill's car for the trip to Chicago. It was a fine fall day. It was cool but sunny. At about 4:00 in the afternoon, John was going over the checklist, as their gear went into the trunk.

"Well, Bill, it's all here. We should be ready to go," responded John with some pride in his work.

Bill looked at everything and nodded in approval. They closed the trunk.

"John, it's always good to have you as a teammate," said Bill, giving John a big thumbs-up.

They again made their way to Chicago. Bishop Frazer was telling Bill and John that if they just stopped this ritual, without arresting the key players, they would have done nothing. Mark was telling them they had to break the cycle, and then the Halloween ritual would mean nothing to Satan.

"You're pretty certain of this, are you, Mark?" asked John, looking over his left shoulder.

The bishop stretched out some and said, "Oh yes, John, many other religions do human sacrifices; if the chain is broken properly, it can't be done for a least a year."

John's frustration with religion was starting to show a little when he turned away. He was thinking, *Why can't we just get along as we should and let the spirit world do its own thing?*

The sun was setting fast as they left the city limits, and now they were on the open four lanes.

The sun had long-since set when they came up to their exit. When they were a block away, Bill asked for his night goggles. Bill pulled over and shut off the lights. With the goggles on and working, he reached under the dash and turned off all the lights of the car.

"What are you doing, Bill?" asked Mark, seeing him reach under the dashboard.

"What am I doing here? I'm shutting off all my lights, so we'll not be seen in the distance ahead or behind. This has saved my butt a hundred times in my life."

"Don't you ever forget to turn them back on again?" asked Mark, wondering about that sort of thing.

Bill smiled and said, "Once in a while, but when I can't see my speedometer, then I remember."

Bill pulled back onto the road and headed toward the building they were staking out. John had the GPS in his hands, and then they found the shrubs that were across from the door to that ritual room they found. The standing shrubs would hide the car well and still let them see some. There were no working streetlights to bother them. John gave a loaded gun to each of them. Bill then said to them, "Use these if you must, to defend yourselves, but not before. If they try to run away, use a warning shot to stop them. Is that understood?"

John and Mark nodded their heads.

"We have about an hour before the ritual is to start, and I don't see any cars yet, but we should see light inside the building, through the windows," said Bill as he reported what he was seeing. He looked up and down the building with his night goggles.

An hour had passed; there were no cars. There were no people walking around outside and no lights inside to give them away. "This is really strange, guys; we should have seen something by now," said Bishop Frazer.

To Bill, it didn't seem right. John was thinking the same thing as Bill. Then John said to them, "We better drive around that building; maybe we chose the wrong room?"

Bill started the car and drove slowly down the road. There were no other cars parked anywhere. Bill turned the corner and drove the width of it. Then, he turned again down the length of the building to where they had been a few days before.

There were no cars anywhere and no people, no nothing. Then Bill stopped the car and started swearing profusely, "That Goddamn bastard tricked us! He chose another site for this!" Bill hurriedly drove up the block and then down the block on the other side—nothing. There were no cars, no people anywhere, not even a stray dog.

"What time is it now?" asked Bill in a very frustrated tone of voice. "Eight thirty-something, from what I can see here," answered Mark, trying to see his watch. They drove up and down several other blocks and found nothing even further. Finally, Bill pulled over and stopped. He removed his goggles and said, "We might as well as go home; they really tricked us this time. We could spend the next two hours looking and find nothing."

Bill spotted a patrol car and stopped to talk to them, but the officers knew nothing of the location or reports of anything unusual. So they put all their gear away and drove to Bill's office for the night.

Later that night, Adam returned to his apartment, and he was feeling electric inside. He could now fully plan for Halloween freely and with no pressure in his planning. He went to the refrigerator and gave himself a nice cold beer to celebrate his last qualifying ritual's success. He strongly felt inside that changing the ritual location at the last minute would lose any police, if any were tracking them. Adam sat in his easy chair and was really glowing inside. The beer made it even better. He lowered his beer in salute to Satan, for he felt that it was he who had given him that idea. He felt his sudden change in plan better trained his followers in following orders and the chain of command, just like the military.

And the thirteen women had worked out just fine; they all got naked at the right cue, in their qualifying for Satan's bride. *What a victory for Satan tonight,* thought Adam, *and on to Halloween night, when Satan chooses his bride and then is the world leader forever.*

Again, he lowered his beer to Satan in salute to him and to his future. He took a big swallow of beer and went to his desk. He unlocked the drawer, pulled out a folder with his Halloween plans, opened it, and found what he was looking for. He had signed up for vacation that week and got it, and many of the followers did the same for the celebration in mind. He felt that to find the girl, the right girl, would be a problem, so he would have to look earlier and just keep her until Halloween. Chicago was never a problem for hiding people, but traveling four hundred miles with a kidnapped child was. So with that solution in mind, he moved on to the next problem—lodging for the extra members. He knew that his house up north could handle about half of them, so the other half would have to make arrangements. He felt that calling each of the motels in town, reserving rooms with special passwords, and paying some in advance should do the trick.

The thirteen women could stay with him. Adam had found them through an occult newspaper ad he ran, and they were eager to try out for it. But because they were Satan's brides, the thirteen women would receive special treatment by him, for he felt that any mistreatment would upset Satan. Adam, taking another drink of his beer, thought on this matter. He made a note of this in his folder, that he better explain this to his followers so there was no misunderstanding on the matter. He didn't want any bad feelings on this matter, for his followers were very important to him, as they always were.

The next matter was food; thirteen women and he, plus servants, would eat a lot of food, and he was talking about three full days maybe. He got up and walked around some. He couldn't remember if there was a caterer big enough to handle that kind of load. He went back to his desk and made a note of that in the folder.

With that thought in mind, he put everything away for the night and locked the drawer. Once he finished his beer, he shut off the lights and called it a night to remember.

Later, Bill, John, and Mark pulled up to Bill's office. Bill was feeling like he had let someone down and someone had died for it. The other two men felt that too in Bill and tried to cheer him up. Then Bishop Frazer took him to the side and had a personal talk with him about faith. He explained to him that all great people in history and in the Bible had moments of serious doubt and failure in their lives. God was always there for him; all he needed was faith and to believe in it.

"Tonight, you failed, and we know that someone died in the end. But never give up and never give in. Success always has a price to be paid. You, my friend, are going after the ultimate prey in your life; he's smart and resourceful, and he doesn't care about the life he takes. Don't let him take yours as well, my good friend. Give it to God." Bishop Frazer said more after that and then went to his car and left. Bill stood there and watched as he drove away.

John, watching the whole thing, wondered what he had said to Bill as he stood by his car. "See you tomorrow, Bill. Get some rest, please," said John, still wondering as he got into his car. Bill stood there and watched John drive away into the night. Bill sat down on the hood of his car and wished he had a cigarette. He sat there about a half an hour and thought it all over. After thinking it all over, he felt that what Mark had said to him was right; this didn't have to be a train wreck, just a bad bump in the road along the way. Finally, he got into his car and went home for the night and some rest.

The next morning, Bill was a little late in opening his office. As always, he did his usual routine in the morning, but this time, he turned on the radio. He wanted to hear what was said about the previous night. He went through the mail that he kept and looked it over as he listened to the radio. Then he went over the schedule of work he had to do for the night.

After making some coffee, he sat down again to go through the answering machine to hear if anything was important. There was nothing new from Kathy or Amy on the machine. There was a call for more work and a number to call. There was nothing else important, just some telemarketers.

Later that morning, Mark entered the office and made himself at home there while Bill was talking to a client. Bill didn't notice that Mark had brought the rolls with him. After another ten minutes on the phone, he hung up. "Morning, Mark. You sleep well last night? And thanks for the rolls," Bill greeted him, seeing that he did help himself to the coffee.

After another half hour, John entered the office and greeted Mark and Bill. He helped himself to some coffee, pulled up the other chair, and sat down. "Mark and I were going over last night together. And from the radio that's playing, there's no word yet of another killing," reported Bill, bringing John up to speed.

"Well, that really is good news, Bill, but I wouldn't count on that just yet," said John, with a note of caution in his voice.

Mark and Bill looked at each other, knowing that John was right in that comment. Mark then decided to tell them both of the final decision he made last night. "Well, after last night, I decided to work with you through Halloween night. To me, it seems that this Adam is not your average man. He's smart and gutsy, and he doesn't care about whose life he takes. I believe he's completely sold out to Satan, and if there is any part of him that's human yet, it may be hard to find."

Bill leaned back in his chair and then said, "But I was under the idea you were going to be with us anyway to the end."

The bishop sat back, chuckled some, and said, "Yes, yes, I did say that, didn't I? But after last night, I had a chance to see what you were up against and why your evidence is so scant. You ever go deer hunting anywhere here in Wisconsin? You can have the best of everything with you and never see a deer. Like you there, you have some evidence; in deer hunting, you might have a small runway or a deer rubbing there but no deer. You can sit or stand there all day and see nothing and if it's really bad, all week. What I'm trying to say is, you have some good ideas, friend, but I'm going to show you how to get into his head!"

Bill and John looked at each other for a second and then at the bishop. "So if I understand you correctly, you're saying we have the right stuff but not the right location. Am I saying this right?" asked John, not believing his ears.

The bishop chuckled and said nicely, "Something like that. Bill and I are Christians, and you are not. Don't take that wrong way, John, but we hear the world around us differently than you do, believe it or not. The spirit inside us hears things differently than you do, and we understand them differently than you do. And this is how we are going to get this Adam character; we are going to jam his frequency, and we are going to put the fear of God in him!"

Bill and John looked at each other again, not really sure what to say. Bill leaned forward in his chair and was about to say something when Alice entered the office.

"Well, we do have a houseful here today," Alice greeted everyone warmly and smiled.

The three men greeted her warmly, and the bishop offered his chair to her. Once she was comfortable in her chair, she opened her purse and showed Bill her bill and offered to pay it. Bill quickly readied himself to help her, as she paid him cash up front. After a few minutes, Bill handed her the receipt. John offered her a cup of coffee and she accepted. After a small drink, she said, "From what I paid today, you men have been busy with my brother; can you tell me what you found? And I have some other information for you, but fill me in first, please."

Bill started first in explaining what they had been doing for her and then everyone else. Alice was indeed surprised with all that they had done for her. After about ten minutes, she was relieved to hear so much was done for her. "I'm really speechless. You guys have been busy. But it was on the radio, just a few minutes ago, that they found the body of that girl in Chicago, and she was killed the same way," said Alice with some emotion in her voice. Then she took a look at each of them.

Bishop Frazer explained to her again that they had been there the previous night, but Adam tricked them and did it someplace else. The bishop reassured her they were now getting very close, and they were going to get closer.

"Your brother is very clever, Alice. You mustn't give up; believe me on that. When we find his true weakness in this, we will have him, and that's money in the bank," said Bill with much confidence.

Mark and John both agreed with that statement and nodded.

Alice was still feeling a bit shaken, knowing another little girl had died because of her brother. "I know it's not your fault at all that she died last night, but that makes three in all. My brother needs to pay for this evil thing and then some!" she said angrily and her voice had some trembling in it. Everyone could feel her pain and frustration, and they were going to help her.

Bishop Frazer broke the silence that followed her statement, saying, "What else did you want to tell us, Alice?"

She felt stronger now, for she knew that they were there to help her. She said, "I'm going on vacation the week of the twenty-fifth to the thirty-first of October, and I want to see him get what he deserves—and the rest of them too!"

Everyone was somewhat shocked by this, but at the same

time, they couldn't blame her either. Each of the men looked at one another, not totally sure how this would work out. This meant a slight change of plans for all of them. "Okay, Alice, this is my rough plan, and Bishop Frazer there is going to inform us with his spiritual information. John there, I'm sure he already knows his part in this, and you and I, we'll stay together, so you can hear firsthand as it goes down. From now on, till Halloween, this may get very expensive for you. So I'm telling you up front and on the level, so it is of no surprise. Is that understood?" asked Bill in a very businesslike tone of voice.

Alice nodded that she understood; her outward appearance showed she had already thought it through. "Like I said earlier at the restaurant, you are the warrior, something like the Phoenix bird; I know you will get them," said Alice with great conviction in her voice.

Bill then started to explain his overall plan to all of them and where he wanted to start first. He spoke of getting the sheriff's attention up there at Park River. Bill then stressed why that was so important to the overall plan he had in mind. Then he went on to explain that with something less than twelve days on the calendar, they had lots to do and get done. Bill was about to say more when the phone rang.

It was Lieutenant Wilson on the line. He said they were right, even though they had little evidence to show for it. Bill informed the lieutenant that they had staked out that building the previous night, but they changed their plans at the last minute. The lieutenant understood that might happen in cases like this. Their force had found the same thing as before, no evidence at all, and the body had no blood in it. The lieutenant went on to say that this time, they had received a phone call next from a pay phone before eight in the morning, reporting the body. He went on to say that they also had information, not released to the press. Bill then told the lieutenant that they were going to be in northern Wisconsin, following the case up there. Then Bill left his cell phone number with the lieutenant. Bill also gave him the address of Adam's place in northern Wisconsin. Then they finished up and hung up together.

Bill smiled as he put down the phone and then said to Mark, "Mark, you were right. I can really see your value to the team." Bill then went on to explain to them what had been said on the phone in great detail.

They were greatly pleased with that information, especially Alice, who now saw their work starting to pay off. Bill again went on about his plan up north and then asked them what they felt would be important to their case. John then went on to explain the manpower problem in surrounding the place. Bill wrote that down on a notepad. "You, Mark, what do you see as a problem?"

Mark went on to explain with the photos of the pit to hell, "If this ritual is the one that I think it is, we're going to need lots and lots of holy water to ruin that opening and possible dead bodies."

Alice looked shocked by that information. Bill wrote it down on the notepad. He then added that he felt that making the sheriff believe and get behind them was necessary, and he wrote that down.

Bill then told them that after the twenty-second of October, he was closing the office and they would be up north thereafter, ending the case. Then again he reminded Alice that this was going to be expensive. Bill said in closing, "I figure if we leave around 10:00 a.m. on Thursday morning. We should be there around four to five in the evening. We have lots to do, lots to get done, and lots of people to make believers of." Bill sat there for a moment, waiting for any questions, and had none. Then he helped himself to one of Mark's rolls.

Alice knew she was coming along and then thought of the little things she had to do as well. "Bill, my vacation is from the twenty-fifth, not the twenty-second," stated Alice, with some fear for her job.

Bill thought a moment and smiled. "Don't worry about that, Alice; all good PIs can handle that. And better yet, I'll see that you'll get paid for that too!" Bill asked Alice for her employer's number and wrote it down. Then he picked up the phone and dialed. Bill waited until he was transferred to the right department and then explained who he was, his association with Lieutenant Wilson, and who he was calling for. Bill ran his charm a mile long and explained why Alice Johnson needed to be off from the twenty-second on through the thirty-first of October. Bill ran into the usual bumps in the road, and then it was cleared for her and with pay. Bill thanked them warmly and hung up.

"Now, Alice, you're cleared for the twenty-second on and with pay!" stated Bill with a big smile on his face.

Alice sat there in total disbelief at what she had just heard; she was speechless. She rose from her chair and gave Bill a big hug. "I don't believe this! How did you do that? I've never heard of it before!"

Bill, feeling really good about himself, then explained the law to her and that she was known to the lieutenant. "No employer can stop you in that; it's a little understood or known law of the land. Some will just give you time off, but others will pay you for that."

Later, on October 20, Adam Johnson settled in for the evening in his apartment after a long day at work. It had been a very busy day of trading, and he saw on the board that many of his investments had done very well, though they were handled by others. As he sat in his easy chair, he started to think of it some. This year would be about the same as the previous year, and the previous year was a very good one. He left his chair and reached for a beer from the refrigerator. He went back to his chair and opened his beer. He drank some slowly, now thinking of a few changes in his plans for Halloween. He would be taking Wednesday and the rest of the week off, while the others came up Friday night. The thirteen women would be up late Thursday afternoon through Halloween and maybe Sunday. The caterer was now set though Sunday until noon. At least he had most of the big-ticket items done. But there were a lot of little things to be done. He had just taken another drink of his beer when the doorbell rang.

Going to the door, he was thinking, *Who could this be?* He opened the door. There were two police officers standing there.

The taller one spoke first. "Are you Adam Johnson?"

"Yes, sir," said Adam in a positive tone of voice.

The shorter officer then spoke. "We understand that sometime time ago, you purchased roughly sixty garments from an occult store. What type of religion are you in?"

Adam had known this day would come someday. He said, "Yes, I did purchase sixty garments from that store, for the followers and myself, and yes, I'm a Satanist!"

The two officers then looked at each other, not knowing

what to think of it. The taller officer then said, "May we come in and look for any weapons that you use at your rituals?"

Adam also knew that would be next, and he waved the officers in and closed the door.

"This is probably what you are looking for, and you can check it out, if you want," said Adam in a friendly manner. He opened the door next to the front, for it was a storage closet, bent down, and went through some stuff. He came up with a dagger in a leather holder and a short sword, also in a leather holder. The officers' eyes opened some at the sight of that, as Adam passed it to them to take with them.

The two officers again glanced at each other, and the shorter officer said cautiously, "May we run these downtown to have them examined for a couple of days?"

Adam smiled warmly and said, "By all means, sir. Take your time with it. Just bring it back before Halloween. My followers and I want to use it again on that day. But I can tell you now that the blood on it is pigs' blood and maybe a stray cat!"

The two officers were shocked by that information. Again, they glanced at each other, and the taller one said, "And where do you go for your celebration? I hope it's outside of the city."

"Yes, sir, just south of the Illinois-Wisconsin border on a farm in the country. Hey, it works for us, men!" stated Adam happily as his voice rose some.

The taller officer then wanted information on that farm, as to the owner and what town and where. With that, the two officers left and Adam closed and locked the door. He leaned against the door and laughed gently to himself. Again, he knew this would come someday.

He went to his easy chair, sat down, and enjoyed his beer, which was now a little warm. Then he laughed again and called the two officers a couple of putzes. He finished his beer and went for another. He sat down again. Then he thought, *I think I better tell five or six of my closest members about this and set up an alibi for the next time.*

It was the morning of October 22, and Bill unlocked the office at 8:30 in the morning. He hurriedly went through his routine. He was trying to make a list of things to do before he went up north and when he came back again. Then he thought of the transmitter and Kathy and Amy. He decided he better put that on the list to do after, before the police really got involved there. He didn't want to explain it to them and answer all their questions. He went through the mail one last time just to be sure not to miss anything. He left the office open, ran down to the bank, and paid some bills before he went away. When he returned, John was helping himself to the coffee. He looked well rested.

"Good morning, Bill. I saw that you were getting ready," said John casually as he then sipped his coffee gently.

Bill returned to his chair and carefully put the paid bills in the proper drawer. "Good morning, John. How's the coffee today?" responded Bill, taking time to greet him.

"Everything is good, Bill. I see you've been busy?" said John with a casual tone in his voice.

Bill again returned to his list of things to do before and after. John handed him his coffee in a mug, and Bill quickly drank some. John just watched Bill work and said nothing to bother him. After several entries, Bill then sat back and looked at it.

"Say, you're really going to sew this thing up, aren't you, Bill?" asked John, seeing the completed list in Bill's hands.

Bill nodded and said, "Absolutely, and I believe we both know the reasons why."

At this time, Bishop Frazer entered the office and saw them both there. He said, "Morning, gentlemen. I see you're taking care of business as usual."

Bill and John greeted him, as Bill made another entry on his list. Mark helped himself to the coffee and then walked over to the window and looked out.

Alice entered the office next and greeted them all. She had been looking forward to this day. Bill now noticed the time and said, "Morning, Alice, I hope you're all set and ready, for we all are going to be gone for some time now."

"Yes, I'm ready, and I have something for you as well," said Alice, feeling happy and excited about the trip. She opened her purse and handed out a thousand dollars, paid in advance, for the trip.

Everyone was a little shocked by this. Bill took the money and then pulled out the proper paperwork. He filled out the paperwork needed and handed her a receipt. "You really don't have to do this, Alice; we know you're good for this," said Bill, feeling a little uneasy with the event.

"Oh, I wanted to, Bill. This will give you some capital to work with, while we're away. I know you will put it to good use," replied Alice with a grin that reassured everyone in the room.

Bill decided to put the money in his wallet with the money he was taking with him. John looked at his watch and nodded to Bill. It was a little early, but that was fine.

"Well, I can tell from the two of you you're thinking about

going," said Mark, while he glanced at them, and then he looked at his watch.

The four of them slowly walked to the door of the office, as Bill followed behind them. Bill carefully looked over everything and locked the door. He had everything in the trunk already. John, Mark, and Alice each had a suitcase, and it was a tight fit to close the trunk lid. They all got into Bill's car and were on their journey north.

They reached a fine motel in Park River, as the sun was at the horizon for the day. Bill paid for four rooms for the next four days. The man at the desk was more than happy for the business. He told Bill about a good family restaurant. Once they were settled in for the night, they went downtown for something to eat.

The next morning, John knocked on Bill's door to see if he was up. It was about 7:00 a.m., and Bill hurried his shower to let him in. John turned on the television set, and Bill finished his shower. After a while, Bill came out ready for the day and John was watching the news. It was about the last ritual killing in Chicago. At the end of the newscast, it was stated that there were no new leads to the senseless killing.

"You hear that, Bill? No new leads. So much for our help, but they now do believe us at least," remarked John as he turned off the set.

"That may be true, John, but Adam will be here any day now. And we know we'll have to be ready when he does arrive," replied Bill as he looked into his bag of gear. When he was finished checking it, he took it with him and John followed behind.

"Morning, Mark. Sleep well last night?" asked John, seeing he was by the car.

Bill nodded at Mark in a friendly manner as he opened the trunk and placed his bag inside. He closed it again just as Alice was closing and locking the door. Then she walked toward the others and greeted them, feeling somewhat excited about the day. After breakfast and a tankful of gas, they went in search of the police station in town.

When they found it on a side street, they got out of the car and walked up the steps into the station. There was an officer at the desk, just finishing up a phone call.

"May we speak with the sheriff, please?" John asked rather politely.

"Do you really need the sheriff for this matter?" asked the officer behind the desk.

"Yes, we do, and the matter is for him to decide," said John with a little more determination.

"Well, I'll see if he has a moment. Wait right here, please," the officer said as he left his desk.

They waited for a minute or two, and then the sheriff walked toward them.

"Good morning, I'm Sheriff Roger Kief. How may I help you?" stated the sheriff rather politely but in a businesslike tone of voice.

Bill came forward and shook his hand, and then he introduced everyone and himself. Bill went quickly into why they were there and how his department could help in arresting Adam Johnson. At first, the sheriff stepped back, and then Bill showed his badge and told him that he was a PI investigating the matter.

"Please follow me to my office," said the sheriff, in a professional tone of voice. They followed the sheriff into his office and closed the door. He said, "Now let me get this straight;

you're saying he has killed three people, and you have spoken to Lieutenant Wilson of the Chicago PD already concerning this?"

"Yes, sir, he felt the same way as you there, until the last murder took place on the day we said it would," stated Bill firmly and rather flatly.

The sheriff paced his office for a moment, not really sure of what to do next. Suddenly, he went to his desk, sat down, picked up the phone, and called the Chicago PD. After a moment, he said, "Lieutenant Wilson, please. This is Sheriff Roger Kief." Lieutenant Wilson came on the line, and again, the sheriff introduced himself. The sheriff questioned the lieutenant about Bill Radner and his party, who were now sitting in his office. The lieutenant informed the sheriff that Bill and party were the only sound lead they had so far as to who was doing the killings and that they were withholding their names from the public. The sheriff sat there in some disbelief and ran his fingers over his balding head. After another several minutes, the sheriff hung up, and it looked like his mind left him for a second.

"All right, he says you're the real deal here, but now you have to convince me," said the sheriff rather bluntly, looking for someone to answer next. John then went on to explain from the beginning to the present the work they had done.

Bill told him of the underground church and the rifles and ammunition that were also there. Then the bishop spoke of the church's involvement with the case. Alice told the sheriff that she was confident that her brother really was a killer. The sheriff sat there for a moment and looked at each one. And then he said, "This is not enough for me to raise the devil here. If you have something, then show me! I don't know how you got the lieutenant there to believe this. But any good lawyer would throw this out the window."

Bill, having heard this before, understood his disbelief. He stated flatly, "Sir, Adam Johnson is not your average man; he's brilliant and cunning, and he doesn't care about your life. And he doesn't care about your opinion either, as long as it's on his side of the fence. He's fooled the best in Chicago, and he's fooling you as well. I agree, we don't have much here, but unlike you, we know it's the truth!"

The sheriff sat there for a moment and didn't say a word, for he didn't like being called a fool. "All right then, let's see some of your proof!" said the sheriff with an attitude in his voice.

"How much time do you have then, Sheriff?" asked Alice, with some hope in her voice.

"Why? Where do you want to take me?" asked the sheriff, with disbelief in his voice.

"We must go to Adam Johnson's place, if you want to see it," said John, with some caution in his voice.

"Fine then, let's see your proof," said the sheriff with reluctance.

They all left the office and walked forward, past the desk clerk. The sheriff said that he would be going with them. The sheriff then added that he could be a while. The sheriff told Bill that he would follow in a police cruiser. With Bill leading the way and Alice again giving directions, they all reached Adam's property and the gate into the woods.

John opened the gate, and Bill and the sheriff drove in. John closed the gate behind them. John quickly got into Bill's car and continued on slowly. By this time, most of the trees had lost their leaves, and the cover they once gave was now gone.

They continued for some time, and then Alice told Bill to stop short of the clearing. Bill shut off the motor and got out. The sheriff did the same and got out of the car. He walked up to them and wondered what was next with Bill's plan. John brought out his GPS locator and turned it on. He set it to locate the entry. Once they were at the tree, Alice opened the hatch and pushed the button. The ground opened up behind the tree.

The sheriff was shocked by this and said, "Good heavens, man! In all my years on the force, I've never seen that before!"

Bill and John cleaned away the leaves from the steps down, so it looked like it had before. The sheriff went and got a flashlight, and Alice passed out Bill's and John's. With their flashlights on, they all stepped down into the tunnel. At the bottom of the step, Alice pushed the button to close it.

"Goddamn it; I've never seen it so black before!" said Sheriff Kief with some fear in his voice. Sheriff Kief had no idea how long the tunnel was; Bishop Frazer wondered the same thing. The five of them with their flashlights on broke the blackness ahead and walked forward for some time. At the clear curtain, the barrels and the boxes were there again. The sheriff could see with his flashlight that this was a large room.

"Now, Sheriff, you will have some of your proof," said Bill in a firm voice.

Bishop Frazer and Alice looked at the pit of hell and the pulpit and altar. The rest looked at the rifles and ammunition, the boxes, and barrels of oil. John showed them the box with the swords in it again. They showed the sheriff the dressing room and the steps into the house above. At last, they showed the sheriff the pit to hell, the altar, and the pulpit. The sheriff went back to see the pit and shined his light into it.

"Damn, that thing is really deep, isn't it?" marveled the sheriff.

Finally, the sheriff had seen enough, and Bishop Frazer had seen enough as well. They left.

Once they were outside again, and the tunnel had closed and been covered as well as they could, they returned to their cars, wondering what the sheriff thought of all of that.

"Personally, I'm with you on all of this. This is really strange. But I can't do anything here; I can't stop somebody from being strange or weird. Your proof is enough for me, but the law says something else," said the sheriff with some mixed emotions in his voice.

Then the bishop again explained the church's position on the matter and asked where they could get a truck with about a thousand gallons of water there and enough long hoses to reach the pit of hell. First, the sheriff refused to answer, and then he said, "The National Park Service can do that for you, but it would have to be cleared through me first."

Then the bishop said politely, "Listen to the news tonight and every night, but most likely, it will be from here, another missing girl eleven to thirteen years of age. Sir, that's what that altar is for, a sacrifice for Satan. Sir, one of your citizens is going to be missing real soon, friend, and we can help you and everybody it may concern. Follow our plan, sir, and we can end this once and for all."

The sheriff looked at each of them and at first didn't know what to say, but then he said nicely, "All right then, you can talk to them there, but you still need my permission first. Is that understood? If, and I mean if, somebody comes up missing, where can I reach you at?"

They exchanged information, and everything was now

understood. They left the property, everybody in Bill's car. They followed the sheriff back to town, and they were going to the National Park Service station for information on a tanker truck with enough hose for their project. That was all they could do for that day, and the following day would be something else. After getting better directions a few times, they found the park service station. It was a nice-sized building with many large doors for large trucks to come and go. They drove up to what looked like the office of the building.

Alice was looking content with the way things were so far. She was a little concerned about the rest of the time. Eight days until Halloween, so it was still some time away. *What else needs to be done?* she wondered.

They went into the office and talked with the man in charge; Bill introduced himself and asked the man there if the sheriff had called.

The man said he had. "You may want a tanker truck for Halloween night."

John then went into the details of the length of hose and the pump needed for their work. The man took them into the back and showed them four trucks that might be suitable for their work. John again wanted to know about the length of the hose. John figured about six hundred feet in length at the minimum.

"Yes, we have hoses that long here, but then, we would be at a disadvantage here, if a fire broke out."

John then pointed out, "If possible, you could borrow some from other park service stations around you."

"Yes, we could. That may work, but what's this all for?"

All Bill could say at the time was that it was a police matter. The man then went on to explain that each truck could pump 1500 gallons of water to a fire anywhere. "Just switch trucks and run again, as long as there are trucks and water."

Once the Bishop was satisfied, and the rest of their questions were answered, they left.

It was the evening of October 23, and Bill was back at his motel room listening to messages from Kathy and Amy. They both told of the police visiting Adam's apartment and finding nothing. Amy told of Adam's plan to work the twenty-eighth of October and then drive up that night. Kathy said she had heard from the receiver, Adam talking on the phone and saying that the thirteen women would be up Thursday and the rest would follow Friday night. After he was through listening to the messages, Bill was thinking he was a little early in coming up there. He figured Adam would be up earlier than that. He called Kathy and asked her several questions. The most important was if there were any more missing girls eleven to thirteen in age. Kathy said that there weren't any new reports. Bill talked for several minutes more and then thanked her warmly and hung up.

He then called the sheriff of Park River, and the sheriff informed him that the state police would not help because of a lack of evidence with the case. The state police notified the governor, and the governor would send the National Guard to the scene—if anything, it would be a good training exercise for the troops up there. Sheriff Kief went on to tell Bill that he was free to contact the officer in charge, for what he needed to end the situation at the Johnson home.

Bill now knew that Adam would be up Wednesday night, so he would have time to kidnap one there. *Could it be as simple as that?* he thought. Bill pondered the question in his mind. *Adam,* he thought, *what's going on in your mind?*

The next morning, after breakfast, they headed to the northern tip of Wisconsin and checked out a National Guard unit up there for possible soldiers for Halloween night. In the evening, they settled back in their rooms again and learned that they needed permission from the sheriff and to be there a day or two early to be ready.

There was a message from Kathy. She said that she had heard on the receiver, Adam talking on the phone, saying that a junior member of the group had become ill. And from what she heard on the receiver, she would be on medical leave of absence through Halloween. The illness was not life-threatening; she just needed medication and rest. Then Kathy went on to say that Adam wanted her to find a child and maybe bring her up with her. And then the message was cut off because of time. Bill called Kathy and talked with her on the phone and learned the rest. When they had finished, Bill knew that Adam was good and even better at planning than he figured.

Sunday, October 25, was a cold and cloudy day in northern Wisconsin. They finished breakfast and drove back to the motel. Bill had them all come to his room for a meeting. Bill set up his new coffeemaker and made coffee for everyone.

"What's this all about, Bill?" the bishop wondered, thinking out loud for everyone.

John watched the coffee brewing for a second and then looked at the rest of them. "Yeah, Bill, what's up today? And why the meeting?" asked John, wondering who was now curious about this meeting.

Bill just went about passing around cups, rolls, and napkins and waited for everyone to be comfortable. With the coffee done brewing, he filled everyone's cup and then began the meeting.

Bill started out his meeting with the news from Chicago, the news from Kathy and Amy. Bill went on in telling them that Adam was coming up late Wednesday night from work. Then Bill told them that the thirteen women for the ceremony would be up Thursday sometime around noon and would be staying at Adam's place through sometime Sunday. Bill then went on to say that the followers would be coming up late Friday night and probably help Adam in setting up Saturday morning and preparing for Saturday night. There was also word that some of the followers were taking vacation that week and would be there sometime in the middle of the week for the celebration. "The dates at this time are unclear, so we don't know at this time. There is no new word from Lieutenant Wilson of the Chicago PD. I have been informed that the police have gone to Adam's apartment and questioned Adam already, but they went home pretty much empty-handed. Adam did give them an old dagger and sword to check, and they came up with animal blood. Adam is keeping his head cool and steady at this moment and doesn't seem to rattle easily at this time. Just recently, I had word that one of Adam's followers had come down ill and would be off for the week of Halloween … and now this is the big part, my friends. I'm thinking early Tuesday, very early in the morning, we are going to Chicago to pick up our transmitter and receiver from those locations, for two reasons—one so that the police don't find them later on in their investigations of Adam himself, and two, once Adam is up here, there will be no more information from his apartment to report. I think you can understand that, and the rest you already know from our planning of the last couple of days here. As you know, our man Adam is brilliant and cunning; he's very good at not making mistakes. He's the ultimate gamester at this time to be following; we can't afford to make a mistake ourselves. If we make a mistake at this time, our cover is gone, and we will never catch him."

"I'm sure Bishop Frazer understands what I'm saying. When you're in the hunt, one mistake can cost you badly."

For a brief moment, there were no questions from anyone, and then Alice spoke up. "Is my brother really that good, that nobody is after him?" She was somewhat surprised with his report.

Bill thought a second and replied, "Alice, that's not a bad question. To keep it simple to understand, when you're looking for someone and you're following your leads, the closer you get, the easier it is. When dealing with a criminal, it's something of the same thing, for once you find them and start to track them, you build a profile of events. You start to understand how and what they think and, most important, why they think it. You can measure your success by what they do and with your notes. When your percentage of right guesses is good enough, then you can plan ahead and make good moves in confidence. Now your brother Adam is more than very good at covering his tracks and is using his job and his clear record with the police to fool them. So there are three things he uses against them. The fourth thing is he's a more than capable leader; he's a natural leader. He builds confidence in his followers, and they do whatever he wants with no questions. I hope I answered your question, Alice."

His friends were somewhat surprised by his answer. They could feel that Bill understood Adam better than they thought; all he lacked was information to go on. Bishop Frazer then spoke up with his question. "How do you plan to capture his group Halloween night and save the child?"

Bill paused for a moment and then answered, "That's really a two-part question, Mark. For one, my friend, you play the big part of that question of the child. John and I, with the National Guard, will be controlling the followers and Adam. Your part in this will be to determine what is best before and after we capture them. Only you can answer that for us, for the safety of the child. Then we can build around that information. The four of us will be in the underground church with them but hiding. The National Guard will be divided—some in the front and the rest in the tunnel. But we must be careful with the tanker truck, not to get it there too soon. We run the chance of someone seeing it. Another problem is the trees blocking the entry to the tunnel; some will need to be cut down and moved. John mentioned six hundred feet at least of hose. The real problem is noise and no real cover. So all of this will have to be at night; there is no other way. But your part is probably just as important; your understanding of the ritual is necessary to save the child. Your remedy is also important, before and after, you probably know which prayers would be most effective in this case. I'm going to give you free reign on that, as well as advice and any personal experience you wish to share."

Bill waited for any more questions. There were none, so he ended the meeting. Bill knew that they had things to do yet but decided it could wait until Monday. Alice walked up to Bill, for he was quietly standing by himself.

"You gave a good meeting, Bill. You shared much more than you know," said Alice politely, for she wanted to talk to him privately.

"It was an up-to-the-moment type of meeting, so everyone knows where we are," stated Bill modestly; he wanted his friends to have information. Alice, now feeling somewhat out of place in the group, motioned for Bill to step outside with her.

They all grabbed their coats and stepped just outside the door. Alice said, "Bill, I just want to let you know privately that when this is all over, I'm thinking of moving to Raleigh, North Carolina. I have some family there, and they promised to take me in till I get settled again. I had been checking out a fine hospital there, and they say they are interested in me."

Bill looked a little surprised at her confiding in him. He saw that she was interested in him. "Don't you have anyone or any family members here close by to help you get through this rough time for a while?"

Alice, now seeing that the feeling was there as well, smiled faintly and then said, "No, I don't, Bill. My family is all over the country. My distant family in Raleigh are probably the closest ones I can call family and have contact with."

Bill was starting to feel a little uncomfortable. He said, "Being with family who cares is probably the best thing you can do for now. Your real friends here will always be there for you. We will never be too far away from you; just call."

Again, a faint smile appeared on Alice's face. They studied each other for a second, and then they went inside.

The rest of the day went along in a restful way for everyone. Monday, October 26, after breakfast and filling up the car with gas, they returned to the motel. Bill entered his room and called the sheriff to see how everything was at this date and time. The sheriff stated that he was still on his side, but the law said no at that time. Bill reported that he had gone to the National Guard unit up north, for the needed manpower. Bill stated that the colonel there would need to hear from him forty-eight hours in advance to make it happen. The sheriff felt that was fine and thanked him, for the sheriff didn't have the manpower for this operation. They talked for some time about other loose ends and then hung up. Bill then called Lieutenant Wilson in Chicago. He was terribly busy but just stated that there was nothing new to report. Bill went on to report what he and the sheriff had done, and they hung up. Bill then left messages with Kathy and Amy. He left a message with Kathy that they would be there early Tuesday morning to pick up the receiver from her. With Amy, he left her a message of many thanks.

He also went on telling Amy to stop by Kathy's apartment, for there was something left for her. With that work done for the time being, he picked up his jacket and went for a walk outside. Again, it was cloudy, and the wind was cool. He felt cold after a while. He enjoyed his walk that day; it was a healthy way to clear his mind of the planning yet to be done. After an hour of just walking, he looked around and really started to notice the town for the first time. It was nice and friendly, and the people just wanted to help him. It was not busy or hurried in any way; it was a place to call home. It had the usual things, like schools, ball games, a library, a small hospital, and work, to make a living. But none of the things one would have found in a much larger city. That later became a problem. This little town also had good fishing and hunting nearby for those who would enjoy it. Even though it was getting cool outside, he felt warm inside with the thought of good, steady people around him. He returned to his motel room and removed his jacket. He thanked God for small towns like this one. For he now felt refreshed and renewed inside, ready for the problems ahead. Bill was napping peacefully when a knock came at the door.

He went to the door and opened it. It was his group, and Bill let them in.

"Bill, my friend, it's almost one o'clock in the afternoon, and we are getting hungry," said the bishop, speaking for the rest of them.

"Well then, I'll have to fix that; I can't let that happen, can I?" said Bill casually as he looked for his jacket. At the restaurant, Bill informed everyone that at 9:00 p.m. that night they were going to Chicago. He then explained that they had to get their equipment out quickly, before the police started looking. There was some grumbling at first, and then Bill reminded them they could sleep most of the way.

It was a little after 8:00 p.m. the same day, and everyone was knocking on Bill's door. Bill greeted them, and they wanted to go, because they couldn't sleep anymore. Before they knocked, Bill had just been resting on the bed. He was fully dressed and ready to go. They left the motel before 8:30 p.m. and were on the road. They drove east for at least thirty-five miles until they hit the interstate highway. They were making good time.

October 27 was a Tuesday morning, and they made good time to Chicago. They filled up with gas and began slowly making their way to Kathy's place. They were somewhat ahead of schedule and had some time to burn. They rang Kathy's doorbell at the agreed time, and Kathy let them in. She had coffee already made for them and even a nice breakfast. Kathy was happy to meet Alice, and the three men could see that Kathy and Alice were friends in the making. When it was about time to go, Bill gave Kathy three hundred dollars for her time and trouble. He gave her an additional three hundred to give Amy. Kathy was happy with her reward and thought Amy would feel the same way. Bill and everyone brought Kathy up-to-date with their activities up north. He told her they all felt it would be done Saturday night. As they were leaving so Kathy could go to work, Kathy wanted John to stay behind for a second. The four of them waited outside the door; they kind of smiled at one another. When John appeared, there was a glow about him, and he looked pleased with himself. John gave Alice a slip of paper. It had Kathy's telephone number and address on it. "John, old buddy, you look like a new man there. Maybe someday I'll have to tell you of the birds and the bees," joked Bill. He laughed some as he put his hand on John's shoulder.

They arrived at Adam's apartment building and waited until it was safe to enter. John looked at the time and said, "It is eight eleven, Bill. Same as last time?" John acted casually, thinking it would be different this time.

"How many of you want to go to Adam's apartment?" asked Bill, wondering. Too many would be trouble in the making. Bill, looking in the rearview mirror, saw Mark shaking his head no. Alice also shook her head no. They waited another ten minutes, until Bill saw the last of the tenants leave. At this time, Bill and John left the car, and Alice and Mark just sat and waited for them. The elevator doors opened to the fifth floor, and some people got in as they got off.

"I hope that's not a bad sign?" whispered John cautiously to Bill as he pointed out the door.

Bill quickly picked the lock, and he was in. He quietly closed the door. John went for the transmitter, and Bill went for the dagger in the prayer room. Bill quickly put on his gloves, as before. They went to the altar to see. Again, there was no dagger, so he made everything look as it had been before. John had the transmitter in his pocket. Bill took off his gloves, and together, they listened at the door. John locked the door as they left and checked it again. They stepped off the elevator into the lobby, and the same two people were there.

They asked, "Who are you? We haven't seen you before."

Bill quickly flashed his badge before them and said, "Police, routine check. Have a nice day."

They walked down the sidewalk to make it look like a routine patrol to everyone watching. Bill and John watched as they got into their car and pulled away. When they were out of sight, they returned to their car with the other two wondering what that was all about.

"We almost had a problem in the lobby, so I flashed my badge fast so they couldn't tell I was a PI," stated Bill, rather concerned as he looked at each of them in the car. They left the parking lot and made their way back home.

They returned back to Park River about 7:30 p.m. and bought a bucket of chicken with all the trimmings. They enjoyed their meal in John's room with some chicken left over. Mark nodded to Bill that he wanted to have a word with him.

"Bill, how close was that this morning?" asked Mark with some concern in his voice.

"Don't know, Mark. I really don't know. The few times I've done that, to avoid trouble, it usually works fine. To most people, that would tell them to leave you alone. But you know that everybody is not everybody!" responded Bill with caution, still wondering about it.

Bill was casually watching the news on television later

that night when there was a report of a missing child, taken from a large city in central Wisconsin. The news cast gave all the information. The abduction looked similar to what Adam would do. Bill thought Sheriff Kief would be looking for him the next day and that would be a sure thing. Bill grabbed his coat and went to each of the rooms of his friends, but the lights were already out for the night. He returned to his room and thought that was probably not a bad idea.

Wednesday, October 28, nobody woke Bill, so he showered and got ready for the day. He opened the window curtains and saw that a dusting of snow was on the ground. He thought to himself that winter started earlier up there than it did at home. He turned on the television and listened to the news for a while. The girl had been found, and she was safe. From the newscast, it seemed it was all a misunderstanding of the parents and the child. Bill's mind was now drifting to the problem at hand. He was thinking, *If you pick him up for kidnapping, with no evidence of murder involved, Adam will be out in twenty to twenty-five years.* Then he would start all over, somewhere else, and he would get away with murder. Even if the followers were arrested, they would play dumb, for their loyalty would make them stick to a story. Any well-paid attorney would ensure that much, in a case like that. Bill knew in his own mind that Adam had thought of that already and had probably made arrangements like that as a backup story. He started to wonder, *What if I was in his shoes? What would I say, to twist one thing for another?* Bill was thinking about this problem. *I heard many stories on the PD side of it, but never quite like this one.*

Bill knew Adam was very cunning. *How do you make thirty-seven people agree to murder and feel good about it at the same time? Could he be mass hypnotist of some kind? Or could he have given some charismatic speeches that brainwashed them all, over time?* Even in organized crime, those who did this type of crime were just rotten to the bone. Something in them just went terribly wrong; murder was no problem for them. But these were successful people, who just enjoyed bloodletting to a God of some type. In Bill's mind, this somehow it didn't add up just quite right. He then remembered Bishop Frazer; these were people who didn't quite fit into society, and they didn't feel as normal people did. *But how do you get so many in one place at one time and all click together?* Most were married, with kids; all had good-paying jobs and just about everything one could want. He then thought that most people would die for that good of a living. So how did Adam make them all change at the same time? Was there something in the beginning with those early rituals that promised them something that they couldn't say no to and they got hooked? At that moment of thought, the answer seemed easy; they wanted the world and all its wealth and power, anything one might ask for and more.

Bill was starting to think along another line of thought when someone knocked on the door. He opened the door. It was Bishop Frazer, and he let him in.

"You see that snow, Bill? It looks like an early Christmas to me," said the bishop with some humor in it.

"Yes, it sure does all right. Make yourself at home," responded Bill, trying to make light of it.

"If we go fishing today, I think we'll need an ice pick," said Mark, humoring Bill.

"Well, I know it's too early for ice fishing, and I don't have a license," said Bill, making a small joke to Mark.

Bill and the Bishop talked for a while and did some joking with each other, and then Bishop Frazer said, "Bill, on Sunday, you mentioned that you were going to give me free reign of the spiritual side, is that correct?" asked Mark in a more serious tone of voice.

"Yes, Mark, I did say that. Is something wrong?" asked Bill.

"No, Bill, I just want to know how far and to what length?"

"Well, Mark, on the force, we did nothing at all, but this time, I want to do it right, even if Sheriff Kief protests at it," stated Bill confidently.

"Last night, I was going over the ritual on my laptop, and the child is to be killed after the thirteen women become pregnant. And Satan and his bride are to stand by the altar as the priest then slays the child, collects the blood, and offers it to Satan and his bride. And that is to be their marriage drink that joins them. Instead of a wild orgy that follows the ritual, Satan will declare himself ruler of the world and set off to make it happen in his spirit and sudden darkness," stated Bishop Frazer flatly in a serious tone of voice.

The two of them had been sitting in silence for a while when there was a knock at the door. Bill opened the door, and the rest came in, all commenting about the snow. Bill looked at his watch and then glanced at Mark and the rest.

"Let me guess now, you're all hungry," responded Bill, seeing they agreed with that.

After breakfast, they returned to the motel, so Mark could gather some of his gear and return to the tunnel. The snow was slowly melting as the sun broke through the clouds, and it warmed some. Back at the tunnel, Bill eyed the trees that needed to be removed to let the truck in with the water.

John and Bill both seemed to agree on the number and how far the truck had to go. John reminded Bill that they needed a large tarp to cover the opening, so the wind in the tunnel didn't move the clear curtains. John pointed out the curtains would move and let everyone know if the opening was open and wind was getting into the tunnel. They entered the tunnel and closed it like before until they reached the other side. This time, the ventilation was working and made a soft rumbling sound in the large room. The clear curtain did move some but not a lot, just enough to prove John's point of the wind in the tunnel.

Alice and Mark stood by the pit, while Bill and John went to see if they were really alone. When they returned, Mark stepped back from the pit and made himself ready from his kit. He passed some of his equipment to Alice and Bill, as John held the flashlight. First, he blessed the open room and sprinkled holy water wherever he could, and then he returned to the pit. He blessed the pit, the altar, and the pulpit and asked God to make them holy and something for good and not evil. And with that finished, he went to the center of the large room and asked Bill to hold a special prayer book. With John and Alice holding their flashlights on the prayer book, Mark paged through book until he found the right prayer. Bishop Frazer then started out in Latin and spoke clearly and with authority. He raised his arms toward heaven. John understood some of what he was saying. Mark was asking for divine intervention of some type, but the rest he could not understand. It was a long prayer that lasted for several minutes, and Mark bowed at the end of it. Mark closed the book when he finished, and Bill whispered to kill the lights and remain silent for a minute.

In the deep darkness, they listened for any sound, wondering if anyone had heard them. They waited and listened. In the blackness, a door opened, and a light from the house broke some of the darkness by the dressing room. Somebody walked down the steps in the light from the house and waited in silence. The only sound was from the soft rumbling of the ventilation system that filled the room. The four of them stood in silence and could see a person faintly in the light from the house above. After what seemed to be forever in the blackness, the person walked up the steps and back into the house and closed the door. The four of them continued to wait silently for another minute and then left to go back into the tunnel. Once they were out, they cleared the steps of leaves, closed the door, and hid the opening the best they could. The house was much more visible to them than before, so they were careful in their leaving. No one said anything until they were safely by the car in the woods.

"Oh my God, guys! That was close. I thought we'd had it there for a minute!" responded Alice, covering her mouth with her hands.

"Yeah, me too, that was cutting it pretty close for me also!" stated Bill, wondering what that person thought.

"From the shape in the light, I thought it was a woman, maybe a servant or a cleaning lady?" responded John, thinking out loud.

And then Bishop Frazer added, "I think the blessing worked; we were protected that time!"

"I hope so, Mark. That was too close for me and the rest of us for that matter," stated John, thinking it might not be over yet.

"Well, all I know is, we better get out of here, before

whoever it was finds us for sure!" said Bill cautiously, not looking for any more close calls. They all climbed into the car and left. Once they were on the road, there was a sigh of relief.

They talked back and forth all the way to Park River. It was getting close to noon, so they decided to get something to eat. Once they were back in their motel rooms again, Bill lay on the bed holding his cell phone. He looked for any messages and found none. He was feeling a little discouraged by the lack of information on what Adam might be doing. He was about to put his phone down when it rang. Quickly, he answered. It was Amy, and she informed Bill that about half of them would be in Park River that day sometime. They would be staying in motels until November 1 and then would head back to Chicago. Adam would be on his way up there that night, sometime around midnight, to ready the place. Bill asked Amy about any child for the ceremony, and she replied she didn't know at that time. Then she said she had to hang up because somebody was coming. Bill smiled as he closed his phone. Now he had something to work with again.

Bill started to think that right then, they could be at this same motel and they would not know it. He got off the bed, went for his jacket, grabbed his room keys, and stepped outside to see. Any car with Illinois plates would be suspect there. He would see what kind of person owned that car. It was almost half past one in the afternoon, so Bill got into his car and drove around all the motels in the city. There were not many. After about thirty minutes, Bill had spotted four cars with Illinois plates at motels on the other end of the city. Bill knew he had his binoculars in the trunk of his car, so he went to Adam's place. After a while, he reached Adam's property and stopped short of the tree line and the lawn. Bill backed up for a ways and pulled into a driveway in the woods on someone else's property. Bill looked at the jacket he was wearing. It was a dark color. He thought it was good, for it would offer protection.

He got out of the car, locked it, opened the truck, and found his binoculars and listening device. Then he closed the trunk. Bill walked into Adam's woods until he was about even with the east side of the house. Through the binoculars, he could see the cars were from Illinois, and there were some people moving from the cars to the house. Bill set up the listening device and recorder to record what he was hearing. Then he put on the headphones and listened in.

"Rob, you're sure you didn't overmedicate that little girl you brought up with you?" asked one of the followers.

"Oh hell no, Jeff. She'll be out for another four hours and have a headache; that's all. Don't worry," said the other follower as he closed the trunk of the car.

"Rob, all I'm saying is that she's been out of it all the way up here and now you say four more hours and a headache?" said the first follower.

"Yeah, yeah, it's stuff from a hospital to put patients to sleep for long periods of time; that's all. I used it on the policeman at the warehouse, and he lived, remember?" said the second follower.

Then they were in the house, and Bill turned off the listening device. Bill waited over an hour more, and nothing happened. He thought he'd better go now, for the sun was setting fast. Once he was back at the car and everything was put away, he left with the knowledge they had a little girl in that house. Bill was entering the city limits of Park River when his cell phone rang. It was Sheriff Kief on the phone. The sheriff was telling Bill that another child had been kidnapped from Chicago, a twelve-year-old.

Bill asked the sheriff if it was a blonde with blue or green eyes.

"Why, yes. How did you know?"

"Because that is their sign of purity and perfection for Satan; it is what they want for this sort of thing, Sheriff."

"How do you know that they have a child already?"

"Because I have it recorded for you already."

"How, and from where?"

"I'll be in in about five minutes, and you can listen for yourself, okay?"

"Fine, I'll be here for that, bye."

Bill pulled in at the sheriff's station, opened the trunk of the car, and got the listening device. He closed the trunk.

The sheriff waited for him at the door. "You have it there?" stated the sheriff, in a demanding tone of voice.

"I sure do, Sheriff; let's play it in your office," stated Bill in a businesslike tone of voice.

They entered the sheriff's office and closed the door. Bill readied the player and gave the headset to the sheriff. Bill played it back for him, and the sheriff nodded and said, "Good, good, that's damn good." He handed the headphones back to Bill and smiled. He walked around his desk and sat down. He looked at Bill. Bill then began to lay out his plans for the sheriff. The sheriff listened with some doubt on his face, but he listened. "Sir, there's a family who wants their child back in one piece, and the PD down there is looking for her right now."

Reading the sheriff's expression, Bill reached into his pocket and pulled out his cell phone. He dialed Lieutenant Wilson's office in Chicago.

Bill explained the situation in Park River to Lieutenant Wilson, as the others listened on Bill's speakerphone. The sheriff had to walk around his desk to hear well. Bill drew out his plan for the lieutenant, explaining what he wanted to do there in great detail. At first, the lieutenant was hesitant, but then Bill informed him that in addition to kidnapping, they'd be able to lay murder charges as well. The lieutenant was now getting it better and saw the idea as very good. So Bill explained in detail once again, so it was well understood to both parties, and they all knew how it would go down with everybody the winner. Bill then reminded the lieutenant that the parents and the rest of the PD should know the child was safe for the time being and they wouldn't harm her yet. The lieutenant understood what he was saying and said he would handle it from there. The lieutenant and the sheriff talked for a while and then hung up.

"That plan of yours, are you so sure of it?" asked the sheriff flatly, not completely sure he liked it.

"Yes, absolutely, Sheriff. We have the ritual with us. We understand what is supposed to happen step-by-step in it. You will be with us, and the National Guard will surround the place. The park service will then come with the water, as I said. And we will arrest everybody before they harm the child."

"I hope you know that you are risking a child's life to get murder charges on the rest of them," said the sheriff flatly with some anger in his voice.

"And I hope you know that, in twenty years, he'll be out of jail from kidnapping charges and will do it all over again and kill more children someplace else!" stated Bill flatly, in the same tone of voice.

"You're risking more than I would at this point. You better be damn right about this; otherwise, my ass is on the line here, you understand?" stated the sheriff flatly, in a slightly rougher tone of voice.

"You're speaking of risk here. I've worked murder cases before, sir. I know about risk. You always have to go the extra mile to get a murderer, and you should know that, sir. This man we're after is no different; it's about evidence, sir, to get that man behind bars, where he belongs," stated Bill firmly with knowledge in his voice.

"Fine, fine. We'll talk tomorrow, toward the end of the day."

Bill picked up his gear and left respectfully. He went to his car. When everything was put away, he drove away to the motel. When Bill drove up to his room, everyone came out to see him by the car. They wondered why he hadn't said anything about his leaving before. Bill waved them into his warm room and explained all that had happened, even with the sheriff. Again, he reminded them that Amy had called and that Adam was coming up that night around midnight. And the thirteen women would be there late the next day. "There is a child there now, as we speak."

"You didn't go into full detail with our spiritual plan, did you, Bill?" wondered the bishop with concern in his voice.

"No, Mark. I think that is still a mystery to them yet," returned Bill, feeling happy about that.

"So tomorrow, Bill, you are going to have the National Guard called up for Halloween night?" asked John, now thinking ahead some.

"Yes, we must. We have no choice in the matter," replied Bill, nodding as he said it.

"You said Lieutenant Wilson liked your plan. Will the sheriff want to follow it?" asked Alice, feeling happy for his success in the matter.

"Well, the lieutenant wasn't happy at first, Alice, but after I explained to him the difference between one charge and the other charge, then he liked it better," said Bill, in a slightly joyful mood.

"You mean kidnapping and murder charges, don't you, Bill?" replied John in a more serious tone.

"Yes, that's correct, John, the difference between knocking on the door and taking the child or getting him red-handed and about to do it firsthand. It's a bigger risk for sure, but he'll be in jail a lot longer," added Bill, in a more business-like tone of voice.

THURSDAY, OCTOBER 29, BILL GOT UP A LITTLE LATER
that morning, but he still had time to ready himself for the
day ahead. After a while, when he was ready for the day, he
pulled the curtain open on his motel window. Again, there
was a dusting of snow on the cars and the ground. He turned
on the television to hear the morning news and made some
coffee for himself. Bill, after so much time there in that motel
room, was starting to like it. So far, as he listened to the news,
there was no word from Chicago about the child.

He was slowly drinking his coffee when someone started
knocking on his door. He got up and opened the door. It was
Alice, and he let her in. "Morning, Alice, would you like some
coffee?" asked Bill in a polite tone of voice.

"Yes, please," responded Alice nicely as she removed her
jacket.

Bill motioned for her to sit down on the edge of the bed.

"What do you have in mind today, Bill? Is today going to
be busy?" asked Alice, wondering as she now tasted the coffee.

Bill then explained the day ahead and what they had to
do, but the big thing was the sheriff, the National Guard, the
water truck, and staking out Adam's place for a while.

"By the sound of that, we'll be busy for much of the day then, Bill," added Alice, now thinking it over some.

"Not really, Alice. Most of it is right here in town and not that far away," responded Bill, starting to enjoy her company.

"You know, Bill, when my brother is in prison for some while, why don't we just go away to someplace nice and really get to know each other?" responded Alice, smiling at the thought of it.

Bill felt somewhat uncomfortable at first, but then again, it sounded very nice. "It would have to be sometime later, Alice, and that does sound nice when you think of it some. But not right now either, there are professional rules, which I must follow for some time; it would have to be later," responded Bill as he then thought it over some.

"You mean, there are rules that you must follow just for going away and having fun?" asked Alice, starting to see his life was complicated with rules.

Bill then slowly and carefully explained the rules and said that these rules were pretty much the same rules police officers everywhere had to follow. Alice only saw it as a code of honor, and they would have to wait some. There was then a knock on the door. Bill got up to see who it was. It was the rest of the group, and they were looking for breakfast.

After they had breakfast and got some gas for the car, they again returned to the motel. When Bill was by himself, there were no new messages from the informants. Bill's new problem was not Adam, but Alice; he knew their lives mustn't get twisted together and more was at stake than a weekend romance.

Bill then called the sheriff, and he said he was free for a little while, so Bill grabbed his jacket and locked up as he left his room. He went to the other rooms and told them to get ready as well. Inside the sheriff's office, the sheriff's outward appearance was one of reluctance, but he was willing to go along with it. Bill asked the sheriff to call the National Guard for fifteen soldiers to be ready and waiting at the sheriff's office with three of his men at 6:00 p.m. Saturday evening. The sheriff placed the call to the National Guard, and everything was set. The sheriff had the call on speakerphone, so everyone heard what was said. Sheriff Kief was now more willing than he had been a few minutes earlier. He asked about the park service and the tanker truck. Bishop Frazer then stated that they would need that truck and seven hundred feet of hose for their plans with the tunnel and that church underground. On speakerphone, the sheriff placed a call to the park service, and in about five minutes, that was ready for them as well. They were to be at the sheriff's office at 6:00 p.m. on the thirty-first. At this point, Sheriff Kief wondered what his role was in all of this. Bill explained that his role was to be a witness and make the formal arrests with his deputies.

The sheriff was quite clear in his point of view that this was a waste of time. But he was going to go along with it, for if Bill and his party were correct in their plan, he would be a hero. Bill, John, and the bishop all made known to the sheriff that they had the ritual as well and that the child would be safe at the point of arrest with the group.

"I damn well hope so, for you and for me, and the same goes for the child!" stated the sheriff, rather roughly.

"The plan is not that complicated, Sheriff. It's the question of timing and of communication, to make it all work right, as it should; that's all!" stated Bill, in a rougher tone of voice. Then he added, in a calmer voice, "We all want the same damn thing here, sir. We all want evidence, a complete arrest of the group, and the child sent home alive and well. We want a murder charge on everyone in that group, starting with intent to murder. And let the DNA tests on the dagger prove the rest. We need your complete support and confidence in us, working with you to make it happen."

Sheriff Kief saw and heard that they were committed to what they said and basically, they all wanted the same thing as he did, just more.

The sheriff stood up, shook each of their hands, and agreed to the plan in full.

"We will all meet here at 5:00 p.m. on the thirty-first, and we'll make last-minute adjustments, so everything is set and ready," stated the sheriff in a calmer and more agreeable voice.

Again, they all shook hands. They agreed to be there on the thirty-first at 5:00 p.m., and Bill and his group left respectfully. As they all got into the car, everyone was smiling and commented that everything was nearly set for Saturday night.

"Now all we need is an electric chainsaw, to cut some trees this afternoon," stated Bill in a casual tone of voice as he started the car.

"What do we need that for, Bill?" asked John, wondering about the saw.

"An electric saw makes little noise, and remember those trees we counted before together? We have to get that truck in there," responded Bill as they headed for the department store.

John was now thinking about the trees and the truck. They couldn't just pull them out. With the saw in hand, an extra battery, and a shovel too, they returned to the car. They went to the motel and charged the batteries for the saw. Then they went to get dinner so the batteries would charge up completely for the afternoon. When they returned, the batteries still needed more time yet to charge. So they agreed to wait one more hour, and they would leave together. Alice went with the bishop into his room, and Bill went into John's room to talk about that afternoon. Later, with the batteries fully charged, they drove out to Adam's property. Bill and John then revealed their plan for that afternoon to Alice and Mark. Alice and Bill would saw down some trees, and John and Mark would set up the listening device and use the binoculars and watch. Alice carried the GPS, which John set up for her, and Bill had the saw, batteries, and shovel. The sky was becoming overcast, and the sun was not as warming as before. The wind was stirring up the trees. It was still peaceful to hear, but if one didn't move much, one began to feel chilled. John and Mark were now leaving Alice and Bill to go to their place, and Alice and Bill went down the road. Alice took the shovel from Bill as they walked together.

"That wind sounds pleasant in the trees doesn't it?" said Alice in a softer voice.

Bill then listened for a moment and said, "Yes, it does. I used to walk in the woods like this sometimes as a child, when my dad and I hunted together for squirrels."

After a while, they came up to the tree stand, and Alice pointed in the tunnel's direction. John was not a woodsman; he kept the house barely in view, so they would know where they were going. Mark enjoyed being in the woods and used to hunt often in his younger days. It took longer for them to travel to their location. John thought of the car that was parked in the woods but out of sight from the road.

He couldn't remember if Bill had locked it when they

left it. John stopped and took off his backpack to find the walkie-talkie. John then called Bill and asked him that question. Alice answered that he did and that everything was fine. Once again, John and Mark continued until sometime later when they reached their location with the house and driveway. There were many cars and people stirring in front of the house. John set up the listening device, and it was working properly, recording everything. John and Mark then started watching with their binoculars and saw that the thirteen women must have arrived not that long before them. John then turned off the headphones and put it on audio so they could both hear and record. John noticed that the women, dressed in warm clothing, were pleasant to the eyes. He could see why they had been picked.

John then found his notepad and started writing down information on everything. A little later, there was talk of the little girl. They learned that she was in a room, eating and watching television. Then John thought of the camcorder and started filming the activity as well. John was wishing he had thought of it sooner, for this scene wouldn't last much longer. Alice and Bill were making progress in their tree removal; the saw was quiet enough for their work. Alice proved to be a good worker in removing the brush that had been cut down. All that was left was the bigger trees, but the saw was on the small side. It just took longer to cut. Bill cut them as close to the ground as possible, so the truck could get over them easily. They made a good team, and with the last tree cut down, all that was left to do was the cleanup. With a fresh battery in, Bill cut the trees into small pieces so they both could move them. With their job done, now there was plenty of room. Five very small trees had been removed, but there was still plenty of undergrowth to cover for them and for the tanker to be in position in the tunnel with its hose. Bill and Alice sat down and talked. After a while, Alice got more personal again. John and Mark recorded everything to the last person to enter the house. John shut off the camcorder. The listening device was not strong enough to listen through the house, so they shut it off. John and Mark just sat and waited until something happened. It was now getting late in the afternoon, and it was slowly starting to get dark. John and Mark started to make their way back to the car. Bill called on the walkie-talkie and stated that they would meet them at the car. Bill was starting to get up when Alice gave him a long and passionate kiss.

"Don't you love me enough, Bill?" asked Alice, wondering why he stopped.

Bill stood up and looked at her for a moment. He said gently, "I can't do this, Alice. This is bad for both of us, even if we wanted to. We will both lose everything. Think ahead, Alice, please, will you? Later, Alice, please later. Think of the damage you will do to everyone around you. Please try to understand and don't let your heart get in the way."

Alice sat there, trying to clear her mind. She put her emotions away, as she did at work, and saw the truth of his words. She put her head down and nodded slowly. And then she said in a calm voice, "You're right, Bill. It's just that I never felt this way with anyone before. I feel somewhat foolish in a way. Forgive me, please. I should have known better."

"Later, Alice, sometime later, please. There will be a time for that but not now. Please keep your head straight and clear. Another day will come, I promise you," answered Bill, trying to clear this matter up quickly.

They returned to the car together and said nothing to

each other. They waited in silence until Mark and John returned, and then they left the woods.

Bill woke up late again that day but still early enough. Nobody would notice the fact. After a nice shower and shave and fresh clothes, he was ready for the day. He was thinking he needed to go to a Laundromat and wash clothes. A pile was forming in his room, and he felt sure the same was true for everyone else as well. He turned on the television to hear the news and weather and opened the curtains some. He looked out the window—no snow this time, just cloudy and a little windy. Some of the leaves on the ground rolled in the wind.

Bill noticed John walking toward his room, and Bill opened the door before him.

"Geez, Bill, you must be psychic this morning!" said John, somewhat amazed by the door opening so soon.

"Morning, John, I hope you slept well," responded Bill, greeting his friend.

John started making the coffee for Bill as Bill checked for any messages he might have and found none. They were quietly enjoying their coffee when John looked out the window and spotted Mark coming their way. Bill waited by the door for John to say when.

"Now!" stated John suddenly.

Bill rapidly opened the door before Mark knocked.

"Oh! My dear God! Not so early in the morning!" said a startled Mark, totally caught off guard.

Bill and John just laughed. Mark, seeing they were just having some fun with him, started to laugh with them. After sometime, as they waited for Alice to show so they could go downtown, Mark questioned Bill, "Did you and Alice yesterday have a different point of view?"

Bill, feeling it was private but knowing it was best not to lie to a friend, said, "Yes, Mark, we did, but I hope I put an end to it."

Mark sensed it was personal, but he already suspected one or the other wanted more than the other would give. "If I may say so, Bill, she wanted something special from you?" asked Mark in a careful manner.

Bill understood his question. He just nodded. Mark and John looked at each other and got the point.

John then said, "And then you rejected her?"

Bill just nodded to that question.

Mark, knowing it was not good to go too far in this matter, said no more about it.

"So, Bill, what's on the calendar of events for the day?" asked John, changing the subject totally.

Bill thought no more on the first subject. He then added, "First, we better all think if we forgot anything here."

Mark then said, "With most of our work now done, is there anything else?"

"Yes, we did that yesterday, so today is easier for us. But tomorrow we will be busier; we don't want to miss anything," stated Bill clearly, for he knew everything must be right.

There was a moment of silence when Alice knocked on the door. Bill let her in, and she greeted everyone with a "Good morning."

Together, they went downtown, as this had become their usual routine.

After breakfast, they stopped by the park service station and checked on the truck and the necessary hose. The ranger told them, "It's being taken care of." He went on to say that it would be there in the morning for them. In the afternoon, after lunchtime, they prepared for the trip to Adam's place;

then they were in Alice's room, talking of what they hoped to learn that afternoon. John pointed out all this collecting of information was for trial purposes. "Sometimes, it helps us as well." With the meeting done, they left for Adam's property to set up for the afternoon. Once safely on Adam's road into the woods with the gate closed, they drove slowly to where they had parked the car before. Bill and John explained to Mark and Alice the use of the listening device and the camcorder. He told them they would be with them shortly.

"Mark, you know where we were before?" asked John, wanting to know if everything was understood.

"Yes, John, I've a pretty good idea where we were yester-day," stated Mark reassuring them that he understood the location.

With that, Mark and Alice walked into the woods, with Mark leading the way. Bill and John watched them make their way deeper into the woods.

"Bill, I don't fully understand what we are going to do here," said John, a little curious as to why they were not fol-lowing them.

Bill just smiled and said, "I have the transmitter and re-ceiver here in my pocket. And once properly placed, if we can get close enough, we are going to record them."

John looked a little shocked at first, for he knew this was a high-stakes game Bill had in mind. Once they reached the tunnel, John approved of the work they'd done the day before. "Not bad, Bill, not bad at all," said John, looking at the work.

They stooped down, for they could see people on the north side of the house through the woods.

"I hope they didn't see us, John," said Bill, wondering out loud.

John watched their movements carefully and then whispered, "I don't think so. If you look at their hands, I think they're there just drinking beer and smoking and talking."

Carefully, they watched the people for a while, until they felt comfortable with their movements.

"I sure hope Mark and Alice are recording this for us, Bill," whispered John, "for this could be useful information."

"Yeah, I hope so too. I wish I could hear this too, right now," responded Bill. "Hey, we have the walkie-talkie with us; let's see," whispered Bill, just now thinking of it.

"Damn, I almost forgot it too!" said John, wondering why he hadn't thought of that.

John went through Bill's backpack and found the walkie-talkie. He called Mark and Alice. Alice reported that they were listening and filming the situation on the north side of the house. Then Mark stated that they were just talking, not saying a thing about the ceremony. John then told them to just listen and stop filming until something was said. Alice then added that if there was nothing new, later, they would continue to their next location. John told Alice that would be fine and he felt that would be a good plan. Then Bill went to the tree and opened the tunnel, and Bill and John entered it. John had Bill's night-vision goggles in his backpack. Bill took them out of John's pack and put them on, so he could see. Bill then closed the door of the tunnel. Bill closed John's backpack in the darkness. Bill led John by the hand in the total darkness. When they were about halfway into the tunnel, they could see light at the other end and hear something that sounded like voices. Slowly, they moved closer toward the light, and the voices began to become clearer. Bill let go of John's hand and then whispered to John, "Stand here. I'm going to ready the transmitter, and I have the tape as well. Now I'm going to leave you here, and I'm going to place this device closer, so we can listen in the car, okay, John?"

John tapped Bill on the back, and then Bill moved closer to the light.

The voices were much clearer now, but with his goggles, he saw nobody. Bill edged much closer. He had to turn down his goggles to see better. The voices now were clear and understandable. Very carefully, he edged closer to the curtains ahead of him now. So bright was the light in his goggles that he raised them up on his forehead and used his natural eyes to see. Again, he edged closer to the curtains. He could see someone moving at the other end of the room ahead.

There was some light where he was, and Bill looked around and placed the device on a wiring conduit and wrapped the tape around it, so it would not fall. With that done, he backed into the total darkness again. He could still see the opening and hear the voices, but he was in a far safer place. He brought his goggles down and over his eyes again, turned around, and again adjusted his goggles. He could now see John farther in the tunnel. Bill walked as silently as he could up to John and then whispered to John that it was him. Bill took the lead again, and John kept his hand on Bill's backpack until they opened the outer door again.

Once all the leaves were again cleared off the steps, they closed the door of the tunnel. They knelt down and looked at the house and the people outside.

"I think that's as close as I want to get to those kinds of people," replied John. Then he glanced at Bill.

Bill looked back at his friend and then at the house and replied softly, "I know what you're saying, John."

They slowly made their way back to the car and tried the receiver; it was working beautifully. As they were listening, they heard Adam telling everybody there that the ceremony would be at 10:00 p.m. the following night. "With food and refreshments for everybody, and feel free to enjoy yourselves ..."

John made a quick note in his notebook with that message from Adam.

"John, we have a problem to solve here. That's how we are going to hide ourselves, behind the barrels, and watch the ceremony and not be seen."

John thought for a minute and said carefully, "We need a distraction of some type, something for just ten seconds would be enough."

Bill was thinking of the lights and then said, "We'll have to talk to Alice about the breaker box; maybe we can temporarily kill the lights remotely, so we can get in."

John didn't quite like the plan; he felt it was too risky, and it would be too easy to be seen. John was thinking more of a few rats. "Why not something simple, Bill, like a few rats on the loose? They would work just fine."

Bill thought for a second and said, "That would steal their attention all right, and if there is a pet store here, that would be cheap too. But how do we get them placed and remotely?"

John thought quickly and then said, "We can set them by the rifles and then let them loose, but at the same time, it means another trip into the tunnel to place them, probably later tonight."

John noticed the time and reminded Bill of it, so they left the car and locked it. They went into the woods.

Carefully, they made their way deep into the woods. John

noticed Mark standing behind the tree with the listening device. They walked up to him and got down low. Mark and Alice were watching the women in front of the house. They were loosely in a group. They seemed to be talking, just getting fresh air.

"Any word about the child in the house yet?" asked Bill, questioning their conversation.

"No, not really, Bill, just little bits here and there, but nothing that is any good to us yet," whispered Mark, answering his question. John noticed that they weren't filming. Alice was watching with the binoculars. Bill walked away from them. He had his cell phone in his hand and was making a call. After about five minutes, he joined the group again.

"What was all of that about, Bill?" asked John, wondering about the call.

"Oh, I just ordered three rats and a remote collapsible cage to let them go," stated Bill, thinking the whole thing was funny.

"Where in the hell did you get that from, Bill?" wondered Alice as she put down the binoculars.

"Twin Cities, Alice, and they'll be here tomorrow morning, about 2:00 a.m., in fact, at the sheriff's office," stated Bill with a hint of laugher in his voice.

They watched for another thirty minutes, and the women went into the house, for the sun was going down and it was getting cooler.

"Well, I think we better be getting in also and maybe get the north side cleared out also!" stated John, starting to feel the chill of the falling sun.

"Yeah, why not? We did well today. Let's go in then," replied Bill as John started to lead the way out of the woods.

Everything was back in the car. As Bill unlocked the car, his cell phone rang in his pocket. It was Sheriff Kief; he wanted to tell him that everything was set with the National Guard and the park service. He reminded him to be there at 5:00 p.m. the next day and run over all last-minute details in their planning. Bill said a few words about what they were doing, called it a day, and hung up.

"That must have been the sheriff on the line, Bill," wondered Alice out loud as she held the car door open in her right hand.

"Yes, it was, and he informed me everything is now ready for us," replied Bill as he put the phone away.

Once back on the road, as they were heading back to town, it was fully dark out again. Bill went to tell John in the car that they'd be at the sheriff's office to pick up the rats and go to the tunnel again before anybody got up.

"Great, Bill, there goes a good night's sleep," answered John, wishing he hadn't said anything about the rats.

After getting a bite to eat, they returned to the motel, and Bill reminded him that he'd be getting him up at 1:15 a.m. to get the rats.

SATURDAY, OCTOBER 31, AT 1:15, THE ALARM WAS RING-
ing loudly in Bill's ears. He hit the snooze on the clock,
but it only rang again, so he got up. Bill had barely gotten
dressed when there was a knocking at the door. It was John
at the door. Bill opened it for him.

John looked barely awake himself, but he was ready to go.
They had been waiting at the sheriff's office for half an hour
when the truck came with the rats. Bill paid the bill, and he
had the rats, the cage he wanted, and the remote. John told
Bill not to feed or water them until they got there. In about
twenty minutes, they were at Adam's property again, but this
time, Bill turned the lights off. He drove to the edge of the tree
line and the lawn to see if all the lights were off. The lights
were off at the house and in the garage. Bill then backed up
the car, turned the car around, and then drove to Adam's gate
into the woods. Once they were safely in the woods with the
car parked in a safe area again, they went out to get their gear.

John had the GPS working and put covers over the flashlights to lower the risk of them being seen at night. They
slowly made their way to the tunnel. John whispered, "This is
it." They stood a moment and looked toward where the house

should be. It was dark on the north side as well. Bill pulled out the receiver and turned it on. John and Bill were shocked to hear sounds on the receiver. "What are they doing down there, Bill?" wondered John, listening to the strange sounds.

The receiver was picking up moaning, sounds of plea-sure, sounds of laughter, and faint sounds of people moving around.

"There's an orgy going on down there, and they're drunk as well!" whispered Bill, now wondering how long this was going to last. They turned off their flashlights, waited, and listened as the time passed in the night.

The receiver had been quiet for about ten minutes when Bill turned on his flashlight. It was 5:18 a.m. Bill and John were quite chilly in the morning air. "Let's try it now, John," whispered Bill, for he'd had enough chill for one day. John found the tree. The tunnel opened up, and they went down into it. When safely at the bottom, they closed it. Bill went to get his goggles out of John's backpack and put them on. He could now see in the dark. Bill whispered that John could leave his flashlight on, because light didn't bother him much. Together, they slowly made their way into the tunnel. It was cool in the tunnel but not as cool as outside. They were feel-ing warmer as they moved some. There was light at the end of the tunnel, but no sound was heard. They were the only two in the tunnel. As they approached the end, the light was brighter. Bill turned off his goggles at that time. John turned off his flashlight as well. With stealth, they stood behind the curtain enough not to be seen.

They could hear the distant laughter of at least four people. Two men and two women, it sounded like to them, and they sounded drunk. Bill took a quick peek through the curtain and saw the four of them on an open sleeping bag, and they were naked. They were at the center of the room, next to a support pole that was in the center of the room.

"All we can do now is wait," whispered John, thinking this might not last.

Bill discovered that he could see them at ground level, at the bottom of the curtain, and John did the same.

After about forty minutes, they made love one more time, and then they talked a little and got up. All of them walked away naked, leaving the open sleeping bag on the floor. Bill and John waited in silence, as finally the lights went off around them. The only sound was the ventilation system rumbling overhead. By this time, Bill had his goggles on again. Nothing moved.

Bill whispered to John, "Wait here, and I'll check it out."

In about five minutes, Bill returned and said, "It's safe, John. Let's do it and get out of here."

Together, they carefully chose a point next to the rifles and ammunition that still offered cover for the rats. They fed and watered them, and the latch worked as it should. They left. Bill stopped by the pulpit and checked; nothing was there yet.

This time, they left the tunnel quickly, after a careful inspection and cleaning. They then closed it. The sun was now at the horizon, and day was breaking again when they reached the car.

"Damn, Bill, all this sleuthing is hard on the nerves," joked John as he removed his backpack.

"Yeah, I know what you mean, friend, but let's face it; we had fun," joked Bill, getting John's attention. He turned on the receiver again, but all that remained was the rumbling from the ventilation system.

"Is it quiet down there, Bill?" asked John, noticing Bill listening to it again.

"Yep, the only sound is the vent system down there," replied Bill, this time turning it off.

Once again, they were on the road and going back to the motel for some much-needed sleep. At the motel, Mark was just leaving his room. He walked up to the car. "You're just getting back, at this time?" asked Mark, somewhat amazed.

John then went on to explain their situation and why it took so long for them. Bill gave Mark the keys to the car and some money and said, "Here, take care of this today; I think we need some sleep for tonight."

Mark looked a little surprised by this, but John waved that it would be fine for them to go.

Alice then came out of her room. Mark waved the keys at her, and she said, "What? Just the two of us this morning, Mark?"

He then explained what had happened to them and why it had taken so long the previous night.

John woke just before noon, but this time, he felt a whole lot better than before. When he was ready for the day, he left his room, walked over to Bill's room, and knocked. Bill was already up and talking on the phone. He was pacing back and forth in his room. John could tell whoever it was, was important to Bill.

After several minutes, Bill hung up and then said, "That was Lieutenant Wilson on the phone. He's thinking he might send up some FBI agents to help arrest those murderers down the road."

John wasn't sure if liked that or not. "Do we really need them, Bill?" he wondered out loud, not sure what to think.

Bill thought a minute and then said, "To tell the truth,

John, in the law's eyes, yes! That's how the system works, and I can't change that."

John shook his head in disbelief and then helped himself to the coffee.

At this time, Mark let himself in, for the door was still open some. Both men greeted Mark as he entered Bill's room, and Mark said cheerfully, "Well, I see the night owls are awake."

"Oh yes, Mark, we are, and we're planning a bigger night tonight!" responded John cheerfully.

Bill then stated to Mark that they might have some FBI agents with them later that night. Mark was like John in his thinking and wasn't really sure if he liked it. "Well then, we'll cross that bridge when we get there, I guess," stated Mark, not really sure what to think.

"And I received two text messages from our informants, and they were the same in detail—all followers will be there tonight. You know what that means, don't you? A full house," stated Bill with sureness. He grinned slowly.

"You think we can hear it on the receiver, Bill?" asked John, wondering about it some.

"No, John, we're out of range some, and it's underground as well," responded Bill with a sureness that was visible.

"Well, it was just a thought," replied John, wishing the opposite were true.

"Hey, guys. I'm hungry. Want to take me out for lunch?" answered Alice laughingly with a big smile on her face.

They all greeted Alice cheerfully, and Mark said with a smile, "My, my, aren't we chipper today?"

"Well, today is today, and after tonight, we can again go home and go back to normal," responded Alice with a grin.

"Well, we can't argue that, Alice, but to tell you the truth, I kind of like it here," stated Mark, feeling sure of himself.

Bill stepped in and explained the latest news, so she knew as much as the rest. She nodded and smiled. "Good, good, everything isn't that far away."

After lunch, they all went out for a walk in the park. There was a river running through it. The day was sunny but cool with a light breeze that stirred the leaves on the ground. "It's nice here, Bill, no problems or concerns; it's just nice," replied Mark easily, sounding relaxed and almost carefree.

"Yeah, I know what you mean; maybe we've all needed this for a while. Not the daily pressures and troubles, just some time to breathe easily for a while," replied Bill in the same tone of voice as Mark used. John and Alice were by the river by the small bridge that crossed the river. Bill and Mark watched them for a while.

Mark said easily, "Look at that, Bill. They're acting like kids would by the water. Days like this are precious. Don't you agree?"

Bill glanced at Mark and just smiled and nodded his head, for it was fun to watch. He was thinking of Mark. He said, "Why don't you retire here and make the best of it for yourself?"

Mark nodded and said, "No, I can't, Bill. I'm not seventy-five yet. I can't even transfer; my job is till sickness or age or death. All I can do is quit and lose my pension, and I'm too old to start over, Bill."

Bill thought about that and said, "That's too bad, Mark. Everybody needs time away from things, even a bishop like you. Maybe a winning lottery ticket will do."

Mark just laughed and nodded his head, and they continued to walk together.

After a while, Bill and Mark noticed John and Alice were starting to tire from their fun. Everybody went back to the car. They went for something to eat; this would be the last chance for food for a while. In the car, John and Alice were still laughing and making jokes with each other. Mark and Bill just smiled at each other as they went to the restaurant, for it was now in the middle of the afternoon. After they ate and returned to the motel, they rested for a short time.

While Bill lay on his bed and thought of many things to keep track of, he thought most of the communication problem between the soldiers, the park service, and them. Everybody had to be there at the right time to make the plan work. If they had walkie-talkies, that would be fine, or they could keep a deputy with them with a walkie-talkie. He did feel confident about Mark and his hand in this.

Alice might be the only wild card in this game. She might react differently, for she still loved her brother. For the most part, he felt this was the simplest way of doing this. Bill knew the sheriff would be all right. This would give the sheriff a big feather in his cap when they were through. He didn't like the FBI in this much, for they were too much of a take-charge type of people. And they really could mess this whole thing up for everybody. Bill only hoped that they came later, not sooner. Bill rested his eyes for half an hour, and when he woke, it was time to go and begin a long night. The others were leaving their rooms about the same time as Bill. When they arrived at the sheriff's station, it was before 5:00 p.m. They waited in the office for a while, for the sheriff was busy with a local matter. When it was their time to be in the sheriff's office, Sheriff Kief wasn't in a good mood. But to the surprise of everybody, he excused himself for his tone of voice and manners.

Bill was thinking this was to be a big day for him and his troopers. The sheriff was confident that everything would be there at 6:00 p.m. at the station.

Sheriff Kief noticed that Mark had a small bag on his lap as he sat there. "May I ask why you need that, Bishop?" asked the sheriff flatly as he pointed at the bishop's bag.

"Since this is a church matter as well, I'm going to do my part. I'm going to do more than one thing in this matter for God and for the church," stated the bishop, confident in its importance.

The sheriff was indifferent in the matter and said, "Fine, just don't get in the way!"

From that point on, John, the bishop, and Bill were strictly business. The sheriff was good at organizing arrangements and asked the bishop what he and the others needed to do. Sheriff Kief was deeply interested in the ritual and the step-by-step progression, for the sake of the child. Bill informed the sheriff that the FBI might be there, and he felt the same as everybody there. Bill told the sheriff the soldiers could carry the hose into the tunnel with them as they entered it, so it would be ready at the same time. The sheriff felt that was fair and it would be no problem to do it quietly.

Bill spoke of the communication. They needed to work that out as well. Sheriff Kief was stating that a deputy at both ends on the same channel would pass the word along. Bill kind of figured on that much of the plan himself. Then the sheriff added that there would be several prisoner trucks to carry all the people away—first to the county jail for the night and to be booked and then back to Illinois. There, they could do as they wanted. A deputy knocked on the door and stated the park rangers and the soldiers were there now. The sheriff smiled as he looked at the clock on the wall and said, "Damn good, it's eighteen hundred hours. Bring in the park supervisor and the officer in charge of the soldiers."

After several minutes, the ranger and officer came into the office and stated who they were. Bill drew out a rough map of the area with all the woods, the house, and the underground complex that was there. The captain of the soldiers asked many questions, where he wanted his soldiers to be at. He gave his ideas as to what he thought was better.

John asked, "How many soldiers do you have tonight, Captain?"

"Twenty, sir," replied the captain in a military tone of voice.

It was finally decided to have two at the back door and two at either end of the house; the rest would be evenly divided at the front door and the tunnel. Then the captain wondered how to get behind those barrels to know what was taking place so they would know when to call in the troops. Bill held up a remote and said, "We have three excited rats to let loose at the push of a button for a diversion."

"Not great, I must admit, but if we get there early, it will work for us," stated the captain, thinking it had a chance.

Bill went on to explain that they had a remote camera as well, so they could watch behind the barrels. They would be able to see the whole thing and record as well. "Bishop Frazer, how long do you feel this opening service will take, before they bring the child in to be sacrificed?" asked the sheriff.

The bishop thought and then answered flatly, "I would say thirty to forty-five minutes, depending on how much ceremony they want to perform before the sacrifice."

"Now why do we have a water truck?" asked the sheriff in a matter-of-fact voice.

The bishop smiled and said with confidence, "Sir, you are dealing with pure evil here. The whole thing is an act of evil. And bringing in the devil and his hordes, in time, will destroy your nice little town. That water will purify the place and the people and will protect you and your town in the future to come. And if I may say so as well, nonbelievers like you, sir, just think you can make it all go away, but you can't. Instead, you will bring in all kinds of crazy people, who sound good to the ears but are as worthless as a gum wrapper."

For a second, the sheriff and the bishop just sat there and eyed each other in silent communication.

Finally, the captain broke the silence by stating, "How soon do you want us to get started on our mission here, sir?"

The sheriff finally took his attention away from the bishop and looked at the soldier. "You will have to ask Bill there; in a manner of speaking, he's in charge here." The sheriff just waved his arm at Bill.

Bill turned to the captain and said, "Seven thirty should be fine, for the ceremony starts at ten, or twenty-two hundred for you. If you have any more questions, let's hear them before we go then."

The captain had some interesting ideas, which caught the others by surprise, and they were used as well.

The bishop stood up and looked at the time. He said, "It's time for me to go to work. Bill; is the car unlocked?"

Bill reached into his pocket and gave Mark the keys. With that, Mark left the office. Alice was quiet through most of the meeting and just listened to everything that was said. They were thinking of ending their meeting when she said politely, "Can I please have a minute with my brother before he is taken away?"

The sheriff was just starting to stand and said nicely, "Yes, you may, Alice, but he will be under a guard's watch."

Alice nodded and smiled slightly. She slowly stood up and waited for the rest to leave. With that, those who were sitting rose to their feet, and together, they left the office.

Bill and John were outside first, followed by Alice and the sheriff with two of his deputies. They all stood and watched as a park service man opened the top of the tanker truck. The bishop on the other side waited for it to be opened. The bishop gave the man his blessing book and a flashlight, so he could read the blessing. Again, he spoke in Latin and gave the water God's blessing three times. It took several minutes to be completed. With that done, the bishop had the man seal up the top of the tank of water, and they both climbed down.

"That's the craziest damn thing I've seen yet today, but okay, it's your show here," stated the sheriff, feeling it was a waste of time.

Getting off the ladder, Mark walked around the truck, and the man gave him his material again and a flashlight. Mark then walked up to Bill and the rest and said, "That's the strongest I can make it, for what we're doing here tonight."

Bill patted him on the shoulder and gave his thanks for the work done.

"Well, if you want to be there at seven thirty, we better be starting out soon. Otherwise, it could be damn crowded down there, and your rats might get tired," stated the sheriff with a bit of attitude in his voice.

Bill looked at the sheriff and said, "Sir, we are well set up here, and I do appreciate the work you've done for us here tonight, but don't worry about the rats. We used them before in the past at other jobs; they will buy us the time we need."

The sheriff didn't agree with the rats at all, but at the same time, he knew people hated rats and it had a chance of working. The sheriff gave the order, and they all got into their vehicles, with the sheriff and deputies leading the way. It was like a parade in the evening as they drove out of town. As Bill, John, and the rest followed, they felt everything was understood well.

Mark and Alice were in the backseat of the car, and nobody was saying much.

"Mark, you have everything you need, at the right time, after the arrests are made?" asked Bill, just trying to break the silence.

"Yes, I do, Bill. In fact, I have more for this, if we need it," replied Mark, sounding ready and prepared. As they approached the gate leading into the woods, the water tanker took the lead and went in first. Then came the hose trucks, Bill's car, and the police cars. When those trucks were in proper position before the clearing, they were to kill their lights and stop together.

At this point, all the brake lights were taped over, and the drivers of those trucks were given night-vision goggles to see. The National Guard didn't go in at the gate but drove down the road, turned around, and came back. They were to stop before the gate, with all lights off, and did so perfectly.

At this point, the captain of the National Guard gave orders as to where he wanted his soldiers to be, and their position was known to all. The captain then explained the communication situation, and the second in command was ordered to handle the communication outside. Only the captain and the second in command were to be talking back and forth. Once everything was understood with the soldiers, they started out through the gate and into the woods. The moon above was rising, offering some light for the troops to see by.

John was helping the water tanker back in to be close to the tunnel, which was cleared for the tanker. After several attempts, the tanker was in the proper position. Bill, by this time, had his backpack and John's in his hand. The hoses were slowly put together by the park service, as the National Guard reached them. Bill turned on the receiver for the sheriff and everybody who wanted to hear. From the voices on the receiver, it sounded like four or five people.

"When do you want to go in and release your rats, so we can set up down there?" asked the sheriff in a matter-of-fact tone.

Bill walked over to the park service and talked to a couple of them and then the captain. With that information, he walked back to the sheriff and deputies. "I would say we take a restroom break and then we go in," stated Bill, with confidence in his voice.

The captain, seeing that they were going in, readied the tarp to throw over the tunnel opening. When everybody came back, John showed the deputy which tree had the switch that opened the tunnel. Bill gestured for the deputy to open the tunnel, and he, John, the sheriff, Alice, and Bishop Frazer went in. The opening closed behind them. Bill had his night-vision on and working. John and the sheriff had their flashlights on. Bill waited as they put covers over their flashlights to reduce the light.

Finally, everybody whispered, "Ready," and then they started for the other end.

When they were about halfway, Bill noticed somebody walking up to the curtain, and he whispered, "Lights off!"

They waited until whoever it was walked away, and then they came back with a laser light to scan the tunnel. They were forced to get very low to the ground. Finally, that person finished checking the tunnel and walked away. "Damn, that was close, Bill. Did you figure on that too?" whispered the sheriff, feeling relief that it was over.

"Yes, I did, Sheriff, but not with a laser light," whispered Bill flatly, happy at not being noticed.

They lay there for several minutes, and the men returned again with their laser light. Time passed, and the person never returned again. "Okay, let's go," stated Bill in a whispered tone of voice. The voices were now clear and easy to understand. They could hear the voices of five people working. They stopped and checked the time. Bill indicated that he was going up to check ahead. The sheriff thought that was nuts and gutsy. It was not a practice he taught his men. Bill removed his goggles and carefully looked through the curtain. He saw that they were now in the back of the room. He waved the others forward, and Bill, on all fours, crawled behind the barrels. Then, one by one, they followed until all five of them were safely behind the barrels. John was the last one. He kept the curtain as still as possible. Safely behind the barrels with a row of boxes on top and barrels that were double-stacked, they hid. John opened Bill's backpack and brought out the camera and tablet player. John set it up and carefully placed the camera where it would be less likely to be seen. With everything now working properly, they watched the five people set up through the camera.

"Hell, that's a nice toy you have there," stated the sheriff with interest in his whispered voice.

Bill felt pleased that he liked it so much and said, "Thanks, Sheriff. It's the easiest way to watch."

They noticed Adam enter the church and seemed too approve of the work they'd done.

He walked around, paying attention to the markings on the floor and the circles drawn. He tested the sound system, their cameras, and lastly, the lights. The look on his face was approving, for the time was drawing near. Lastly, three women brought out the girl, and they were explaining to the child what she was to do and how to walk out with them. The child looked tense but not really afraid and didn't appear in or near tears. The five of them looked at each other as this took place.

Shortly, Adam stood by watching the three women and the child as they did their jobs well. Finally, the three women and the child left the room, with Adam walking toward the exit. He stopped and looked around one last time and then left as well. Bill looked at his watch, but he couldn't read it clearly, so he picked up a flashlight. With a roll of tape in his jacket, he taped over the flashlight even more. Pointing toward the floor, he turned it on, and it was only a point of light, enough to see his watch.

Bill now looked at his watch again. It read 8:35 p.m. "In less than an hour and a half, this room is going to get busier. Let's carefully barricade ourselves in a little bit, if possible," whispered Bill with caution in his voice.

"What's the point, Bill? We'll still be easy to see if someone checks to see back here?" whispered the sheriff, wanting a better reason.

John listened to both sides and knew Bill was right. He whispered, "If we don't cover ourselves better, were dead here, so what's your problem, Sheriff? Bill and I have done this many times in the past, and we're here. We know what we're doing. Just make it look like it belongs."

The sheriff reluctantly helped the others by taking boxes that would not be seen from the front, and their barricade was up. Bill nodded to John and the bishop. It looked good, and they were better protected from visitors. Bill looked at his watch again—8:55 p.m. A crowd was forming, all dressed in black gowns with black hoods over their heads. The ceiling lights were bright enough for them to see clearly.

Alice watched with interest, as more and more people started to fill the large room in front of them. They moved carefully outside the circle and avoided stepping inside it. After a few minutes, the child appeared again, but this time, in a black gown and hood made for a child. The child was led to the altar with the three women again, and the women were carrying something in their hands. Bill looked at John and Mark, and they looked at each other. Bill carefully reached into his right jacket pocket and pulled out a syringe. Mark and John saw the syringe in Bill's hand and automatically knew whom it was for. John had warned Mark earlier when they were by themselves that this might be necessary for Alice.

At this time, Adam appeared on their viewing screen. He walked up to the altar with the three women and the child. Adam was wearing a black gown with priest's markings on the shoulders and a pentagram on a golden necklace around his neck. He stood in front of the pulpit, facing the altar, with the others. Adam did a blessing over the altar in some old Latin language. With that done, the child then disrobed and was naked before the altar. The three women in black gowns helped the child onto the altar. The child lay flat on the altar with her arms by her side. The three women set their objects on the altar as well and opened each one, as Adam went behind the pulpit and brought out paintbrushes. He gave them to the three women.

With this activity taking place on the viewing screen, Alice was shocked badly, and they could all see it on her face. She watched more on the screen as the three women continued to paint the naked child's body. Mark had trouble seeing what type of markings they were from the screen in John's hand. The sheriff at this time was concerned with the fear Alice was displaying.

By this time, all of Adam's thirty-seven members were there in the room, standing and watching the painting of the child. They all stood silently in the room, just watching, and started to hum something in a low tone. Adam raised his arms above his head and again spoke in old Latin. It sounded like he was offering a word of thanks to Satan for this child he was about to offer.

The fear on Alice's face was even more evident. There was more disbelief, and she looked as if she wanted to do something about it. The sheriff watched her closely for any sudden moves or any word that might come out. With even more intensity, she watched the screen in John's hand. They could hear the humming fill the room. Suddenly, Alice had enough. She started to spring to her feet, but the sheriff grabbed her and covered her mouth very tightly. She fought strongly, but a murmuring was all that was heard. Bill grabbed her, and the sheriff saw that he was trying to talk to her. Alice leaped to her feet suddenly, but tripped over the sheriff's legs. She fell badly on the hard floor and knocked herself out cold. Bill and the sheriff made Alice comfortable on the floor behind them and out of the way. "You must've figured on that too, Bill.

How long will she be out of it?" whispered the sheriff with a hushed question.

Bill gave a faint smile and said, "Yes, I did figure on this as well. She had to see this much of it for her own information. The bump on the head isn't bad, maybe a half hour and she'll wake up with a headache."

The sheriff shook his head approvingly. He was somewhat amazed at how he knew this in advance and how to take care of it. "Well, in two hours, this will be over with, and she should be calmer by then," whispered the sheriff, with more confidence in Bill and his group. Bill and the sheriff again returned their attention to the screen and saw that the women, who were painting the child, were about finished with their work.

"Bill, those markings are very old, but they are used for sacrificial offerings, such as this," whispered the bishop with a knowing tone of voice. Bill looked at the bishop and nodded that he understood what he had said. The sheriff understood as well and watched with more interest than before. John, at this time, had never seen anything like this before except on television. John was feeling glad that everything was being recorded and could be watched again in the future. John's basic belief was that these were all crazy people doing crazy things—something like cavepeople would have done thousands of years before. And somehow, it was still going on, even in the twenty-first century. When the markings on the little girl were completed, Adam came up to the altar and inspected them. Then he looked at each of the women and nodded with approval. He then raised his arms and thanked Satan for the work done. The child at this time was calm and relaxed on the altar. After about five minutes, one of the women tested the paint for dryness.

The child rose up, sat on the altar, and looked at the rest of them, who were still humming on the floor. The child then slid off the altar, and one of the three women put the gown back on the child. With the child now covered, she left the altar and walked with the three women through the followers to a room in the back. At this point, the child was ready for a later ceremony. Bill looked at his watch with the help of his flashlight and saw that it was 9:15 p.m. The bishop noticed that they were now getting ready for the ceremony to begin.

"They're getting ready for something now, Bill. Adam is waiting for something to happen, and then it will begin with the main ceremony at 10:00 p.m.," whispered the bishop, now understanding their ceremony.

John, Bill, and the sheriff, at this point, glanced at each other and wondered what was next. At this time, the followers broke into two groups and formed straight lines. They left enough room for someone to walk through the groups, past the circles on the floor, and to the altar. Two women, each carrying a basket of black candles, entered from the room behind the groups. And they proceeded to pass out the black candles to each member of the groups. With that done, they went back and came out side by side, each holding a large black candle, which was lit.

The two candle-bearers lit each candle of the members on both sides and then walked forward to the altar. They stood there with their candles lit, facing the members. Adam, at this point, blessed them with their candles and then stood by the altar and faced the membership. He blessed them as well. Adam and the two candle-bearers waited for something to happen. A member then came up from the back room with a huge unlit black candle and stand, approached with a slow but honorable step, and placed the huge candle and stand between the pit and the altar. There was no music playing, just the sound of the humming and the ventilation system that was working.

Bishop Frazer found this to be very exciting and interesting. The other three men were just amazed by the ceremony itself. Once the huge black candle was placed, the two candle-bearers together lit the huge candle. Once it was lit, Adam loudly clapped his hands and the humming stopped. The lights went very dim in the room. The candlelight filled the room, along with the faint light coming from above them. One could still see clearly in the room. The member who had the huge candle then went to the room behind the two groups and returned with a cache case at his side. Once up to the altar and Adam, he bowed and gave the case to him. They bowed to each other, and the member went to the rear again. Adam, as high priest, went to the huge candle, bowed, and said something in old Latin again. He bowed again and then went to the pulpit, stood behind it, and turned on his reading light. He opened the cache case, brought out his prayers and message, and placed them on the pulpit and the cache case lower. Bill looked at the time again with the flashlight. It read 9:50 p.m., and John, Mark, and the sheriff noticed it as well.

"It's about to start, Bill. This should be an oath, or something to that order, before the big ceremony," whispered the bishop with excitement in his voice.

The sheriff, from the look on his face, seemed to be enjoying the ceremony. Finally, he said in a hushed tone, "Right now, I could arrest them!"

Bishop Frazer, having heard this, whispered, "Just wait and see, Sheriff. You will want to later!" The bishop noticed the sheriff's lack of knowledge in this matter and didn't want to say any more on it.

Adam began with a satanic prayer as an opener. It was clearly understandable to all, and after each verse, they followed with, "Hail, Satan." The speaker system was of good quality, and it was very clear. The opening satanic prayer lasted for five minutes; it was then followed by their version of the Ten Commandments, which were the opposite of God's. And after each commandment, there was, "Hail, Satan." With the last commandment read, there was another prayer and an acknowledgment, and then the overhead lights went out. There was only candlelight; otherwise, the room was black and silent. Again, Bill looked at his watch, and it was 10:00 p.m.

The sheriff whispered, "This must be the big event now; this should be good!"

John just sat and watched the screen in front of him, and then he glanced at everyone and gave a faint smile. There was a minute of silence in the large room, and then Adam, the high priest, raised his arms and blessed his members openly to all. Then he lowered his arms and waited, as the brides of Satan slowly stepped forward between the two groups on the floor. There was a single bride, and then the others followed, two by two, forming a row of brides from the pit of hell to past the altar, all facing the high priest. They were dressed in black gowns with red hoods and walked in a stately way.

When the last bride took her place, Adam read another satanic prayer over them and blessed them all. He read each name of the person to the membership. In closing his prayer, he finished with, "May you live forever in hell as your home. And may you find it better than heaven, mated with your partner, serving Satan as your god. For all power and honor and glory belong to Satan, who is God forever."

And everyone said, "Hail, Satan."

John, Bill, Mark, and the sheriff looked at each other and shook their heads in disbelief at the closing prayer. At the end of the prayer, the lights went much brighter, and it was easier to see everything. The lights were about the brightness of early morning as the sun broke the horizon.

Adam then stated, "My friends, normally we enjoy candlelight, but this is special tonight. For tonight, you will see Satan, our god, and twelve of his top demons, as they mate with their brides. We will share in power over a new world order, and you will have a role in it. And now we begin the ritual of all rituals, and tonight you will be gods as well."

Bishop Frazer whispered angrily to Bill, "That is the most damnable thing I ever heard of in my life. God himself will never settle for that sort of thing to go unpunished."

The sheriff then took his microphone and whispered into it, "Prepare up there. Ready all stations. My next message is to enter. Is that clear?"

"Roger that, sir," was the reply that came back.

Adam then glanced at each of the thirteen brides and clapped his hands once. They removed their hoods from their heads. John now noticed that they were all beautiful women indeed. Adam did another blessing over them and then started the ritual of all rituals. Adam spoke in old Latin again. Mark couldn't quite understand it all. To the surprise of everyone, and Adam as well, the lights dimmed some and went bright again. Then there was a groan from the pit of hell and some smoke. Then the room shook some, like a small earthquake, but Adam continued with the ritual. When he finished with the first part, he clapped his hands once, and the thirteen brides removed their gowns and stood naked before Adam.

Again, he proceeded with the ritual for about a minute, looked at his members, and clapped once. All the members stepped inside the circle on the floor with their candles. With that done, Adam stepped aside, took sea salt, and made a circle behind his pulpit. He stood in the center of it and then continued the ritual, with even greater authority, his voice higher and more direct. Smoke from the pit of hell was now continuous, and a wind from nowhere started to blow inside the room. It was not enough to blow out the candles, but the flames of it flickered. The bishop was now watching with an intensity Bill had never seen in him before. The smoke was slowly filling the room, as the wind stirred it all around. Adam stopped and again clapped his hands. Everyone said, "Hail, Satan."

The smoke now had an odor of sulfur to it. It bit the nose some. Adam waited and looked at the pit of hell. For the time being, the smoke had stopped, as did the wind. And everyone waited and watched for the appearance of Satan himself.

After a minute or two, a loud moaning came from the pit itself. Suddenly, the head of a man appeared from the pit and continued to rise up from it. Slowly, the whole man appeared and floated in the air above the pit. Then he moved past the pit and landed on his feet. The man was naked and was somewhat muscular in build and of average height for a man, with a red tint to his skin. The man said with a booming voice that filled the room, "I'm Satan, your god, and you are my servants, and together, we'll serve one another for all time." Satan then looked at each of the naked brides before him—he was not hurried—and chose one. Pleasure appeared on his face, as he looked into her eyes, and this made her look uncomfortable. He quickly turned his attention to the pit and ordered the rest to follow him.

First, there was a rush of smoke from the pit, and then one by one, the head demons appeared from the pit. All were naked like Satan himself. They looked human in facial appearances, but their sin was showing on their faces, looking haggard and lustful at the same time.

"Oh my God, this is the worst thing I have ever seen in my life, and so many at that too!" whispered the bishop with fear in his voice. The other three men looked at him and seemed to feel the same way. Again, the bishop whispered, "Please understand me here. No army can stop them. There're too many now!"

The three men looked at each other in silence and could only feel they were in trouble this time. Twelve demons came out of the pit, all naked and with red-tinted skin and all similar in height, with a muscular build like Satan himself.

Each one picked a bride and stood in front of her. Lust was on each of their faces, as they now looked at Adam, for the next ritual to begin. Adam clapped his hands, and the lights went bright again. He gave a short sermon about a new hour and a new day dawning with Satan as leader. And then in old Latin, he gave them their marriage ritual, blessed them, and called them husband and wife. At this point, they forced their wives to the floor and mated with them there. The groans and the screams from the women were petrifying, and the membership in the circle was alarmed by what they saw. They wanted to run but couldn't, for breaking the circle would mean their death.

The groans and screaming continued. Suddenly, from the ceiling, fourteen glows of light appeared. The brightness of the room hid the brightness of the lights. It settled to the floor behind each of the mating couples on the floor. Adam, in total disbelief, froze behind the pulpit and was speechless. The members in the circle were now frozen in fear, for they knew in their hearts that they were doomed. The glow of lights slowly changed into fourteen angels with swords in their hands. Some of the angels were men and some women; all were extremely beautiful in appearance. Their gowns were of brilliant white.

Bishop Frazer then remembered the prayer he had offered there and whispered to Bill, "Bill, remember that prayer I did there? It's now being answered! It's being answered!" whispered the bishop with much thankfulness in his voice.

Bill then remembered that day and nodded. He gripped his arm happily. John also remembered it, but now he couldn't argue about God anymore. God and his angels were in front of him, and he couldn't deny it anymore. The sheriff watched in total disbelief and didn't know what to say. So much had happened already and now this too.

His mouth was open; his mind couldn't fathom what he was seeing. There was groaning and screaming filling the room, and then the angels made ready. The fourteen angels raised their swords to God and then pointed the tips outward and down. They raised their swords up and then thrust them into the demons and the women below. The sudden groan of severe pain and screaming filled the room and every ear. The room shook from the screaming, for there was power in Satan's and his demons' voices.

The last angel thrust a sword into Adam's heart. Adam

was frozen, unable to move a muscle. He collapsed over the pulpit and died quickly. The angels removed their swords from their victims' bodies, again pointed them to heaven in thanks, and disappeared. Satan and the demons rushed to the pit of hell and were gone in a few seconds, leaving the bodies of the dead lying there in a pool of blood. The sheriff quickly got on his microphone, called in everybody, and rescued the child. They brought in the water hose. The members stood in their circle, frozen in fear with what they had seen before them. They knew it could have been them there on the floor. Bill looked at Alice, lying on the floor, and wondered about her. He thought that he had better revive her. He reached into his other pocket and found the smelling salts.

The sheriff saw the soldiers enter from behind the circle on John's screen. The members in the circle were on one hand happy to see them, because of what had just happened in front of them. But, on the other, they knew they were going to jail for a long time.

Bill and the sheriff both knew now as they looked at each other that they could reveal their position and didn't have to hide anymore. Bill looked at John and said in a normal voice, "Keep the machines recording, John, but watch over Alice for now, please?"

The bishop stood up and stretched himself out. He followed Bill and the sheriff around the barrels and out to the floor. At this time, the other soldiers came from the tunnel next to the barrels with the water hose in hand and carrying their rifles at attack position. The bishop had the soldiers place the hose by the pit of hell. The soldiers, after dropping the hose, stood ready with their rifles. The members in the circle quickly raised their hands but didn't try to run, for they knew they were surrounded. Fear was evident on their faces, for the law was now against them and Satan was not going to help them.

"Which one of you Satanists would like to explain the whole story now?" asked the sheriff frankly, with assertiveness in his voice. The sheriff looked around the members and spotted two well dressed men entering from the dressing room with the child dressed in a black gown.

The captain of the soldiers was having his men handcuff the members, while the other soldiers stood with rifles ready. The deputies appeared from the tunnel and walked toward their sheriff. At this time, the two well-dressed men approached the sheriff.

"Special Agent Zdun, Special Agent Marth, we're from the Minneapolis branch FBI. We saw the angels kill the women and the creatures run into the pit—in fact, we saw everything, ah, Sheriff who?"

The sheriff was a little nervous with these men, for he had never had much time with them before and answered, "Sheriff Roger Kief, sheriff of Park River, and these are my deputies with me."

Special Agent Zdun then said in an official tone, "We were called in by Lieutenant Wilson of the Chicago PD, who informed us that the kidnappers and murderers would be at this address, and we could assess the situation here."

Bill heard the agent say that as he walked closer from behind the deputies. The sheriff then introduced Bill to the special agents and said that he was pretty much in charge of this operation and he was instrumental in setting it up. The two special agents recorded everything from the beginning of that operation and what he wanted to do at the end of it. Bill also explained Lieutenant Wilson, how he was connected to the lieutenant, and why most of this was on Bill's plan.

"Mr. Radner, what you have done here was neatly done, simple in design, and well thought out. We both thank you, sir." With that, they all shook hands and continued with their questioning.

John was with Alice as she came to and said, "What happened when I was out, John?"

John, knowing that he would have to tell her of her brother, then said, "Oh, Bill has much to tell when he's here."

Alice's mind was slowly clearing after hitting her head on the floor. She said, "What I wanted to do, at that moment, I would have knocked myself out too. Where's Adam?"

John, fearing this would come at this moment, replied softly, "Alice, I'm afraid your brother is dead. I'm sorry."

Shock came over Alice's face, and she cried bitterly for some time. There wasn't much John could do but hold her and be with her at this time.

Bishop Frazer was examining each of the fourteen people's eyes as they lay dead. It was as he had feared. He knew he had to take action at this important time, or this was not over at all. The sheriff walked over to the bishop and wondered what he was doing, for he never saw anyone do this type of examining before.

"What in God's name are you doing, Mark?" asked the sheriff, in a matter-of-fact tone of voice.

"Sir, look at each of the eyes in these bodies here. We're not done here yet. Go on; look, please. I dare you to look, and you tell me, please!" demanded the bishop in a stern voice.

The sheriff looked into the bishop's eyes. He could tell he wasn't fooling. He bent down and looked at the eyes of one of thirteen women. "Crap, what is this, sir? That's not right!" shrieked the sheriff, with fear in his voice. The sheriff and deputies then looked at all the eyes of everyone lying there on the floor and Adam's. "Man, what is this crap anyway, sir? All those eyes are coal black! Now what happened here? You tell me now, damn it!" shrieked the sheriff, again with fear in his voice.

The two agents and Bill all turned around, wondering what this was all about. One of the deputies then explained to them and pointed at the eyes. With that, they looked at all the eyes of the dead. The FBI agents were at a loss for words in this matter. The bishop then spoke up. "Put the dead women in a pile, one on top of the other, and I will bless them and spray them with holy water. Or everyone will come back to life, with Satan's spirit, and evil will reign over the earth. This is no joke!"

Agent Marth then said, "You got to be kidding, sir. The dead can't walk again. They're dead. By what authority do you have to say what you're saying?"

The bishop had dealt with this matter many times in the past, doing this work for the church, and he showed his papers from the Vatican.

Both agents read the papers and were surprised by the information. They handed them back. The two agents stepped aside and talked with each other. They talked for a minute or two. When they were finished, they turned and one said, "First, let us collect the names of each, if you have them, and second, you may continue, with us as witnesses. And third, since this is of national importance, we will film it and report it to our superiors. It will be handled from that level."

With that, Bill went to the pulpit and found the paper

with each of the names of the thirteen women and handed it to the FBI agents. They looked it over, smiled, and nodded their approval.

Alice was feeling better at this time, and John helped her back to her feet. "You think you want to see him now, Alice? Or would you rather see how it happened first?" asked John, as easily as he could say it.

"No, I think I want to see him first and say my good-byes," replied Alice with some pain in her voice. John led her around the boxes of protection and around the barrels until Adam's body was visible on the floor. She then ran to her brother on the floor and sobbed some more over the body. Again, John held her. Everybody could feel the pain she was feeling as she sobbed over her brother. Bill felt really sorry for her at the time but felt he should leave it alone for the time being. Bill told the agents who she was and described her relationship to the deceased.

Mark walked slowly up to Bill and took him aside. Then Mark whispered to Bill, "Bill, we don't have that much time with this. I have to bless and spray holy water on them, now or never!"

Again, Bill could see that Mark was very serious about this matter. "You mean they're not dead yet, Mark?" he asked with some amazement in his voice.

"Bill, friend, these bodies here on the floor don't have any soul or spirit—if you will, they are open vessels for Satan to use any way he wants. But remember, each one is pregnant, and he wants those children in his name. The sooner we do this, the safer we will all be, now and forever," Mark pleaded, with seriousness in his voice.

Bill looked at all the dead women lying on the floor, for

they were not covered yet. "All right, Mark, let's get this done right away. I'll find the captain and get some men here," stated Bill with some authority in his voice.

The members were slowly walking away and up the stairs in handcuffs, still wearing their black gowns. There was some talking among them.

They walked through the house and then to the prisoner truck, for there were several. Once the last followers were inside, the doors were locked and the trucks pulled away and to the county seat jail.

The sheriff called for several coroner vehicles to carry all the dead bodies away. The families had to be found to identify the bodies.

Bishop Frazer slowly walked up to Alice, who now had control of her feelings again. He wanted to show her something. "Alice, you must see this. I know it's going to be hard, but please trust me. It's important for you to know," stated Bishop Frazer as softly as he could.

Alice nodded, and then the bishop opened both of Adam's eyes at the same time. They were as black as coal. Alice wanted to cry but couldn't. She only nodded her head. The bishop then closed Adam's eyes again and then said to Alice, "Alice, I must move this body over there with the others. They will be blessed and then showered with holy water. Satan can still use them if I don't do this ritual; they will be the walking dead for all time. Please let me do this."

Alice again nodded that it was okay, for Alice knew Satan had controlled her brother this far. Mark waved to the soldiers to carry Adam's body over to the others where they were piled. Then the sheriff got the signal from the bishop and called on the radio to turn on the pump for the water.

Bishop Frazer walked around the barrels and found his bag. He returned to the piled bodies. As the bishop opened his bag and prepared, Bill walked up to him and offered to help in any way he could.

"Oh thank you, Bill. Yes, hold on to this, and I will begin the blessing. Later, please help me with the hose," replied the bishop as he made himself ready to begin.

The bishop began the blessing in Latin with his arms raised. The blessing was somewhat long, and from Bill's understanding, it was complete. Bill, not knowing much Latin, could tell that he wanted God to forgive them of their sins in life and help them find eternal rest. The bishop, the blessing finished, lowered his arms and appeared to be somewhat satisfied with it.

The two agents watched from a distance with the child nearby. They had been asking the child questions. It appeared to Bill that they had a question. When they made eye contact, the agents walked toward them. "We would like to film you as you spray the holy water on the bodies, if you don't mind, sir," one of the agents said, not offering the reason why.

Mark looked at Bill, who was still holding the bag of prayers, and then gave his approval. Mark went through a dozen prayers in his bag before he found one that was suitable for his needs. "Bill, you can now put that down and rest your arms. It must be getting heavy," responded the bishop, seeing Bill was starting to look uncomfortable.

Mark then blessed the hose with the water in it. He turned and again blessed the bodies. With that done, he put that prayer in his bag and closed it. He nodded to the agents that they were about ready, and the agents prepared their camera to begin filming. The child next to the agents was watching with interest and even seemed to be in shock.

At this time, John and Alice picked up the hose and readied it for Bill and Mark. The bishop took the lead position with Bill behind him and John and Alice holding the rest of the hose. The bishop nodded to the agents to begin filming the scene. They nodded back. The bishop turned on the water to a saturating spray that covered a wide area of all the bodies. With the bishop praying as he hosed the bodies, saturating them, a fire appeared on the pile of dead bodies. The flame was about six feet tall, but there was no smoke from it. Everybody was amazed by that. The sheriff and deputies stood there and had trouble in their minds, trying to explain it. The heat from it could be felt by all who were close to it, but nobody was hurt by it. Only the bodies being sprayed with the holy water burned. They held the hose on the bodies and the flame, as it started to consume the dead bodies. The body of Adam started to move, for it was only next to the pile of bodies. Adam's body was in flames as it tried to get up. Everybody was in fear and wondered what could have happened.

Adam struggled against the holy water and the flames that consumed his body at this time rapidly. Tears ran down Alice's face as she watched, still holding the hose with the rest. Another body started to move; it was at the top of the pile of bodies, but the consuming flames damaged it so badly that it was of no use. Rapidly, the flames ate the bodies. After several minutes, there was nothing there, not even a trace of water.

The bishop shut off the water, and for the time being, they put the hose down. The FBI agents at this time stopped filming as well and, with the child, walked toward them. They shook the bishop's hand and the hands of the rest, as the sheriff and deputies came near as well.

"Where are the bodies? Are they in hell, or did they go to heaven? And where is all the water, which should be all over the floor?" asked the sheriff, sounding more confused as the night passed.

"Sheriff, please … everybody, please listen to me. They have already been judged, and they are now dead. They are not in heaven or hell, but there is no more tomorrow for them. The Father will have the water and will use it again," stated the bishop, answering the question as simply as possible.

"What else do you plan to do tonight, Bishop, before you are finished here?" asked Agent Zdun, looking surprised by what had unfolded before him.

"I'm going to spray this room yet and the rest of the water into the pit and then seal it forever, and I'm done tonight," stated the bishop with a faint smile.

"My report tonight doesn't fit a normal profile, though we have it on film here, the missing bodies and then no coroner's report. We may be witnesses here and have seen it. This report can't go through normal channels, so it will go to a special branch of the bureau. They will study it," stated Agent Zdun flatly in a professional tone.

The rest of the night, the agents, the child, and the sheriff and deputies watched as the bishop and the others worked together and blessed everything in the room and finally as the pit was sealed forever until all the holy water was gone. The park service reclaimed their hose and placed it neatly back on the trucks as they made ready for the trip back to town. They all agreed to meet at the sheriff's office at 1:00 p.m. and finish all details of the case there.

After another hour, with everything done, Agent Marth said professionally, "Agent Zdun and I will meet you at the sheriff's office as stated earlier tonight; we'll need a better explanation of what happened here tonight for our superiors at the bureau. And for right now, this child here needs a bath, a doctor, and rest. We'll meet tomorrow."

The sheriff and the deputies then talked to Bill, John, Alice, and Mark. The sheriff explained that the National Guard had left early with the prisoners and the park service had just reported they had left as well.

"What about the house and everything, Sheriff?" asked John, wondering about the property.

"I'm going to leave two county deputies in charge of that. It will be light work, but it must be done. Do you have anything you think we should do, Bill?" asked the sheriff with some politeness in his voice.

"No, Sheriff, I think that will be fine for now. If I think of something later, I'll have it tomorrow," stated Bill with politeness as well.

"Sheriff, how do you report my brother, dead or missing? Just how do you report something like this?" asked Alice, wondering about her lost brother.

The sheriff thought for a moment and said politely, "Good question, Alice, but I think when the FBI gets done reviewing this matter with the missing bodies and everything, they will probably be telling me."

Bill thought of the coroner's vehicles. He wondered if they were still coming. "Sheriff, did you cancel the coroner vehicles? There is no need for them now, sir," Bill said with wonder in his voice.

"Yes, they were, Bill. The FBI did that for me. I just failed to mention it, sorry. And by the way, Bill, your car is in front of the house with the keys in it," replied the sheriff in a normal tone of voice.

Bill then remembered that earlier that evening, John wanted the keys for something but now couldn't remember when. Bill, John, Alice, and Mark made their way to the tunnel that had the dressing room and the stairs that led up to the house. Once they were inside the house, they again noticed how nice everything was—the fine paintings, the light fixtures, the fine carpeting, and everything else—but Adam had just thrown it all away.

It was like a monument to foolish desire, for he first gained it all and then quickly lost it. Once they were inside the car and started to pull away from the house, John reminded Bill of the rats in the basement.

"Do you feel they had enough water and feed to make it till tomorrow, John?" asked Bill, having almost forgotten them down there.

"I think so, Bill. We did give them plenty earlier today, but they will need it tomorrow," replied John, still thinking of it.

"That will have to be the first thing then we'll do in the morning. Agree, John?" answered Bill in a reassuring tone of voice.

Again, they were on the road back to town. They were all tired and could use some rest. Nobody was saying much. Bill said to Alice as he drove the car, "I'm sorry for your loss, Alice. Did John explain how it happened?"

Alice, at first, said nothing, for it still hurt much inside. "No, but he promised to play it back for me, so I will know what happened to him."

Mark said, "I think we all did our jobs very well tonight,

especially you, Alice, with the strength and courage you showed, even after a terrible loss. Always remember to keep the faith and take courage with you."

For the rest of the trip to the motel, it was silent in the car. Everybody returned to his or her room for the night. Bill lay in bed for a while. He couldn't sleep at first. He was thinking of all that had happened to them earlier. There was no way they could have saved Adam or the others; it was completely out of their hands. If they would have stood up and interrupted the angels' business, the outcome could have been everybody's worst nightmare. He had never had this happen to him before—for that matter, very few had ever been in this position where something supernatural stepped in and changed everything.

The next morning, Bill rose up about midmorning and went about his routine before starting the day. He was about to leave his room when there was a knock at the door. Bill opened the door. Everybody was there, and he greeted them.

"Hey, we're hungry, Bill. How about some food?" suggested Alice in a cheery mood and tone of voice.

"Well, we can't let that happen now, can we?" responded Bill in a similar tone of voice.

Bill noticed that everybody was feeling good and in a somewhat happy mood that morning. It made him feel there was hope again and everything would work out in time. As they drove into town, John noticed the wreckers who were removing the followers' cars from the motels.

After a good meal, they drove out to Adam's house, and after getting clearance from the deputy, they removed the rats from their hiding place. The police were everywhere and were doing their part in finishing the case. The news media were there as well, trying to get any news they could. But they weren't getting much of anything from the officials at that time. The news media swarmed around them for a while because they were there. They said nothing at all except, "Just talk to the sheriff." Once back at the car, with the rats in the trunk, fed and watered, they made their way back to the motel. At the motel, Bill reminded Alice to call her employer and explain that she would need leave for the death of her brother. Later, Bill and John left the motel to get some rolls at a grocery store and return.

While they were in John's room drinking coffee and eating rolls, Mark and Alice entered the room.

"I see that things are slowly returning to normal again. May I help myself to a roll?" asked Mark, happy to see his friends looking relaxed.

Alice joined in. She seemed more like her usual self again. She enjoyed everyone's company. Later in the afternoon, they returned to the sheriff's office, and there were many officials waiting, including the two FBI agents. At the right time, everyone was led to the basement, where there was a makeshift conference room waiting for them.

The room was large enough to handle all the officials who were there. The sheriff was cordial and fielded many questions from the officials. At the end of his time, he asked Bill to stand up and stated how Bill had played the most important role in solving the case. The sheriff even admitted that it was Bill who had convinced him to see the truth about Adam Johnson and the other followers.

The rest of the meeting was long and revealing. Alice found her answer when she asked the sheriff about her brother. She learned that at the national level, her brother would be listed as deceased, but at all other levels, he would be listed as missing. They also learned that the child was currently on her way back home to her family, thanks to the FBI. The thirteen women's families were being notified at that time. Adam's property would be held for further investigation until it was released to the public. And the thirteen women would be reported the same way as Adam, for the same reasons.

The weapons Adam and the followers had on the property were still being looked into as to motive at that time. The thirty-seven followers would be transported to Chicago in the morning, where they would be jailed while awaiting trial. The meeting lasted over two hours, with the news media waiting for them. Bill and the rest were able to leave with not much trouble. They went to a restaurant to enjoy their meal.

John then said, "You know we could leave for Milwaukee tonight, but it will be very late when we get home?" John slowly looked around the table, as everybody looked around at each other.

Alice felt that she should answer that and said, "Personally, I feel we have the rooms paid for tonight already; let's make the best of it and leave in the morning."

Mark thought most would feel the same and said, "I feel I have to agree with that statement as well."

With that, they agreed to stay the night and leave in the morning. The next morning, everybody was up early and packed up. After a meal and a stop for gas, they headed back to Milwaukee. It was in the middle of the afternoon when they arrived at Bill's office. They all removed their luggage and took it back to their cars again. Mark and John each said they would be in touch and then went home. Alice stayed behind and thanked him warmly for all his help and more. They hugged and kissed warmly, and she left as well.

Bill left his luggage in the car and slowly walked around, thinking of the past week and how it had all ended. Finally, he thought maybe it had all ended better than he'd thought it would. He got into the car and went home as well.

Slightly over two weeks later, John was at Bill's office, enjoying rolls and coffee with him. It was later in the morning, and things were fairly quiet.

"You say that Alice is to be in this morning to settle up with you today?" asked John as he started to sip his coffee.

Bill quickly drank some coffee and said, "That's what she told me three days ago, John, and I have it on record here."

John eyed another roll and picked one. He said, "You know, she's been really quiet since we last saw her."

Bill thought for a moment and said, "Now that you said that, you're right. I know she wanted to settle up, and she wanted to say something as well. But I don't know what."

A while later, Bill was finishing up a phone call, and John was waiting. Alice stepped into the office and greeted them both. John pulled up the other chair for her, and she made herself comfortable.

"Well, well, Alice, I must admit it's good to see you again," said Bill, greeting her with a handshake.

John was once again happy to see her. He said, "So bring us up-to-date and tell us what you've been doing since we last saw you?"

Alice proceeded to explain everything about the property and the FBI asking her questions, wanting to know if she knew this or that. She went on to say that work had been good and then stopped for a moment. "I'm taking a new position in Raleigh, North Carolina, and I will be doing the same job that I'm doing now. The pay is somewhat less, and the hospital is a little smaller, but I will be working only two shifts, not three—mornings and afternoons. They give the newer nurses, fresh out of school, the three shifts."

Bill and John both congratulated her on her fine move and offered her a roll and coffee.

After a while, Alice went through her purse and brought out the bill. Bill readied himself with the ledger and his metal box. Alice paid in cash. Bill counted the money and put it into the metal box. Then he wrote out the receipt and gave it to her. Alice put the receipt in her purse and came out with more cash. She gave both John and Bill a bonus for their work.

She took a moment to find the words to say what she wanted. She said, "I will always be grateful for all you did for me and Mark as well. I couldn't ask for more if I wanted too. You all have done so much already. You all gave me a new walk in life, and I appreciate that. You were right about saying no to me up north, Bill, but now I know what to look for on that subject. I will give you the number in a second here, and I want you to feel free to call as well. I don't ever want to say good-bye. I want to be friends forever."

A tear ran down her face as she opened her purse and gave them a slip of paper each with her address and telephone number. She gave each a hug and kiss. She slowly walked toward the door but stopped when she reached it, paused for one last look, and left. There was a long moment of silence between them, and they just sat there and looked at each other.

After a while, Bill broke the silence. "In all my years of service to the public, I never ended a case like this or ever felt this way before. I know I will miss her."

THE END.